# ROYAL BOROUGH OF GREENWICH

## New Eltham Library
## Tel: 020 8850 2322

# PeL under pressure

## MARK HEBDEN

HOUSE OF STRATUS

Copyright © 1980, 2001 John Harris

The right of John Harris to be identified as the author of this work
has been asserted.

This edition published in 2001 by House of Stratus, an imprint of
House of Stratus Ltd, Thirsk Industrial Park, York Road, Thirsk,
North Yorkshire, YO7 3BX, UK.
Also at: House of Stratus Inc., 2 Neptune Road, Poughkeepsie, NY 12601, USA.

www.houseofstratus.com

Typeset, printed and bound by House of Stratus.

A catalogue record for this book is available from the British Library
and the Library of Congress.

ISBN 1-84232-893-X

*Though Burgundians will probably decide they have recognised it and certainly many of the street names are the same, in fact, the city in these pages is intended to be fictitious.*

# one

The city was like an oven.

In its deep valley under the northern hills the place sweltered and the sergeants' room in the Hôtel de Police was as uncomfortable as the inside of a furnace. The building was new and the architects had clearly believed in the use of solar heating but, planning to extract the maximum amount of energy from the sun on cold days, they had overlooked the fact that the city had quite a few hot days, too. At the last moment, however, they seemed to have panicked and, while making the windows nearly two metres square to let in the sun, they had also arranged for them to turn on a central pivot so that it was possible to lay them horizontal to allow the breeze to enter the offices as freely as possible.

That day, unfortunately, there was no breeze at all and, despite the early hour, it was already so hot nobody was eager to start work. Certainly no one was anxious to be out on the streets and they clung to the sergeants' room as if it were a life raft and they were drowning, all of them hoping nobody would be stupid enough to rape anyone else, rob anyone else or assault anyone else until the heat wave broke and the city grew cooler. They already had enough to keep them occupied.

Sergeant Nosjean sat at his desk in his shirt sleeves, staring at a set of photographs spread in front of him. Some were in close-up; others had been taken far enough back to include the furnishings of a shabby room. They showed the bound

1

shape of a young man lying on the floor and were sharp enough to show the worn patches in the carpet.

The young man's name was Jean-Marc Cortot and he was a student at the Faculté des Sciences at the University. He had been found the weekend before in his room, naked and bound hand and foot, with enough rope round him to moor a North Sea oil rig. His room-mate, one Philippe Mortier, had returned home to discover him, his face bruised, his body scarred, quite dead.

There were marks on Cortot's arms that indicated he had injected himself recently – and had been doing for some time – with heroin. There were no other wounds, however, beyond the bruised face and the scars on his naked back, and Dr Minet, the police surgeon, had made it clear very quickly that none of these was the cause of death.

Nosjean's chief, Inspector Evariste Clovis Désiré Pel, involved in investigating on behalf of the Chief a bit of sharp practice at a police sub-station at St Clément-sur-Tille, had turned the enquiry over to Nosjean, for whom, though he would have died rather than admit it, he had a very high regard.

'Bend your brilliant mind to it, mon brave,' he had said. 'Why was he tied up after injecting himself with drugs? Who gave him the drugs? And where did they come from? You ought to sort it out in no time.'

At the next desk, Sergeant Lagé was typing a report. He was engaged on a hit-and-run case at Gévrey that looked remarkably like an attempted murder and it was involving him in a great deal of work with a typewriter. He wasn't enjoying himself, because most of the machines in the sergeants' room were cast-offs from the offices of the girl secretaries elsewhere in the building and they were so worn they made typing a job for a strong man. And, since Sergeant Lagé, in the manner of most policemen, used only two fingers, he was feeling the effort right up to his elbows.

Sergeant Misset was studying a map of the city. How, he was trying to decide, had a certain Hyacinthe Baranquin, who was well known for his ability to break into locked shops and offices, got from the Avenue Victor Hugo to the Rue Rioux in a matter of five minutes? Misset had tried it. It had taken him a quarter of an hour. There had, he decided, to be an accomplice somewhere.

Sergeant Krauss was merely reading the newspapers. He was due for retirement any day now and nobody wanted to know him. It had once been Nosjean's job, as the youngest and most innocent member of Inspector Pel's team, to fetch the beer and sandwiches, but, as Nosjean had grown older and more experienced and Krauss had grown slower and more indifferent, they had exchanged duties. There had been no orders from Pel, no instruction from the Chief. It was simply accepted that Krauss wasn't very fast any more, either with his feet or with his mind and, since he was so close to retirement, if he were caught up in something big, it would have caused endless problems if he'd passed from the force by the time it came before the court. Krauss was therefore left alone.

Sergeant Daniel Darcy watched them all with a sort of wary affection. As senior sergeant and Pel's right-hand man, he was cynical enough not to trust a single one of them too far. After all, he thought, they were all human, in spite of being policemen. Misset and Lagé, he noticed, had stopped work and Lagé was now sitting on the corner of Misset's desk, discussing photography. Lagé's son had been in the habit of building model aeroplanes from kits and Lagé had caught the habit from him. Growing ambitious, he had hung them from fishing rods and photographed them against the sky but, unfortunately, the thread persisted in showing and it had so engaged Lagé's mind he had joined a photographic society in Fontaine where he lived to find out how to overcome the problem. The speed with which they had made

3

him secretary was put down in the sergeants' room to the fact that he could use a typewriter, was a sucker for doing other people's work, and had access to the copying machine in the basement of the Hôtel de Police. Lagé's son had long since progressed from model aeroplanes to girls but it had still not occurred to Lagé that the photographic society was making a monkey out of him, and he'd become so keen on photography, he'd forgotten his aeroplanes and went out every weekend with a German Braun taking pictures in the Parc de la Columbière, along the Cours General de Gaulle and the Canal de Bourgogne, and in the neighbouring villages and towns. He had even taken pictures in the prison which, he claimed, provided great contrasts of light and shade. He was always talking these days about light and shade.

'You got any women in your photographic society?' Misset was asking.

Lagé looked surprised. 'What's that got to do with it?' he demanded.

Misset grinned. 'I wondered if that was why you were so keen.'

'We're not all like you,' Lagé said stiffly. Misset was also married – almost *too* married at times, he felt – and with his family growing faster than he could assimilate it, his eye had started roving once more over the pretty girls.

Nosjean listened to them, saying nothing. Though he had a girl and Odile Chenandier would have given her eye-teeth to be his wife, he nevertheless still managed to fall in love with anything female that took more than a normal amount of interest in him. Nosjean was young and, though he was becoming a good detective – much better than he realised – he still managed to remain shy, slightly introspective and doubtful of his own skill. He had met Odile Chenandier when, with his colleagues, he had been instrumental in sending her father away for life and, cowed at home, since

4

meeting Nosjean she had blossomed. The sergeants' room had been taking bets on her for a long time.

Lagé was gesturing. 'Brigitte Bardot,' he was saying. 'That's what she's like.'

'Who?' Misset asked.

'This dame I'm talking about: Marie-Anne Chahu. I've been trying to find an excuse for weeks to go and see her again.'

'If she looks like Bardot,' Misset grinned, 'I'll come with you.' Nosjean frowned at them. With his idealistic approach, his own affairs with girls were invariably meetings of the mind. Which was why they rarely came to anything. Most girls weren't interested in meetings of the mind.

Lagé did things with his hands to indicate bust, waist and behind, and Krauss put down the newspaper to join in.

'Personally,' he said, 'I think I'm getting too old to run after women.

'When you're retired,' Misset said, 'you won't have to run. You'll be able to walk. Slowly. To conserve your strength. What are you going to do, anyway? Get a job with some security organisation?'

'Not me.'

'Not even watchman at FMPS?'

'Not even that.' Krauss smiled. 'I'm going to spend my retirement sleeping. To make up for all the nights on this job when I couldn't.'

'Can't you find anything better to do?'

'I might grow tomatoes,' Krauss admitted. 'I might take my grandchildren out in the car. I've got two. Come to think of it, I might even take them tonight. It's hot enough and there's a *plage* near Fleurey. Paddling pool for the kids, swimming for me and the wife and daughter and a bar for all of us. What more can you ask?'

'This famous Marie-Anne Chahu you're going on about.' It was Misset again to Lagé. With women these days he was like a terrier at a rat-hole. 'Why haven't I ever seen her?'

'You've only to go to Foussier's office,' Lagé said.

'Which Foussier? There are dozens of Foussiers in this city.'

'Professor Foussier. University. Faculté des Langues Modernes.'

'Oh, him!' Misset stared. 'I've been there! That time when the porter was pinching from the lockers. I saw nothing special. Just an old dear with glasses and a bust like a frigate under full sail.'

'You've got the wrong office,' Lagé said. 'That's the University office. He has a private practice. Aviation Studies and Navigation and a few other things. La Chahu works for *him*, not the university.' Lagé looked smug. 'She speaks three languages,' he pointed out.

'So do I,' Krauss said in the thick Alsatian accent he put on from time to time. 'French, German and Obscene. Is she his secretary?'

'She's his personal assistant.'

'Assistant to do what?'

Lagé grinned. 'It's not like that.' He paused. 'All the same, I wouldn't mind having her as *my* personal assistant.'

Misset eyed him enviously. 'How did *you* get to know her, anyway?'

'The photographic society.'

Misset looked at Krauss and grinned. Lagé and the photographic society had become a joke in the sergeants' room.

'I wrote to Foussier,' Lagé went on. 'Asking him to give us a talk. He's an expert on photography, too. I got a telephone call from her. What a voice! My wife thought I'd taken a mistress.'

'I wouldn't mind taking a mistress,' Misset said wistfully. 'What did she say?'

'She asked me to go over and see her. It was that time when I was going to Talant about that supermarket case. I said I couldn't just then, so she gave me her telephone number. She doesn't give it to anyone. I was very lucky. She asked me to let her know when I *could* call. She had something for me.'

Misset grinned. 'Did you get it?'

Lagé grinned hack. 'Foussier couldn't give us a talk but he had one I could read to the members. It was one he'd given in Lyons. He said we could use it.'

Lagé was so full of his own importance, Nosjean couldn't resist taking him down. 'This Marie-Anne Chahu,' he said.

Lagé looked round. 'Yes?' he asked. 'What about her?'

Nosjean smiled. '*I* have her telephone number, too,' he said.

The disgusted expression that appeared on Lagé's face at Nosjean's words was being roughly matched just to the north of the city centre by the expression on the face of one Emile Escaut. Long-haired and none too clean in grubby pink jeans and a navy blue shirt, he was having difficulty identifying his car. He had left it by the sidewalk in the Rue du Chapeau Rouge the previous evening to go to a party and now he was not at all sure which it was.

They were pulling down an old house at the end of the street and the dust hung in the air like a veil, obscuring the view and covering everything within a hundred yards with a thick sepia pall that came from old plaster and the accumulated dirt of years. The parked cars had been covered with it as it drifted on the light breeze and they looked now as if they had lost their brightness, like vehicles in an old and faded photograph.

Eventually, Escaut managed to identify his car, less by its colour than by the dents in it, and moved round it, wiping the dust from the windows. When he came to the rear window, however, it dawned on him it was so tightly shut in by other cars he couldn't hope to move it. There was less than a centimetre or two at either end.

'Merde,' he said bitterly.

Moving to the car behind it, he examined it. His own vehicle was an old Deux Chevaux and the car behind was a large American Cadillac. Staring at it, he allowed his thoughts on American tourists to range freely across the spectrum. They were too tall, too handsome and too wealthy, their cars were too big, and they had no right to block good French cars driven by good French drivers. It was quite obvious there was going to be no movement in that direction. The Cadillac was too wide by a long way. Nor could he bash his way out. The little Deux Chevaux would fall to pieces long before he'd moved the Cadillac enough to get clear.

Moving to the front of the car, he examined the vehicle ahead. It was a large old-fashioned Renault, but this still left it quite a lot smaller than the Cadillac. If he was going to get out he was going to have to do it that way.

He put his hand on the boot of the Renault which was hard up against his own front bumper. The metal was hot under the sun and he sniffed in disgust. As his nostrils wrinkled, he became aware of the smell. It was strong, sweetish, sickly and stomach-churning, and in his delicate state after the party, it made Emile Escaut heave.

'Merde,' he said again.

The smell appeared to be coming from the boot of the Renault and it was enough to make his hair curl. It was something he had never smelled before, like bad drains but infinitely worse than that, something repugnant and obscene, and nauseating enough to make him catch his breath.

He noticed, however, that whoever owned the Renault had pulled the handbrake only over the first notches and it was just possible to move the car against it. Sighing, knowing he would end up exhausted, he got his back against the car and pushed. The effort made his head throb and caused him to break into a sweat. With the best will in the world, he knew he couldn't move it sufficiently to escape.

He was just about to light a cigarette when one of the demolition men approached from the old building just up the road. He was a short man, with a belly that hung over his belt, and he sucked at a cigarette end, a thickset figure with a face so ravaged by acne in his youth it looked like the workings of a quarry. He wore a blue armless singlet and his grubby thatch of hair supported a tartan cap with a bobble on top. Escaut thrust his cigarettes away quickly. The street was empty of passers-by because they were all avoiding the dust, and this man was the first he'd seen.

'Hé!'

The workman stopped and Escaut gestured.

'How about a shove, copain?' he said. 'They've blocked me in and I can't get out. This car'll move but it needs two.'

The demolition man tossed away his cigarette end and joined Escaut behind the Renault. Laying his hands on it, with a cry of 'Et hop!' he managed to move it quite considerably on his own. Escaut watched him admiringly then lent his own weight and they moved the car several more centimetres.

'I might do it now,' Escaut said.

'Yes, you might.' The demolition man dusted his hands. Then his nose wrinkled. 'What have you got in there, comrade?'

'It's not my car,' Escaut said. He gestured at the little Citroën. 'That's mine.'

The workman moved round the Renault, his nose twitching.

9

'I was with Leclerc,' he said. 'I was a sergeant. Aristide Roches, that's me. We went through North Africa after the Germans. I know that smell.'

'It's a bit grim,' Escaut agreed.

'It's more than that. It's a smell I smelled a lot in those days. It comes when it's hot and it's a smell you never forget as long as you live.'

'What is it?'

'More likely *who* is it?' ex-Sergeant Roches said. 'I reckon, mon brave, that it would be a good idea for you to walk down to that bar on the corner there and telephone the police.'

There were a variety of reasons why Escaut wasn't keen to be involved with the police. 'It's not my car,' he said.

Ex-Sergeant Roches gestured at the Renault. 'You can smell that, mon brave,' he snorted.

'I know, but – I don't think I'll bother.'

Roches gestured again. 'Well, if *you're* not going to,' he said, 'I will.'


The demolition work had stopped. The dust had settled. At each end of the Rue du Chapeau Rouge there were police cars, their blue lights flashing. Several police motorbikes stood by the curb and a large dark van waited in the middle of the road. The demolition men sat on their machines, watching, squinting against the sun, and the tapes the police had put up were crowded with sightseers.

A police sergeant with a bunch of car keys worked over the boot of the Renault, his nose wrinkled at the smell. At last, he managed to unfasten it without having to break the lock and as the lid lifted, the smell that escaped was enough to send him reeling back.

'Ach, mon Dieu!' he gasped.

The stench was caught by the people watching from the ends of the street and one or two women turned and hurried away. The sergeant, his handkerchief to his nose, took another look. The body in the boot of the Renault was swollen with the heat, the clothes tight against the flesh. The face had gone from grey to greeny-black, so puffed the features had almost disappeared. The flesh was dark, shining and moist and behind the right ear there was a small hole where the blood, black now, was crusted along the back of the head.

'This isn't a job for Traffic,' the sergeant said, and his inspector, who was watching, lifted his radio and spoke to the Hôtel de Police.

'Pomereu,' he said. 'Inspector Pomereu. In the Rue du Chapeau Rouge. We've just found a body in the boot of a car. Black Renault, Number 9643-QT-21. Looks as though it's been here more than a day or two. Inform Police Judiciaire.' The inspector paused. 'You'd better tell them to bring gas masks and aerosol squirts. The stench's worse than a cow's inside.'

In the sergeants' room, Lagé was staring up at Nosjean. '*You've* got her telephone number?' he was saying.

Nosjean smiled at him. 'Yes.'

'You couldn't have,' Lagé said. 'It's ex-directory. So's the Professor's.'

Nosjean grinned. 'I've got it all the same.'

'She's not that red-headed one that sits in the outer office,' Lagé said.

'I know which one she is,' Nosjean smiled. 'I've been in her office, too. *Right inside.*'

'When?' Lagé clearly didn't believe him.

'Yesterday. I went about that kid who was found dead: Cortot.'

'What's she got to do with Cortot? Cortot was studying electronics. Foussier's Modern Languages.'

11

'He also runs that committee the University set up to investigate drug-taking,' Nosjean said. 'It's an extra-mural activity.'

'Like Lagé with his secretary,' Krauss pointed out.

'Is *that* how you got letters from her?' Lagé asked. 'The drug thing?'

'Yes' Nosjean said.

'Just letters, I suppose. Typed. Signed by Foussier. I've got those. At home.'

'No,' Nosjean smiled. 'I had a note from her in her own handwriting. It was sent here. To me. Marked "Personal". It's in the file. Foussier keeps a watch on kids who get involved with drugs. He knew about Cortot.'

'A fine man,' Lagé said earnestly.

'I think he's a pompous ass.'

'I wish I had his salary,' Misset observed.

Darcy looked up from his desk. 'A bit more attention to detail, mon brave,' he said, 'and you might have.'

'He's an expert in half a dozen fields and a near expert in half a dozen others,' Lagé said. 'Everything from languages to electronics. He makes me want to go in for a few myself.'

'Me,' Krauss said, 'he makes tired.'

Darcy pushed away the papers in front of him, deciding the discussion had gone on long enough. 'If his eminence, Evariste Clovis Désiré Pel, walked in here now,' he said, 'you'd all be back on Traffic in forty-eight hours, escorting kids across the road and making sure nobody pinched the Porte Guillaume. How about getting on with a bit of work? Because nothing's happened lately it doesn't mean it never will. And when it does you'll be complaining there's too much to do. It could happen this afternoon. Or an hour from now. Or in five minutes time. Even now.'

It was at that moment that the telephone rang.

For a second Darcy stared at it, as if startled by its reaction.

It was Control and what they said made him grin and look round at the others in the room. There was something in the grin that made their hearts sink.

'Rue du Chapeau Rouge?' he said. 'Who found it? Are Traffic holding them? Good. What's that? It's a wonder it wasn't found before? Why not?'

They were all watching him, and they saw his face fall.

'Because the smell's enough to turn your stomach?' he said. 'Dieu! Right, I'll tell the Chief.'

He put the telephone down, and turned to the others.

'What did I tell you, mes braves?' he said cheerfully, opening a drawer and stuffing pencils and notebooks into his pocket. 'It's come.'

'What's come?' Krauss asked.

'The incident, mes petites mignonnes, that we were all awaiting with bated breath. It's a body. And a nasty one, too. Nosjean, inform Lab and Fingerprints. Misset, order a car. Lagé, tell Doc. Minet. Krauss – '

Krauss stared at him. 'I was going to take the kids out tonight,' he pointed out.

'Well, now,' Darcy said, 'you're not. It's a murder. You'd better sit on the telephone. It'll save your poor old legs.'

'It's my night off,' Nosjean pointed out.

'Not tonight, mon brave,' Darcy smiled. 'This one sounds a beauty. Traffic have found a stiff in the boot of a car. It's been there for some time, it seems, and it smells like ripe Camembert. I'd better go and tell the Old Man.'

The 'Old Man' had just returned to his office. He had walked from the Palais de Justice and the narrow streets of the old city were hot. His feet ached. They'd been aching ever since the previous evening. There'd been a long session out at St Clément, and when he'd finished they'd felt as if they belonged to several other detectives, all cripples, and like Krauss, all on the point of retirement.

13

The newspapers had already got wind of the questioning and were doing their best to make it appear that the whole French judiciary system was corrupt. '*The enquiry is in the hands of Inspector Evariste Clovis Désiré Pel,*' they announced.

Evariste Clovis Désiré Pel scowled. They'd obviously somehow got his name from his record. Or from a deadly enemy. Seeing his full name in print always bothered Pel. Even when it was only looking at his driving licence. The names had been his mother's choice and he sometimes thought they had been the cause of his father's early death. Perhaps he had worried himself into his grave at the thought of what might happen to a son of his carrying the load of such a label.

Pushing his spectacles up on to his forehead, he sat down, took out a packet of Gauloises, selected one which looked as though it might just be smaller and less lethal than the others and lit it with a sigh. It was Pel's ambition that one day he might stop smoking. He knew he never would, but he liked to make a lot of song and dance about trying. Any minute now, he thought, he would drop dead of a heart attack, or gasp out his last with asthma or cancer of the lung. The facts were clear. He knew them well. The grim truth, unfortunately, was that he *couldn't* stop smoking.

As he drew the strong Régie Française tobacco smoke down to his shoes, he coughed violently, but his eyes brightened and he began to feel better immediately. His depression fell away from him at once and he decided that, with luck and a bit of effort, he might last out the day.

As he stretched in his chair, it seemed almost as if the smoke was leaking out from under his toenails. He began to cough again, racking coughs that made him go red in the face and brought tears to his eyes. When he stopped, he felt a new man.

He was just savouring the feeling of being reborn when the door opened and he sat bolt upright, guiltily aware that he'd been caught relaxing. Sergeant Darcy grinned at him. He knew Pel too well to be put off by his alert expression.

'Job, Patron,' he said.

'What is it?' Pel asked bitterly. 'Something dreamed up by a traffic cop between a bock of beer and a session with his best girl?'

'No, Patron. It's a stiff. And I gather it's a strong stiff.'

'Strong?'

'As a ripe cheese. Traffic found it in the boot of a car in Chapeau Rouge. Seems to have been there for a few days and, in this heat you can imagine what it's like. They suggest gas masks.'

Pel scowled. 'I was just about to go to lunch,' he complained.

Darcy's shoulders moved. 'That's the worst of this job, Patron,' he grinned. 'The tensions. The frustrations. The bitterness that comes with them.'

Pel glared at the sarcasm. 'Any witnesses?'

'The two guys who found it. One, Emile Escaut, who was trying to move the car to get his own out. And one, Aristide Roches, demolition worker, who was helping him. Traffic have them answering questions – so far without much help, because they've never seen the car before, or for that matter each other. Judge Polverari's on the case.'

Pel began to stuff a notebook, pens, spectacles and cigarettes into his pockets, a slight, dark-eyed, dark-haired, intense figure in a shabby suit and dusty shoes. Then, rooting round in his drawer, he found a packet of bismuth tablets and pushed those in, too, in case he started a stomach ulcer from missed meals. A second notebook followed the first then, for safety, an extra packet of Gauloises in case he worked his way clean through the others without noticing.

'Come on,' he said. 'Let's go. Informed Lab, Fingerprints, and Doc. Minet?'

'Patron,' Darcy said sadly, 'I've been doing this job a long time now. They're all on their way, all as eager as you. Nosjean's already gone. Misset's in the office complaining he ought to be home helping his wife with the baby. I've got him standing by. Lagé's following Nosjean. Krauss' on the telephone. I think he's going to be busy.'

'Car?'

'At the front ready for you.'

Unable to find any flaws, Pel grunted.

'I don't suppose you thought to ring my home and tell my housekeeper I won't be in for lunch?' he said.

'I always got the impression,' Darcy retorted, 'that you couldn't care less whether you went home to her cooking or not.'

Pel scowled. His feud with his housekeeper was known throughout Police Headquarters. It had been going on as long as he could remember, and he had only brought it up because he'd been unable to find anything else to complain about. He stared at Darcy.

'Well,' he demanded sharply. 'What are you waiting for? Hanging about as if we had all the time in the world. Let's be off.'

# two

Nobody was very pleased with the body in the Rue du Chapeau Rouge. The odour was appalling and they were all concerned that somehow it would get on to their clothes.

Misset's wife, for instance, had a nose like a bloodhound and could almost tell what job he'd been on by the smell he brought home. She knew when he smoked and when he had a beer – something, in view of their growing family, she wasn't any too keen on – and above all, when he'd been in the presence of another woman. Since Misset's job often included interviewing women, not all of them old and some of them young and more than sprightly, Misset suffered a great deal from her suspicion, and he knew exactly what she'd have to say if he walked into the house smelling of the smell that was coming from the boot of the car in the Rue du Chapeau Rouge.

Dr Minet was moving gingerly. His concern was that, if there were broken bones, he should not touch them. It didn't look as if there *would* be broken bones, but if there were a scratch from a splintered end it could lead to gangrene. His assistants, who were going to have to handle the corpse when Pel gave the word, were even more reluctant. Their job involved touching a great deal that wasn't pleasant but it was not very often they handled anything as unpleasant as the body in the boot of the Renault. The photographers weren't any too pleased either. It was their job to produce pictures from every possible angle. Including close-ups. It was the close-ups which bothered them.

Emile Escaut was standing with ex-Sergeant Aristide Roches. He looked worried as he watched what was going on. He had intended bolting when Roches had turned to head for the bar to telephone the police, but Roches, like any good Frenchman, considered it his right to poke his nose into other people's business where the security and safety of the Republic was concerned, and had deftly removed Escaut's keys from the dashboard. 'The police will want witnesses,' he had pointed out. 'And you're one of them.'

Escaut looked bitterly at Roches, who was standing, plump, square and important, watching the policemen. He touched Darcy's arm.

'Look,' he said quietly. 'My car. That's it. Do you think I could go now? I've got an appointment.'

Darcy eyed him up and down. Darcy looked smart enough to be on guard at the Elysée Palace. Emile Escaut didn't look smart enough to be on guard anywhere.

'Is it urgent?' Darcy asked.

'Well, no.'

'Better wait then. You're the guy who found it, aren't you?'

'No. Not really. I just happened to be here.'

'Live in the city?'

'Four years.'

'Well, just hang on. We'll let you know.'

His handkerchief over his nose, Pel was watching as Minet moved warily about. He was frowning, his dark intense face absorbed, his thin frame alert. Pel didn't like the smell any more than anybody else, particularly as he had a nose like Misset's wife. Darcy often said they should put a lead on him and use him as a sniffer dog. But he had a job to do. Alongside him, watching narrow-eyed, Judge Polverari, the juge d'instruction, also waited. He was small and round and fat and his nose twitched unhappily.

'I think we shall need a large cognac after this, Pel,' he said.

Pel nodded.

'In fact,' Polverari continued, 'I think I'll visit the bar down there now, and think about that Lavergne case. It's a nice comfortable case to think about with this smell around. Blackmail of a beautiful woman. All boudoirs, perfume and scented baths. It's something I'll have to take up with Paris before long, because she lives there. Either way it'll take my mind off this. Have we got the two who found it?'

'Yes.' Pel turned and spoke over his shoulder. 'There's no good reason to hold them, though. They don't seem to be concerned. After I've talked to them they can go.'

Polverari nodded. 'Keep me informed,' he said. He jerked a hand at a small red-fronted establishment at the end of the road whose door was full of people staring at the activities of the police. 'I'll see there's a brandy waiting for you.'

Pel hardly heard him. As Polverari wandered off, still holding his handkerchief to his face, Inspector Pomereu, of Traffic, appeared.

'The car was stolen,' he announced.

'It doesn't surprise me,' Pel observed. 'I can't imagine anyone having *that* in his car from choice. Where's it from?'

'Auxonne. It was reported stolen four days ago.'

'Just about the time our friend was stuffed inside it, I imagine,' Dr Minet said shortly.

'Get hold of the owner,' Pel said. 'We'll need to talk to him.' He turned to Minet. 'What have you got, Doc?'

Minet shrugged. 'Can't tell you yet,' he said. 'I'll need to do an autopsy. But it's a gunshot wound in the back of the head. I can see no other wounds at the moment. You'll have to wait for the report.'

'You can do better than that,' Pel growled. 'It doesn't have to be exact and I won't use it as evidence. I just want an idea.'

Minet looked up. 'Single shot. Small calibre. Somewhere around 7 mm. They placed it hard up against his head before they pulled the trigger. There's scorching of the hair and skin. Under the circumstances, it could hardly be considered an accident.'

Pel rubbed his nose, fought hard to avoid lighting a cigarette, failed miserably and offered one to Minet as a guilt offering. Minet lit the cigarette and drew in the smoke to kill the smell. With a rubber-gloved hand he reached into the boot of the Renault alongside the body.

'There's something here that might be of interest,' he said. 'A button. A very dirty leather button.'

Pel wasn't very interested. He read a lot of detective stories in which people always found buttons and matched them with the murderer's clothing. The buttons *he* found usually came off a workman's overalls and invariably had nothing whatever to do with what he was investigating. He fought for breath as he drew down the first lungfuls of smoke from his cigarette and gestured speechlessly at Misset who was standing behind him, smoking a cheroot he'd just bought at the bar at the end of the road to take away the appalling odour. It was so strong only the bite of tobacco seemed to kill it.

'That's what *we* used to do,' ex-Sergeant Roches said approvingly. 'In the desert. Cigarettes. We used to smoke them all the time. You could almost taste the smell.'

Misset gave him a sour look and, fishing in his pocket, produced a small plastic bag. Minet dropped the button into it.

'Get it down to the Lab,' Pel said. 'Tell 'em we want to know everything they can tell us about it.'

'It probably fell off a suit the owner of the car was taking to the cleaner's,' Misset said. 'The ones I find always seem to be.'

Pel nodded, still fighting to stop coughing.

'Who is he, Doc?' he asked.

Minet shrugged. 'Nothing in his pockets to identify him. I expect we shall have an idea when we've examined his clothes.'

'Is there nothing at all?'

'No. Cheap clothes. That's all. Off-the-peg stuff.'

'Doesn't tell us much. What would he look like? – when he didn't look like this.'

Minet shrugged. 'Short. Thickset. Too fat. About forty. Blue eyes. That's about all at the moment. Hands look as though he didn't work very hard. They're clean and soft, with no callouses. Hair, black – where he has any. There's a mole on his cheek by his right eye and what looks like a scar lower down. Quite a good-sized scar.'

'Made by what?'

Minet looked up. 'Would you like me to say it was done by a knife so we can identify him as a gangster or something?'

Pel gestured. 'It looks like an execution. The single bullet at the back of the head. Pockets emptied. No identity card. Nothing. Why shouldn't he be a gangster?'

'No reason at all.' Minet smiled. 'In fact, a gangster is exactly what he *could* be. That scar could easily have come from a knife. But a long time ago. And he looks as though he might well have lived off his wits because he was too fat and too soft. But that's only a guess, mon vieux.'

'It'll do,' Pel said. He had been jotting down in his notebook what Minet had been saying and now he turned to Darcy who was waiting nearby, smoking like the rest of them.

'Where are the Press boys?' he asked.

'In the bar, Patron,' Darcy said. 'I saw them follow the judge.'

'Get them. This is something we need the jackals on. Some woman might just have noticed her husband hasn't been home for a few nights. He might turn out to be our friend here.'

As Darcy began to move away, Emile Escaut decided to try again with someone else. He touched Nosjean's arm.

'Look,' he said. 'That's my car. Think I can go now?'

Darcy heard him and turned round. 'You're in a hurry to be off, my friend,' he said sharply. 'What's worrying you?'

Escaut shrugged. 'It's this appointment.'

'I've told you once to hang on.' Darcy took another look at him. 'Come to that, haven't I seen you somewhere before?'

Escaut blew his nose on a large red handkerchief. 'I shouldn't think so,' he said. 'I don't get around much.'

Darcy's eyes narrowed. 'Where do you come from?'

'Here. Near the barracks.'

Darcy stared hard at him, his mind clicking away like a machine.

'Take him down to the office, Nosjean,' he suggested quietly. 'And stay with him. He's just too keen to get away and I have a feeling he might have something to tell me.'

'Look – ' Escaut bleated ' – I've done nothing.'

'I never said you had,' Darcy said blandly. 'But you're a witness, aren't you? You found the stiff.'

'Not me! It was the other guy!'

'You were the one who wanted to shift the car, aren't you? How do we know you didn't put it there? Find the other one, Nosjean, and take them both down. The Old Man'll want to talk to them. While you're there, you can dig up the owner of the car.'

The owner of the Renault, a printer called Légeard, was soon turned up. He was understandably annoyed.

'Yes, it's my car,' he admitted. 'It was stolen while I was in Auxonne with my wife. Dieu, the uproar when we had to come back by bus! She has bad legs.'

'I'm sorry,' Darcy said.

'Not as sorry as I was. She's not as bad as she makes out. Mind you, they're bad all right. It costs me a fortune in taxis.' Légeard paused. 'And what about the smell?'

Darcy shrugged. 'We'll do our best to get rid of it,' he said. 'I expect the Lab people will spray it with something. They don't fancy it much themselves.'

'When will I get it back?'

'As soon as possible.'

'What happens about it? Do I get a new car?'

Darcy smiled. 'Not from us, you don't.'

Légeard looked hurt. 'My wife'll never go out in that one again,' he said. 'Not after this. She's already having a nervous breakdown all over the house.'

'Once the Lab's finished with it,' Darcy said, 'you'll never notice. You ever wear a jacket with leather buttons, by the way?'

'Leather what?'

'Buttons.'

'I had one with leather patches on the elbows once.' Légeard frowned. 'What about the blood? I distinctly saw blood on the rubber mat in the boot.'

'You can get a new rubber mat. It's a standard pattern.'

'Who pays for it? Me?'

'I don't think we shall, Monsieur.'

'See what I mean? I'm losing on this all round, aren't I? The insurance company would have paid up if the car hadn't turned up. As it is, they only pay for damage after the first few hundred francs, and as there's only the rubber mat I suppose I'll have to foot the bill.'

Ex-Sergeant Aristide Roches was none too pleased either.

'Look, mon brave,' he said to Darcy. 'I'm supposed to work for Bellecins', the demolition people. They don't pay me for not working.'

'I think they will this time,' Darcy said.

'Can you guarantee that, my friend? They're capitalists. They watch their money.'

'So do I,' Darcy said. 'Always.'

'I'm on the bulldozer.' Roches reached out to accept the cigarette Darcy offered. 'I used to drive tanks with Leclerc. That's how I started on bulldozers. After the war. How much longer am I going to be kept here?'

'Just till the inspector's had a word with you.'

'I didn't do it, you know.'

'Nobody's said you did.'

'I only found it. That kid didn't know what it was. Probably thought it was somebody with a bad case of body odour. I knew straight away.'

'That probably makes you an expert witness.' Darcy was growing a little bored.

'It does?' Roches looked more cheerful. 'Does that mean I'll have to get up in court and tell them?'

'I expect so.'

Roches thought for a while. 'Don't they pay expert witnesses?' he asked.

Darcy smiled. 'If they have technical knowledge,' he said. 'All you've got seems to be a keen sense of smell.'

Emile Escaut was the most annoyed of all. He was a busy young man. Doing nothing occupied a great deal of his time and he objected to waiting at police headquarters to answer questions.

'Why did you fetch the police?' Darcy asked.

'I didn't. I only wanted to get in my car and drive away.'

'Where to?'

'My place. It's in the Rue de Maroc.'

Darcy studied him carefully. 'Share it with anybody?'

'Yes.'

'Who?'

'Do I have to say?'

'It might be a good idea.'

Escaut eyed Darcy for a while. 'It's a girl,' he said eventually.

Darcy nodded. 'I thought it might be,' he smiled. 'Who?'

'Just a girl.'

'Why are you so anxious to keep her name quiet? Nobody gets very worked up about that sort of thing these days.'

'Well – ' Escaut shrugged ' – she doesn't want her father to know. It's normal enough, isn't it? He's against it.'

'Lots of fathers are. On the other hand, a lot of them have got used to the scene. Is it just you he's not keen on?'

'He doesn't think I earn enough.'

'Don't you?'

'*I* think I do.'

'What do you do, anyway?'

'I'm an artist.'

Darcy's eyebrows lifted. 'You don't meet many of those. Make much at it?'

'I'm only just starting.'

'Got a studio?'

'Near the École Commerciale. Top floor of the Lamy Building.'

Darcy smiled. 'That place's about due for demolition, isn't it? If they don't pull it down soon, in fact, it'll fall down. Take care it doesn't happen while you're in it.' He paused. 'This girl of yours. What does *she* do?'

'She's a student. Faculté de Lettres.'

'How old?'

Escaut scowled. 'Old enough,' he said.

Darcy refused to let go, worrying him like a dog with a rat. 'Where's she from?' he asked.

'Here.'

'Then why is she sharing a flat with you?'

'What do you mean?'

'Kids at the university who live here usually live at home.'

'She's different. She's got a bit of money.' Escaut paused. 'The flat's hers really.'

'Is it now?' Darcy smiled. 'That's not what you said at first. Why isn't she living at home?'

'She wanted to be free. Parental ties, that sort of thing.'

'Do her parents know she's sharing it with you?'

'Er – well, no. They think she's sharing it with a girl.'

'Don't they ever come and see her?'

'Yes. But she always insists they phone ahead. Then I move out until they've gone.'

Darcy eyed him coldly. It was a pity, he thought, that investigating the dead man they'd found would necessitate seeing Emile Escaut again. He had decided he didn't like Emile Escaut very much.

# three

The next day's newspapers carried the story. *Le Bien Public* was decently sedate and gave it with the facts and the dead man's description. *France Soir* dressed it up, sparing no details and managing to suggest it was the result of a crime passionelle. *France Dimanche* would do even better at the weekend, without doubt.

Pel stared at the description. 'Forty, blue eyes, black hair, short, sturdy, plump, his hands showed he was not a labouring type. Mole on right cheek. Old scar lower down. Appendicitis scar on lower torso.'

Doctor Minet had worked all night over the corpse, and his report as usual was clear, concise and as short as possible. He set the time of death as four days before, stating that the advanced decomposition was due to the heat. Cause of death: one bullet in the brain. He didn't put it quite as simply as that, but that was exactly what he meant. Somebody had placed a gun hard up against the dead man's head and pulled the trigger.

Reaching for his jacket, Pel headed for the laboratory. It was a sterile place of long white benches and tall green cabinets, lit by fluorescent tubes. The cabinets contained lists of laundry marks, pistol types, tyres, poisons, soils, glass, foliage, wools, cottons, bones. You mention it, the laboratory probably had it. It enabled Leguyader, who was in charge, a small fierce-looking man, as bad-tempered as Pel

27

himself, to hand out his opinions on what was brought to him. He wasn't often wrong.

He wasn't very often co-operative either. He wasn't now.

'I gave you my opinion yesterday,' he said. 'That's as far as I'm prepared to go at the moment. I haven't finished. What's the hurry? The man won't run away.'

'The man who shot him might,' Pel snapped.

Leguyader refused to be budged. 'I'll be finished by this evening,' he said. 'I'll take the report home and you can ring me there. I shall enjoy having my meal interrupted.'

Pel left the office gloomily, driving the ancient Peugeot he owned and wondering when he'd be able to afford a new one. Battling his way through the screeching, honking scrum round the Place Wilson, he concentrated on getting home without the car letting him down. Pel was a naturally pessimistic soul and was always convinced it would conk out and jam the traffic near the Rue de la Liberté where everybody would laugh at him. The engine already seemed to be knocking badly and there was a smell of burning somewhere, and he was hoping against hope he wouldn't suffer the humiliation of seeing it go up in smoke.

His house looked desperately in need of paint and he realised he would eventually have to dig into his savings and get somebody to paint it. Without doubt it would bankrupt him, and he wondered if he could get one of his men to do it for him in his spare time. After all, everybody seemed to be doing two jobs these days – especially policemen, who seemed the most underpaid of all the world's workers. He sometimes wondered even if he might delay his own financial end by getting a job as a doorman at the Hôtel de la Cloche. He studied the house again. Perhaps he could get Krauss to do the job after he'd retired. He'd have time on his hands then and probably be glad of the money. Pel sighed. On the other hand, of course, like most of the things Krauss did, it would be slapdash and the whole lot would probably drop off at Pel's feet at the first sign of bad weather.

Madame Routy, his housekeeper, had the television going. It sounded like the Battle of Waterloo, or at the very least as if she had the whole neighbourhood in there arguing with her. Having a television, Pel decided, was like living the whole of your life with ten thousand other people. There always appeared to be someone having a fight or an argument in the salon, smashing up a car or making love to someone else's wife. Pel wished *he* could make love to someone else's wife.

Madame Routy greeted him ungraciously. 'I've got cutlets for dinner,' she said, making no attempt to rise. 'I'll do them when this has finished.'

Pel spent half his life waiting for something to finish. Madame Routy's day consisted of things on the television that weren't quite finished.

'Don't bother,' Pel said, making up his mind on the instant. 'I've got to go back. I'll eat out.'

She gave him a suspicious look. Ever since Pel had put his best suit on some time before to interview the Baronne de Mougy in the course of duty, she'd suspected him of having a mistress.

He changed into his next-to-best suit. On Pel it looked as if it had been cut by a cross-eyed tinker with one arm. He could never understand it. While Darcy always looked immaculate, Pel looked as if he'd been dragged from under a bus. Perhaps it was because he only had a disgruntled housekeeper while Darcy had a dozen or so adoring females all willing to slave and press and sponge.

Climbing back into his car, he drove to the city centre. He didn't particularly like eating alone but eating alone was better than eating with Madame Routy and the television. The Bar du Destin was almost as dark as a cinema, which was one reason why Pel liked it. Nobody recognised him except the owner. It was scattered about with tired plants among the pernod bottles and was full at that moment of young male students from the university with long hair, tight pants and dark glasses, all stroking the knees of young female students with long hair, tight pants and dark glasses. It was sometimes hard to differentiate. By the bar, a small fat man in high belly-holding trousers was describing the affair in the Rue du Chapeau Rouge. 'I was there,' he said. 'The police were running round like a lot of cockerels with their heads chopped off.'

Pel directed a glare at him over his coup de blanc.

'Probably some student lark,' the little man went on. 'That lot would shove up a barricade if the President wanted to go to the lavatory.' He turned to Pel. 'It was laughable,' he said. 'There must have been two dozen cops standing about, all doing nothing. There'll be a few heads rolling at the Hôtel de Police for this, you see. They were at their beautiful French best, they really were, bullying everybody just to show how efficient they are. You should have been there.'

Pel emptied his glass. 'I was,' he said.

'Well, wasn't it a shambles?'

'No,' Pel snapped. 'It wasn't.'

'Well, they closed up both ends of the street, didn't they? Those people demolishing that house couldn't get on with their job, could they? It was ridiculous.'

'No, it wasn't,' Pel said.

The little man had been on the point of sinking his drink when Pel's hostility finally seeped through. He turned aggressively. 'Who do you think you are, anyway?' he said.

Pel couldn't resist it. 'Evariste Pel,' he said. 'Inspector, Criminal Brigade, Police Judiciaire. I was in charge of the investigation.'

As he left the bar, the students had stopped pawing each other and the little man was standing with his jaw dropped open. The landlord was grinning all over his face.

'What did I say?' the little man was bleating. 'What did I say?'

Pel stood outside to regain his temper then walked round the corner to the Relais St Armand. The Relais St Armand had once been Pel's favourite restaurant. It was inexpensive, kept a chablis that burned the skin off your tongue and served the sort of andouillettes that could only have been made by someone able to work miracles. Pel was convinced that the Relais St Armand had a magician in the kitchen.

He stared at the door. He had not dared go in for months in case he found himself facing Madame Faivre-Perret. Madame Faivre-Perret was a favourite of Pel's, like the man who made the andouillettes. She ran Nanette's, a hairdressing salon in the Rue de la Liberté and ever since he'd solicited her help over one of his cases, he'd had a heavy crush on her that reduced him to a state of nerves, doubt and self-accusation.

Sadly he turned away and headed for the station buffet where he ate his meal in crushed silence. There were times when he felt a desperate need to accomplish something before his buttocks grew lean and stringy. He knew what, too, though he hesitated to let it come to the forefront of his mind and always forced it back into the dark recesses where it didn't make him feel so ashamed. While he was there, a man came in selling newspapers. Pel bought one to find out what they'd decided he'd decided about the man in the boot of the Renault.

They'd improved on the stories he'd read earlier. By this time they'd discovered a woman in Lyons. He couldn't imagine how, because the dead man hadn't yet been identified, and he put it down to the journalistic passion for *femmes fatales.* Everything these days had to have sex in it. Even the cartoons.

There was a photograph alongside the headline of a girl in the arms of a man. She appeared to be wearing no clothes and at first glance seemed to be part of the story of the dead man in the Rue du Chapeau Rouge. At second glance, however, it became obvious she belonged in the trivial affairs of a pop star just below. It was a clever trick and, for people who weren't very quick on the up-take, helped to establish the idea of a crime passionelle.

Pel frowned. The man in the car in the Rue du Chapeau Rouge, he felt, had hardly been a sex symbol – even when he was alive. Just short, balding and forty – like Pel – hardly the type to conduct deathless love affairs.

Finishing his coffee, he headed back to the Hôtel de Police. Darcy was still in the office, standing by the open window. He had it flat on its central hinges so that the maximum amount of air came in. With evening, the city had cooled and the air that swept into the room seemed to come from the hills to the north.

'Nothing turned up?'

'No, Patron. Expecting something?'

'An identification, perhaps. What do *you* make of him?'

Darcy shrugged. 'Whatever he was,' he said, 'he was a small-timer. Cheap suit. Cheap socks. Cheap shoes. He was probably just a third-rate chiseller.'

'It has the look of a gang killing,' Pel said slowly.

Darcy wasn't so sure. 'He doesn't look much like a gangster, Patron, in spite of what Doc. Minet says. Not smart enough. They're flashy dressers on the whole.'

'Perhaps he deliberately remained *unsmart*,' Pel said. 'Keeping a low profile.'

Darcy shrugged again. 'This one's profile was so low his nostrils must have been dragging along the pavement.'

'Has Leguyader come up with anything yet?'

'He's been trying to get you.'

Sitting at his desk, Pel picked up the telephone. Leguyader was his usual sarcastic self.

'I thought you'd be ringing just when I'd decided to eat,' he said.

Pel ignored the sarcasm. 'Have you finished?'

'Yes. I think he was a Parisian. The suit was labelled "Tati", and that's a cheap place. I looked it up. And the dirt on it is Paris dirt. We have it all listed. He smoked – Gauloises. He also wore false teeth and I expect we shall be able to get them identified before long. We have fingerprints, too. Was he involved with drugs?'

'Why?'

'It'd be a good reason to shoot him.'

Pel sniffed. 'So would sleeping with another man's wife. There must be a better reason than that.'

'He had benzedrine tablets in his pocket.'

'A lot?'

'Three.'

'Perhaps he was depressed and needed pepping up from time to time.' Pel knew what he was talking about. He did, too, only *he* merely smoked too many cigarettes.

Leguyader was unimpressed. 'And perhaps,' he said, 'he carried them about to sell to students. This is a university city, and students go in for that sort of thing. Isn't young Nosjean worrying about some heroin addict who was trussed up like a piece of veal? Perhaps they're connected.'

Perhaps they were, Pel thought. It was an idea. 'What about the gun?'

'7.65 mm calibre. Probably a Belgian Browning M1900 FN.'

'And the button? Off a workman's jacket, I suppose, as usual?'

Leguyader paused. 'Not this time, mon brave,' he said. 'It's bone.'

'Bone? I thought it was leather.'

'So did I. But it was bone covered with mud. It's a centimetre and a half across, brown, and with a flower motif carved out of it. It had some green thread through it attached to a fraction of green material. It doesn't come off the corpse. All his buttons were there.'

'So where did it come from?'

'A garage mechanic who did a service on the car? A hotel porter? But not a French hotel porter. When you get it back you'll see the flower's an edelweiss and the green's what's known as jaeger green – hunting green. It's a colour that's common to one or two countries to the east of France.'

'German?'

'Perhaps.' Leguyader was carefully non-committal. 'Or Swiss. The mud on it's similar to that found round Pontarlier, and Pontarlier, as you know, is in the Jura and is the entrance to Switzerland. Some of the dirt on our friend's shoes comes from Paris, some from here, and some from the Jura. You're probably looking for a Swiss mechanic with French connections.'

Pel put the telephone down, then rang Polverari's number. The judge always liked to know what was going on. He had just finished his meal and was in an expansive mood.

'It's always a button off somebody's clothing,' he said. 'But bone buttons with flower motifs sewn to Jaeger green cloth aren't all that common in France.'

Pel wondered if he could manage a few days in Switzerland at the expense of the Police Department. Polverari chuckled and thought not. Pel sighed. A few days in a Swiss hotel would have done him the world of good.

As he put the telephone down, Darcy came in from the sergeants' room. He was carrying his jacket. 'Our friend in the car?' he asked.

Pel looked up. 'Leguyader wondered if he was dealing in drugs. There were benzedrine tablets in his pocket.'

'Perhaps he took them to stay awake. People do.'

'What people?'

'All sorts. Long-distance lorry drivers, for instance. Pop stars.' Darcy grinned. 'Cops.'

'Leguyader suggested he was selling them to students.' As Pel fished in his pocket for a cigarette, Darcy pushed a packet at him. Pel took one gloomily, convinced it was the last nail in his coffin and that he'd never reach home alive.

'It's quite a thought,' he said. 'We'll go into it.'

Darcy glanced at his watch. It was nine o'clock and there was a girl in a flat in the Rue d'Ahuy waiting for him to put in an appearance. He looked at Pel. The poor old sod looked lonely, he thought. Then he pushed his sympathy aside hurriedly before Pel suggested they went to the Bar Transvaal across the road for a beer.

'Tomorrow,' he said firmly.

'Yes.' Pel, who *had* been on the point of suggesting a beer, had to agree. 'Tomorrow.'

As Darcy vanished, he sighed and went down the stairs to his car. It ought to be an exciting evening with Madame Routy, he decided.

# four

The sound of the telephone in the top apartment of the Maison Robiquet in the Rue Réauot just north of the Seine, in the St Denis district of Paris, jarred the silence with the urgency of an explosion.

The Maison Robiquet had been built long before Haussman had opened up the boulevards in the middle of the previous century and should have been pulled down long since. But somehow it had always escaped the depredations of the planners, and the sudden shriek of the bell, hurling itself like a misdirected rocket down the spiral staircase, stirred up all the ancient spectres of all its past occupants and brought the building to a state of quivering awareness.

A disturbed baby began to wail and the woman in the bed in the top apartment fought herself free of the man who was clinging to her, and reached for the telephone.

'That you, Ernestine?'

There was a long silence.

'Ernestine?'

The man tried to push the telephone back on to its cradle but the woman managed to fight him off.

'Yes,' she said. 'This is Ernestine. Who's that? Henriette?'

'Of course it is. Who've you got there?'

The woman in the bed managed with her spare hand to push away the man's arm. 'Nobody,' she said. 'I'm on my own.'

'What are you doing then? Polishing the floor? You're breathing heavily.'

'Dieu!' The woman shifted in the bed. 'What have you rung up for? To discuss what I do with myself in the middle of the night?'

There was a chuckle down the wire. 'I *know* what you do with yourself, ma vieille. I rang up because there's something in *France Soir* that might interest you.'

'I'm a bit busy at the moment –'

'I expect you are. Who is it? That big hunk of man I saw you with in the Café Antique last weekend? He'll probably be interested, too. I would, under the same circumstances.' The voice on the telephone was excited but full of good humour. 'It's on the back page. Last column. Half way down. I nearly missed it. I think you'd be wise to have a look at it.'

The telephone clicked and, staring at it, startled and irritated, the woman in the bed put it back on its cradle. Heaving over, she pushed at the man alongside her.

'For the love of God,' she snapped. 'Keep your hands to yourself. There's something in the paper.'

His head jerked up. 'We're going to read the sports page? *Now?*'

'It's not the sports page.'

'Well, the political news? It's always the same: the Communists are gaining ground. Somebody's thrown a bomb. The President's made a statement. They none of them affect us.'

'Listen, that was Henriette. She says there's something I ought to see.'

'It'll keep.'

She fought herself free and reached from the bed to where the newspaper lay on the floor alongside her, with an ashtray full of cigarette butts, a wine bottle and two dirty glasses. The man heaved over after her, so that the blankets leapt and turned as if a wounded whale were in there trying to get out.

'In the name of God, woman! – '

'Shut up! Here it is. "Fortyish, sturdy, plump. Blue eyes. Balding. Dark hair. A mole on his right cheek, with a scar just below running from the cheekbone to the mouth. Appendicitis scar on torso." Burgundy?' Leaning on her elbow, the woman lowered the paper and stared ahead of her, her eyes blank, unaware of the untidy bedroom and the scattered clothes. 'I ought to ring the police,' she said.

She made a move to leave the bed, but the man grabbed her and pulled her back, holding her down with a strong arm across her body.

'Afterwards,' he said.

'Look, Jacques – '

'Afterwards.'

Her protests grew less certain. 'Jacques – '

'Afterwards.' The word came again, like a litany.

'They've found a body.' There was a long silence. 'In Burgundy somewhere.' There was a longer silence. 'I think it's my husband.'

The following day, Darcy went round to Emile Escaut's studio near the École Commerciale. There was something about Escaut that bothered him. His face looked familiar but he wasn't sure where he'd seen him.

Never the man to let up on a hunch, on his way to the Hôtel de Police he climbed the stairs to the top of the Lamy Building. Several of the apartments were occupied by students and there was a strong smell of cats and drains. Darcy, who always expected some girl to open a door to him somewhere with the old green light shining in her eyes always made a point of wearing spotless linen and keeping himself immaculate, and his nose wrinkled fastidiously. In a city as fair as this, he felt, there should be no such place as the Lamy Building.

Escaut wasn't very pleased to see him. His studio consisted of a few canvases which even Darcy, who was no artist, could tell at once were mere daubs. He was working over a small drawing at a table and, when Darcy entered, he became extremely busy with an eraser. Glancing over his shoulder, Darcy decided that what he'd been drawing was a dirty picture and he wondered if he were in the porn trade.

He sat down on a broken-backed chair and opened the conversation cheerfully, talking about the body in the Rue du Chapeau Rouge. But the questions he asked had all been answered long before and it wasn't really that which was engaging his attention. There was something else that bothered him and little warning bells were ringing in the recesses of his mind. There were things that needed to be checked.

'Well, I'll be off,' he said eventually. 'Have a coffee before I go to the office. You'll have had yours, I suppose.'

'Yes.' Escaut remained surly.

'That's the best of having a little woman to look after you, isn't it?' Darcy smiled. 'Was she with you at the party?'

'Yes.'

Darcy's face changed and his smile vanished. 'How come you were alone when you found that car then?' he said.

Escaut flushed and Darcy pressed the point. '*Was* she at the party?'

'No.'

'Why not? A lover's tiff?'

'No – ' Escaut scowled ' – yes.'

'Make your mind up.'

'She was at her parents' house.'

'Because of the tiff?'

'No. She goes to see them occasionally.'

'But not with you, of course. What did you say her name was?'

Escaut scowled. 'I didn't.'

'No. Come to think of it, you didn't. Perhaps you'd better.'

'Why?'

'Because I'm beginning to be interested.'

'Do I have to?'

'Yes, you do.'

'It's Perdrix. Marie-Bernadette Perdrix.'

'That's an unusual name. Any relation to Georges-Robert Perdrix?'

Escaut tried not very successfully to look blank. 'Who's he?'

'Lives out Chevigny way. Big house worth a fortune. He's head of FMPS.'

'What's that?'

Darcy frowned and his voice grew harsher. 'Don't hedge with me, my friend! Your home's here in this city. You've lived here for four years. You said so yourself. And you've got eyes. One each side of your nose. To get from that flat of yours in the Rue de Maroc to this place, you go past FMPS.'

'Sometimes I go the other way.'

'And circle the city?' Darcy glared. 'Outside FMPS there's Perdrix's name. Right up there. In big red letters. Over the factory gates. Everybody in the city knows who runs it.'

'I didn't,' Escaut insisted.

'Well, never mind. *Is* she any relation?'

'Of Perdrix?' Escaut hedged. 'Well, yes, I think she is. Sort of.'

'*What* relation?'

'Daughter.'

Darcy studied Escaut with interest. 'And you didn't know who Pappy was? You didn't know he's one of the wealthiest men in the city?'

Escaut shrugged. 'I've heard of him, now you mention him.'

'How old is she?'

'Who?'

'The daughter.'

Escaut's mouth tightened. 'Nineteen,' he said. 'That's old enough. I told you.'

Darcy was still thinking about Emile Escaut when the telephone on his desk rang. Picking it up, he listened carefully. 'Who did you say?' he asked. 'Ernestine Miollis? Yes, I've got it. Apartment Nine, Maison Robiquet, Rue Réauot, St Denis, Paris. You think it's your husband, Gilles? You're pretty *sure*? Well, look, can you tell us a bit more about him? To help identify him. What did he do for a living?'

There was a long silence on the telephone. 'Why do you have to know that?' the woman asked warily.

'It helps,' Darcy said. 'To identify. That sort of thing. For instance, if he was a mechanic, he's not the man we found. He hasn't got a mechanic's hands. More like a clerk's.'

'He wasn't a mechanic,' Madame Miollis said slowly.

'He wasn't?'

'He wasn't a clerk either.'

'What *did* he do?'

'Well – ' The woman on the other end of the telephone was remarkably vague and it took Darcy another five minutes to discover that her husband didn't do anything at all in particular. He just did anything and everything. He was self-employed and always had been, occupied chiefly, it seemed, with buying and selling. A firm idea was beginning to sprout in Darcy's head and it seemed to confirm that the man found in the Rue du Chapeau Rouge was indeed Gilles Miollis, the husband of the woman on the telephone.

'We'll need you here,' he said. 'To identify him.'

'It's a bit difficult,' Madame Miollis said. 'I work at this tabac, you see.'

'This may be important,' Darcy said more sharply. 'I'll get the Quai des Orfèvres to come round to see you.'

The voice down the telephone sounded alarmed suddenly. 'I don't want the police coming here! They scare me.'

'Madame, they'll only be bringing you a train ticket. There'll be a woman detective to look after you, and we'll meet you here.'

When Darcy opened Pel's door, Pel was staring at a cigarette, wondering if he dare light it or whether it would send him reeling from the room, an immediate case for the undertaker.

'We've got an identification,' Darcy said.

Pel's head jerked up.

'Gilles Miollis, Apartment Nine, Maison Robiquet, Rue Réauot, St Denis district of Paris. I've had his wife on the phone.'

'What is he?'

'She seemed a bit vague about that. She said he worked for himself and when I asked her what at, she said she wasn't sure. He bought and sold things.'

'What things?'

'As far as I can make out, anything that was going cheap. He did things for people.'

'What sort of things?'

Darcy grinned. '*All* sorts of things. By the sound of it, Patron, he was a small-time crook on the fiddle.'

Darcy met Madame Miollis at the station. She was a brassy blonde who wore so much make-up, her face looked as if it would crack if she smiled, while her false eyelashes were long enough to sweep the ornaments off the mantelshelf. Her dress was too tight and her heels were so high she walked with her knees bent and her toes turned in like a pigeon. The policewoman who accompanied her, however, managed to have all the chic that Paris was famous for. She was slim and dark-eyed and Darcy wondered why there weren't any women police officers like her in his own city.

'How's she taking it?' he asked quietly.

'All right,' the policewoman said. 'I think she's as tough as old boots. I've brought an electric razor her husband used. It's covered with fingerprints.'

Darcy introduced himself. Madame Miollis was staring in front of her in a faintly dazed way. 'I think it's my husband,' were the first words she said.

Darcy didn't argue, but he spent most of his time between the station and the mortuary explaining that the man in Chapeau Rouge had been dead some time when he'd been found and that it might be a little unpleasant. It didn't seem to worry her too much.

The morticians had done a good job on the body and since it had been kept refrigerated for some time the smell had diminished. When Darcy pulled the sheet back Madame Miollis' face stiffened but she didn't wince or turn away, staring at the corpse as if making sure it really was dead.

'Yes,' she said at last. 'That's him. When did it happen?'

'Last weekend, the doctor thinks. On the thirteenth, perhaps.'

'What happened? Was he knocked down?'

'No,' Darcy said, watching her carefully. 'He was shot. In the back of the head.'

He'd been expecting she might show some concern and ask who could possibly have done it, as they usually did, but she took it very calmly – almost, Darcy thought, as if she'd been expecting something of the sort for some time.

'He looks a mess,' was all she said.

Pel had a small pile of notes on his desk when Madame Miollis was shown in. He had vaguely expected a frail woman bowed with grief. Madame Miollis seemed to have recovered already.

'I could do with a drink,' she said as she sat down.

'Brandy?' Pel asked, thinking she might feel a little faint.

'I'd prefer a beer,' she said. 'It's hot.'

'Send Krauss out,' Pel said to Darcy. 'And get the Quai des Orfèvres to watch the house in Paris,' he added quietly. 'We'll probably need to search it.'

Nosjean came in and put a bundle of photographs on the desk. 'From Fingerprints,' he said. 'Off the razor. They match.'

Pel lit a cigarette and looked at Madame Miollis. 'Can we have your husband's age, Madame?' he asked.

'Forty-three last birthday.'

They managed to find out over the beer that Gilles Miollis had never done a regular job in his life and that his income fluctuated a great deal. 'Sometimes he had a lot,' his wife said. 'Sometimes he had nothing. Mostly, he had nothing.'

'You've no idea what he did for a living?'

She shrugged. 'He did odd jobs. Looking after things. Running errands. Buying and selling.'

'Was he often away from home?'

'No. He usually operated in Paris.'

It was the word 'operated' which strengthened Pel's belief. Like Darcy, he had already come to the conclusion that Gilles Miollis was a small-time crook and the word confirmed his view. Like the wives of most crooks, Madame Miollis appeared to have lived with the ambiguity of her husband's life without too much effort, though she had doubtless never considered herself a crook's woman, and had obviously faced the incongruity of her situation with a deadpan expression.

He drew a deep breath. 'Forgive me if this seems hurtful, Madame,' he said. 'But was your husband known to the police?'

'Never!'

'You sure, Madame?'

'Well – '

Within five minutes, Pel had it out of her that Miollis had a criminal record and had passed more than one sojourn in the Santé.

'Did your husband associate with known criminals, Madame?'

She hesitated. 'Well,' she said. 'I think he knew a few.'

'Was he involved in criminal activities himself?'

She sighed and seemed to relinquish the struggle. 'He never stopped, did he?' she said bitterly. 'He was at it when I met him and he never gave up.'

'What sort of criminal activities?' Darcy asked.

'Well, he got sent down for helping himself from the till when he worked as a garage attendant, didn't he? We'd only been married six months then. He got a longer stretch for trying to rob some old woman at Cloisart. He got away with that one. They never found the money. Come to that, neither did I. I expect he spent it on some other piece.'

'Go on.'

'Then he did a bit of receiving and got mixed up with a car gang. They stole cars and changed the number plates. But he was never violent. Not my husband. Except for that bank thing.'

'What was that?'

'They robbed a bank at Orgueuil.'

'Who did?'

'Him and a couple of his pals. At least, the other two did. He drove the car. Somebody got hurt and he got two years for it.'

Gilles Miollis seemed to have been little more than a highly unsuccessful small-timer.

'What do you think he was doing in this city, Madame?' Pel asked.

The plump shoulders lifted.

'Did he have business down here?'

'He's been before, I know. He once told me he was going to Vichy, but I noticed he came back with a case of Burgundy from a place near Beaune, so he must have got it here. In Vichy it would be Bordeaux, wouldn't it?'

Pel sniffed. As a good Burgundian, he didn't acknowledge that there were any wines other than those from his own province.

'Did he come often?' he asked.

'I think he'd been four or five times. Perhaps five.'

'Did he say why?'

'No. He gave me money – when he had it – so I didn't ask questions. I never supposed he'd got it by working hard at anything, but money's money and I had to live. Can I go home now?'

'Wouldn't you prefer to stay at a hotel for the night?'

'I'd rather go home.'

'It'll be late when you arrive in Paris,' Pel pointed out.

She gave him a contemptuous look. 'Paris in the middle of the night's got more life in it than this place in the middle of the day,' she said. 'I'll go home.'

'Think he was smuggling something?' Pel asked Darcy. 'He was the type.'

Darcy pulled a face. 'It's only a hundred and fifty kilometres from here to the Swiss border,' he said.

'Watches? Could it have been watches? Or precision instruments. Money? Currency? Something like that? And, if so, was he executed?'

'And if he *was* executed, Patron, why?'

'Trying to take more than his share?' Pel suggested. 'Why kill him here then?' Darcy asked. 'Why not in Switzerland or wherever he was operating from?'

'We'll probably learn the answer to that when we find what it was he was smuggling. Contact the Quai des Orfèvres. Find out what's known of him.'

'Do we tell the Press he's been identified?'

'Not yet.' Pel pushed his chair back. 'Leave it for a while. It sometimes pays to leave people in the dark. Especially people who make a habit of murdering other people. They get scared and make a move. And sometimes it's the wrong one. I'll see Polverari. He'll not argue. In the meantime, I think somebody'll have to search our fat friend's home.'

This time, since Pel was only anxious to go to Paris, neither the Chief nor Judge Polverari was against the idea.

'Paris is different,' Polverari said enthusiastically. 'Everybody wants to go to Paris.'

'I don't,' Pel said earnestly. For Pel there was only one place in the world and that was Burgundy. Burgundy was a royal duchy, the richest province in France. It provided a wealth of history, an infinite variety of scenery, and a prodigious contribution to art, society and gastronomy. It had also produced Evariste Clovis Désiré Pel.

Coming from Grenoble, Polverari hadn't the same feelings and he gestured expansively. 'Everybody should go to Paris,' he said, his little black eyes bright. 'As often as possible. In fact, I think I'll come with you. You'll need a judge handy and I have to talk to the Palais de Justice there about that Lavergne woman. She's a Parisian, too. We'll make a point of enjoying ourselves. It'll do us both good. Paris is full of vice, and so long as it's kept under control, vice is good for you.'

That evening, the Quai des Orfèvres came up with all they knew about Gilles Miollis. They had a file on him as long as their arm.

'He's been in prison more times than you know about,' they said. 'All small things. Fencing. Robbery. Fraud. Pimping. You name it, he's done it.'

'Nothing big?' Darcy asked.

'Nothing that ever brought him in much money, as far as I can see. He was the errand boy. Always on the fringe.'

'Was he connected with any of the gangs?'

'He was part of the Pépé le Cornet outfit once. But that was a long time ago. He just wasn't clever enough to stay the course.

And he wasn't big enough or tough enough to be used as a heavy. He was even a bit squeamish and backed away from violence.'

'Could he have been the victim of some gang feud?'

The man in Paris hesitated. Darcy could almost hear him shrugging down the telephone. 'You never know,' he said. 'But if he was killed in a gang feud, why dump the body down there in your area?'

'Exactly,' Pel said when Darcy reported back to him. 'He was up to something, and he was up to it *here*. We'd better have a look at this flat of his.'

# five

When Pel turned up at his office the following morning for his trip to Paris he looked like Napoleon III receiving the news of his defeat at Sedan.

He had had a rough night, with Madame Routy listening to the television until the early hours. Since the television was situated directly beneath Pel's room and Madame Routy liked to pull out all the stops, he had had to listen to the programme to the very end, hearing every momentary uproar without the pleasure of knowing what it was all about. Sometimes, he felt, Madame Routy was not just hard of hearing, she was stone deaf; and Pel, who considered himself an insomniac, had thrashed about in bed until he had convinced himself he would never sleep again. In fact, he required very little sleep, but, daily considering himself exhausted by his work, he always made the mistake of going to bed too early. Getting up worn-out made him feel a martyr and feeling a martyr helped him believe he was succeeding at his job.

He gazed gloomily at the cigarette Darcy offered him as they waited for Judge Polverari to turn up, and lit it as if it were the last gesture of a man facing a firing squad.

'I wish I could give it up,' he said.

'Try acupuncture,' Darcy suggested with a grin, lighting up himself and inhaling with obvious enjoyment. 'Or you could have an operation. Have your lungs taken out, for instance. As a last resort you could even have your mouth sewn up.

'I'd stick them up my nostrils,' Pel said bitterly.

When Polverari appeared, smiling with anticipation, it was Nosjean who drove them to the station. Polverari, his arms full of magazines, was all smiles. Pel looked as if he were going to the guillotine.

'Enjoy your trip, Messieurs,' Nosjean said.

Polverari smiled. 'I intend to. I have plenty of sin in my heart and, though I feel that other slates should be kept clean, I'm not so sure about mine. Isn't that so, Pel?'

Pel managed to moderate to fretful the surly expression he wore. He'd probably drop dead in Paris, he was thinking. His cigarettes and his sins would finally catch up with him there. He wondered what his last words would be.

Grinning at his expression, Nosjean returned to the car, deciding he'd been neglecting the dead student, Cortot, for too long. Cortot had been found behind a locked door, from which the key was missing. His room-mate, Philippe Mortier, had had to use his own key to let himself in and there had been no sign of Cortot's key. It seemed to be time to do a little checking with Dr Minet.

Dr Minet welcomed him warmly. He was a fussy little man but he loved his fellow human beings, and though it didn't trouble him much to see them dead on the slab in his laboratory, as he so often did, he much preferred them alive, and preferably young like Nosjean, for whom, in his warm affectionate way, he had a special spot in his heart.

'What was it that killed him?' Nosjean asked. 'If it wasn't an overdose of drugs or any of the marks we found on his body, then what was it?'

'Let's examine it carefully, mon brave,' Minet suggested helpfully. 'Didn't you notice his colour?'

'Yes,' Nosjean said. 'He was a bit blue.'

'Know what that means?' Minet was nudging Nosjean carefully forward so that he'd be able to feel he himself had made the discovery Minet was laying before him.

'Cyanide?' Nosjean suggested. 'They turn blue with cyanide.'

'No.' Minet smiled. 'Not that, mon brave.'

'What then?'

'He was just short of air.' Minet laughed and gestured. 'He choked. One of those cords he had round him seems to have slipped and tightened underneath the larynx. It barely left a mark but it was enough to kill him. In effect, he hanged himself.'

'Committed suicide?'

'What do you think?'

Nosjean finally realised he was being given a lesson in forensic deduction and he applied his mind to it. Suicides slashed their wrists, turned on gas jets, shot themselves, dived off cliffs, jumped from windows, swallowed rat poison, ammonia or sleeping tablets. Or, finally, hanged themselves. Cortot seemed to have hanged himself, but not deliberately. And where did all that rope come in?

'Suicides don't usually truss themselves up first,' he said.

'No, mon brave,' Minet smiled. 'They don't.'

'So, what?' To Nosjean it looked more like an accident after somebody had been playing a joke. Students got up to funny things – like setting fire to people's hair, putting vodka into beer, carrying beds containing sleeping fellow students downstairs and leaving them in the street. Sometimes the jokes went too far and someone got hurt. Sometimes they even died. He wondered if someone had tried to play a joke on Cortot.

'I think I'll go and see that friend of his again,' he said.

'I think,' Minet agreed cheerfully, 'that would be a very good idea.'

51

Philippe Mortier's apartment was in an old house in the area of the Place du Creux d'Enfer. A lot of university lecturers, technicians and students lived in the area, all jammed together cheek by jowl, filling the bars and eating side by side in the little restaurants that catered for them. It wasn't a poverty-stricken apartment of the sort students usually occupied. It had two bedrooms, a living room, a kitchen and a bathroom, which was four more rooms than most students had. But Mortier appeared to have money because his father was a lawyer in Amiens.

'I paid for it,' he admitted.

Despite the money and the background, however, and despite the space, the rooms still resembled most student apartments in one thing at least: there were unmade beds, and dirty plates, cups and glasses about.

'We never seemed to have time to clear up,' Mortier said, picking up books, piles of papers and clothing. 'We always seemed to be busy.'

He pushed a cat from where it was sitting on a denim jacket and lifted the jacket. Underneath it was a plate. Picking up the plate, he put it on the table and indicated the chair to Nosjean.

'Look out for the spring,' he said. 'It'll probably spike your backside. What do you want to know?'

What Nosjean chiefly wanted to know was why Mortier shared the apartment with Cortot.

Mortier shrugged. 'Just to have somebody around,' he said. 'It could have been anybody. He just happened to be there. I wanted company. Kids who have rooms to themselves end up hanging themselves from the banisters. I have three brothers and a sister and I'm used to having people around. He paid his share of the food.'

Nosjean studied Mortier. He was tall with strong features, nothing like Cortot's more sensitive cast of countenance. He was also well in control of himself, while Cortot, from

Nosjean's enquiries, appeared to have been a nervous young man, unsure of himself and his place in society. The two didn't seem to go together.

'Have you decided it's murder or something?' Mortier asked.

'At the moment,' Nosjean admitted, 'we've decided nothing. There are no wounds and he didn't die from an overdose of drugs. But he or somebody else tied him up. So why? Tell me what happened?'

Mortier shrugged and lit a cigarette. 'I'd been to Paris for the weekend,' he said.

'Proof?' Nosjean asked.

Mortier grinned at him. 'My parents were there. They'll tell you. When I came back, he was lying on the floor, trussed up like a Sunday joint.'

Nosjean wrote in his notebook and looked up. 'How long had you known him?'

'Ever since I came to the university here. Two years or so.

'How did you meet him?'

'Music society. Both keen on Debussy.'

'Ah!' Nosjean's tastes still lay in the direction of pop, so he carefully dodged the subject. 'Did you know he took drugs?'

'I'd guessed,' Mortier admitted. 'I was getting worried, to tell the truth.'

'Did you ever see him at it?'

'No.'

'Did you ever see any syringes? Anything like that?'

'No. That's the point. And you can't accuse someone. He must have done it all in his bedroom.'

'Did you ever notice anything strange about him?'

'He seemed to sleep a lot. Sometimes he was irritable and lost his temper. At other times, though, he was perfectly easy to get on with.'

'Have *you* ever taken drugs?'

Mortier hesitated. 'Well, everybody has a go at pot, don't they?'

'I don't,' Nosjean said stiffly.

'Well, you're a policeman. That's different. You're not under the same pressures.'

Nosjean almost laughed out loud. He couldn't think of anything more pressurised than the life of an underpaid, overworked policeman, usually running three or four enquiries at a time. At that moment, Nosjean was checking Cortot's background, an assault at Chevannes and a break-in at Longvic, and was also involved in the new enquiry on the body found in the boot of the car in the Rue du Chapeau Rouge.

He returned to his notebook. 'Cortot,' he said. 'According to the doctor, he'd just had a fix. If he had, why did he end up dead? Why allow himself to be trussed up? That's normally just the time when addicts don't risk their lives this way. It's the one time when they're happy.'

Mortier shrugged.

'How long do you think he'd been at it?'

'A few months, I think. Six? Perhaps more.'

'Where did he come from?'

'Audeux. His father was an insurance clerk.' Mortier made it sound a very indifferent occupation. 'Not much money. But no other children. Perhaps he was lonely. Perhaps that's why he was glad to share the apartment. He moved in here last October when the new term started.'

'So he must have got on to the stuff here at the university.'

Mortier shrugged. 'Well, Audeux is a small place. This is a city. Most cities have places where you can get things like that.'

'Do they?' Nosjean said, interested.

'Well, don't they?'

'Do *you* know these places?'

Mortier gestured. 'No. But people get them, so they must exist.'

'Did he show much interest in drugs?'

'He once said he saw someone giving himself a fix in the washroom in the Faculté des Sciences.'

It occurred to Nosjean that it might be a good idea for someone to keep an eye on the Faculté des Sciences. He made a note of it and looked up again. 'He was twenty-six,' he said. 'That's a bit old for a student, isn't it?'

'Well, yes,' Mortier agreed. 'That's usually the post-graduate age. But he'd been in the Navy, you see? Not his military service. He volunteered. I think he was running away from his home at the time. But when he got in, he hated it and deserted. He did time for it. Eventually he got out on medical grounds.'

'I'd have thought if he was a lonely type he'd have enjoyed being with other men.'

Mortier gestured. 'He was a bit weak. They probably teased him.'

'Did you?'

'No. We got on very well.'

'Have *you* been in the Navy?'

Mortier shuddered. 'Not me.'

'What else do you know about him?'

'He was trained in electronics in the Navy and he'd decided to go in for it properly. I think he intended to go into computers. Something of that sort. There's a lot of money in computers. Perhaps that's what appealed. He'd never had much.'

'What are *you* studying?'

'Humanities.'

Nosjean wasn't sure what Humanities were, so he didn't pursue the matter. 'Know where he got these drugs?' he asked.

'No idea.'

'Know any of his friends?'

'Just the few I saw him with.'

'Can you give names?'

Mortier shrugged. 'Achille Lorre. He's at the Faculté de Médecine. Jean-Pierre Ramou. He's French Literature. Paul-Edouard Hertot. He's Sociology.'

'All different subjects!'

'Yes.'

'What did they have in common then?'

Mortier shrugged. 'Nothing that I know of.'

'Unless,' Nosjean said, 'it was drugs.'

# six

Polverari and Pel arrived in Paris at midday. Depositing their luggage at their hotel, they used the same taxi to collect a plainclothes detective and a uniformed man from the Quai des Orfèvres and took them to the Maison Robiquet.

The Rue Réauot, with its battered walls and narrow corners, was a billstickers' paradise. There were advertisements for night clubs and discos and political parties, even a red Communist poster – still gaudy after several months of exposure – 'Homage to the Heroes of the Commune of 1871. Service at the Wall of Père Lachaise. Sunday 11.30. Beneath, someone had written 'Down with the politicians – even Communists.' Beneath this again, someone else had scrawled 'Save oil. Burn tourists.' The capital seemed to be fit and well.

The caretaker of the Maison Robiquet was an elderly man with one leg who lived in a small room off the hall that smelled like a dog's basket.

'Miollis?' He jerked his stick upwards. 'Top floor.'

The stairs were dark and illuminated by minutière bulbs apparently adjusted to switch off before their time, so that they had to grope their way upwards for most of the way in semi-darkness. As they went, they passed dog-eared cards drawing-pinned to doors: Alphonse Doré, Plombier. Théodore de Ramy, Assurance de la Ville. Odette Brevsky, Corsetière. They were on parade like a procession of failures. The Maison Robiquet looked the sort of place where failures found themselves and they seemed to go with Gilles Miollis and his trivial attempts at crime.

The top floor was lit by a dirty skylight and on the door this time the card said *Gilles Miollis, Affaires de l'Arrondissement.* It was an imposing title for an unsuccessful shyster, Pel decided, but, he supposed, living with Alphonse Doré, Théodore de Ramy and Odette Brevsky, Miollis' pride had obliged him to call himself something, and he could hardly have a card with 'Small-time Crook' on it.

The bell didn't appear to work, so they hammered on the door. When she opened it, Madame Miollis looked in even worse shape than when she'd been in Pel's office. She hadn't done her hair and didn't appear to have washed, so that her make-up from the day before was smeared.

'What do you want?' she demanded. 'I've told you all I know.'

'We need to search your husband's effects,' Pel said.

The look on her face showed her concern. 'You can't,' she said.

'I think we can,' Polverari pointed out. 'We have a search warrant.'

She opened the door unwillingly. The apartment was as untidy as she was herself. The search was careful but, apart from a few small items of jewellery which Madame Miollis claimed were hers but which Polverari insisted on taking away for checking, there was nothing incriminating and nothing to indicate what Gilles Miollis had been up to in Burgundy.

'Did your husband ever go to Marseilles?' Pel asked.

'Occasionally.'

'On business?'

She shrugged.

'Was he ever connected with the Paris gangs?'

Her answer was oblique. 'He was scared stiff of them.'

'How about Marseilles? Did he ever operate down there?'

'No. We once went there for a holiday, and he started working the Vieux Port, but one of the louches – the heavies – came up to him and took him into a bar.'

'Whose heavies?' Pel asked.

'He said he was from Maurice Tagliacci.'

Pel made a note of the name. 'What happened?' he asked.

'There was a discussion.'

Pel glanced at Polverari. It was a notable understatement. They could just imagine the big man leaning over Miollis, all smiles but making it quite clear that anybody who got ideas above his station was likely to aggravate the men who controlled the prostitutes, casinos and big business crime from Marseilles to Nice. It was something the tourists never saw on their summer holidays.

'Go on,' Pel said.

Madame Miollis shrugged. 'We left the following day. I didn't want to tangle with that lot. Not after what happened in the Bar du Téléphone in 1978. Nine dead and one wounded – mown down by sub-machine guns. When they do anything down there, they do it big.'

Pel nodded. Gilles Miollis appeared to have been a very cautious operator.

'Did your husband have a passport?' he asked.

Madame Miollis stared. 'Of course.'

'Where is it?'

She crossed to an ancient dresser of enormous proportions – how it had been carried up the stairs Pel couldn't imagine – opened a drawer and rooted about, tossing out old socks, papers and notebooks.

'It's missing,' she said. 'He always kept it in here. Perhaps he sold it.'

'Why would he do that?'

'Because – ' she stopped dead.

'Well?'

59

She gestured hopelessly. 'You can get a lot of money for a passport, can't you? They change the photograph.'

'Do they?' Pel was bland. 'How do you know?'

'Well – ' she gestured and Pel suspected that Miollis had done a bit of passport selling among his other activities ' – I've read it. In the newspapers.'

'You don't want to believe all the papers say,' Pel pointed out. 'Did he have it with him when he last left home?'

'How do I know? I never knew whether he was going abroad or going to the moon. He didn't tell me.'

'Could you tell when he'd been abroad?'

'Once he brought me back a watch from Switzerland.'

Pel exchanged a glance with Polverari.

'That all?'

'Cigarettes. They were cheap, I suppose.'

As she began to stuff the papers and notebooks back into the drawer, Pel stepped forward. 'We'd better have those, Madame,' he said. 'We might need to examine them.'

Drawing Polverari to one side, he spoke quietly. 'I think perhaps we should bring in sniffer dogs. You don't get killed for the sort of stuff Miollis was normally mixed up with. And he appears to have crossed the frontier more than once.'

While they talked, there was a bang on the door and Madame Miollis turned, her face worried. Pel crossed to the hall and turned the handle. On the landing outside a tall heavy man with dark eyebrows like Mephistopheles was leaning on the wall, smoking. As he saw Pel, he bounded upright, his face dark and angry.

'Who in God's name are you?' he demanded.

He pushed the door open then, seeing the policemen and Polverari, he immediately swung round and began to bolt down the stairs.

'Get him!' Pel screeched.

The uniformed man barged past to clatter down the stairs, with Pel stumbling after him. The big man was younger and was gaining on them fast until he reached the first landing, where he happened to bump into Théodore de Ramy, Assurance de la Ville, who was just coming up. Théodore de Ramy was in his seventies, weighed about as much as a feather duster, and was hardly the man to put up a fight but, because of his age, he carried a walking stick and, as he was brushed aside, it was this that got between the tall man's legs.

He took a nosedive down the stairs on his head just as the uniformed policeman fell over Théodore de Ramy's skinny legs and went down after him. By the grace of God the policeman landed on top and when Pel arrived, the panting policeman was just dragging the big man to his feet, while Théodore de Ramy lay on his back on the landing above, shrieking blue murder and claiming he'd been attacked.

'Bring him upstairs,' Pel snapped.

. The big man with the eyebrows was pushed and shoved and walloped up the stairs by the policeman who was out of breath, and in a bad temper because he had a bruise on his knee and had lost a button off his jacket. When the big man decided to turn and chance it, the policeman's gun was jabbed hard in his ribs.

'Shove him inside,' Pel said. 'Then go down and quieten that old lunatic on the first landing and send someone for help. You'd better leave me your gun, while you're at it, too. This little beauty's bigger than me and he doesn't look very pleased.'

As the policeman vanished, Pel balanced the gun in his hand and made the tall man turn with his face to the wall.

'Alors,' he said. 'Just keep your hands up and think pure thoughts. We will now conduct an enquiry. We're police. Who are you?'

There was a long silence then the big man decided it might be safer to answer. 'Treguy,' he said. 'Jacques Treguy.'

'And what do you want here?'

'Nothing.'

'And that's why you came, eh?' the plain clothes man from the Quai d'Orfèvres asked. 'For no reason at all.'

Treguy gestured. 'I'm just a friend of Madame Miollis,' he said. 'And – of course – Monsieur Miollis. I was just passing.'

'To offer condolences?'

Treguy was quick to take advantage of the suggestion. 'That's it,' he said. 'I heard about him. We were good friends.'

'Then you'll know what his line of business was?' Pel said.

'Line of business? Gilles?' Treguy laughed. 'He hadn't got a line of business.'

'What did he live on then?'

'This and that.'

The same old story, Pel thought. Nobody seemed able to pin down exactly what Miollis did.

'Did you know he had a criminal record?'

Treguy hesitated. 'Well – yes, I did.'

'Have you?'

'Have I what?'

'A criminal record.'

Treguy's face darkened. 'What is this? Are you starting to investigate *me* now?'

'Who said we were investigating anybody? We're trying to clear up a death. *Have* you a criminal record?'

'No, I haven't.'

'Then why did you bolt when you saw the police?'

'I didn't bolt.' Treguy paused, his eyebrows working. 'I – I suddenly remembered I'd got an appointment.'

Polverari laughed out loud. 'My friend,' he said, 'that's the best I've heard in many years of dealing with people like you. You'd better tell the truth.'

Treguy frowned. 'I've been in trouble once or twice.'

'What for?'

'Do I have to say?'

'Yes, you do.'

'I got involved with the police over a bit of – well, I did time. I was only a kid in those days.'

'Did you ever work with Miollis?'

'Not likely.'

'Why "not likely"?'

'He wouldn't know his arse from his elbow.'

Pel looked at Treguy. He was smartly dressed with a good suit and neat shoes. 'Meaning that you do?' he said. 'He was just a small-timer who wasn't very good, while you were in the big time?'

Treguy scowled. 'I didn't say that.'

'That's what you seemed to mean.' Pel peered up at him. 'We'll check up on you, my friend.'

Treguy exchanged glances with Madame Miollis and Pel waited, his eyes questioning.

'We're just friends, that's all,' Madame Miollis said.

Pel watched them with interest. 'Where were you in the last few days?' he asked. 'Can you account for where you've been?'

Treguy thought. 'Yes, I can,' he said. 'No trouble.'

As they talked, the uniformed man returned with two others. The screeching on the bottom floor had come to a stop so they assumed that Théodore de Ramy, Assurance de la Ville, had been sorted out, dusted down and polished within an inch of his life.

'We've got a policewoman in there,' the uniformed man said. 'She's making coffee. I think he'd be quite happy to be knocked over every day of his life if she could come to mop his brow afterwards. He was getting a bit frisky when I left and she'll probably have to hit him over the head with the saucepan.

The tracker dog arrived soon afterwards. It got to work at once, moving excitedly about the apartment, its nose probing the corners, its interest centred chiefly on the wardrobe in

Madame Miollis' bedroom. As they opened the door, it jerked forward, its head among the clothes.

'Get that lot out!'

As they laid the clothes on the bed, Madame Miollis began to cry.

'It was nothing to do with me!' she wailed.

In the empty wardrobe, the dog was concerned with a corner away from the light and, probing under the wallpaper that lined the bottom, they found a small carefully fitted flap that looked as if it had been cut out with a fretsaw. The dog handler pulled out a penknife.

'The usual,' he said.

He lifted out the slotted square of wood with his knife, and putting his hand inside, produced a small flat tin. Opening it, he sniffed.

'This is what he kept it in,' he announced. 'It's heroin. But not much. Just a little.'

Pel turned to Madame Miollis whose tears had completed the ruin of her make-up. 'Was your husband a drug pusher?' he asked.

'I don't know anything about it.'

The plainclothes man glared at her. 'Then why are you crying, Madame?'

'Because you're making my home a tip.'

Considering how it had looked before, Pel felt she hadn't much to complain about.

At the Quai des Orfèvres, they consulted with the inspector in charge of the narcotics squad. He studied the tin and looked at a report in his hand.

'He's not known to be part of the drugs scene here,' he said cautiously.

'But he obviously was, wasn't he?' Polverari said.

The inspector shrugged. 'He must have been involved with some Marseilles crowd smuggling from Italy or somewhere, and broke his contract by taking the money but keeping some of the stuff back to sell himself. We know most of them and suspect a lot more, but Miollis is a new name.'

'What about Treguy?'

'He's a heavy. Not too bright. He runs with Pépé le Cornet's gang. He leans on people for them. He's got a record of violence. Robbery, threats, assault with a deadly weapon. One suspected murder. He came here from Marseilles.'

'Was he ever part of the set-up run by a Maurice Tagliacci?'

The inspector pulled a face. 'He might have been. Tagliacci's a new one. Up and coming. Beginning to worry the usual lot. The police, too. Would you like us to hold Treguy? We can. On suspicion.'

Pel gestured. 'I think you'll have to let them both go,' he said. 'But perhaps you'd better keep an eye on them just in case.'

That night, Polverari insisted they should celebrate the excitement of the day by dining in the city. Since he'd married a wealthy wife, he was never afraid to spend, and eating was one of his delights. He knew a restaurant beyond St Germain des Prés where you could eat roast sucking pig. It was a drab place with bare brick walls and the pig was greasy and overcooked, but Polverari loved it and thought a show would be a good idea to follow. Pel, whose idea of a good time was fishing or a fierce game of boules, was not so keen.

The show turned out to be a place near the Place Pigalle. It was full of tourists and was colourful, noisy and melodious, and contained more girls without clothes than Pel had dreamed existed. Polverari thoroughly enjoyed himself. He was a man who enjoyed every virtue in life but made no bones about enjoying its vices, too.

Back in his room, his stomach queasy from the pork, the wine, the cream that had been poured on the English strawberries, and finally the champagne they'd swallowed at the night club, Pel found he couldn't sleep. Tossing and turning for a while, certain he was going to have a bad night – Pel was always certain he was going to have a bad night – in the end, he sat up and started going through the papers in his briefcase that he'd brought from Miollis' flat. Most of it was gibberish about insurances – Miollis seemed to have been taking care of his old age – rent accounts and little additions and subtractions on deals he appeared to have done. His total profits seemed low. The papers seemed to lead nowhere until Pel noticed a number written in pencil on the corner of one of them – 80-35-01-601. He might not have noticed it but for finding Miollis' body where they had; now he recognised it as a St Seine l'Abbaye number, and St Seine l'Abbaye was in the Côte d'Or area of Burgundy.

He decided to try it, and picked up the telephone. He was answered by a speaking machine. 'This is Archavannes', Hauliers. The office is now closed but if you will please leave a message and your telephone number you will be contacted as soon as the office reopens. Please speak as soon as this message ends.'

As the tape stopped, Pel glared at the telephone in disgust. He hated conducting conversations with machines and for a moment felt like answering with 'And this, if you please, is Evariste Clovis Désiré Pel, Inspector, Police Judiciaire. I will now give you a selection of songs from my extensive repertoire.' Instead he dialled Directory Enquiries.

The operator seemed to be out making himself a cup of coffee, and when eventually he deigned to answer, Pel was in a bad temper.

'Archavannes',' he snarled. 'Hauliers. Telephone number, St Seine l'Abbaye – 35-01-601. Can you give me the full address?'

'One moment.' There was a pause and the voice came back full of enthusiasm. 'Archavannes'. Haulage contractors. St Peuple.'

Pel lit a cigarette and gulped at the smoke as if he had died and the smoke could bring him back to life. St Peuple was twenty kilometres from St Seine l'Abbaye and forty from his office in the Hôtel de Police. He had struck lucky.

He was just about to place the sheet of paper back in his briefcase to be filed, when he decided not to waste time. Glancing at his watch he saw it had not long gone midnight and, if he knew Darcy, he wouldn't be asleep yet. He might be in bed. But he wouldn't be asleep.

He was dead right. Darcy *was* in bed and he *wasn't* asleep. His voice was brisk as he answered the telephone and Pel could tell there was someone with him. He could hear movements, then there was a crash as if something had been knocked over and a soft voice said 'Merde!'

'What was that?' Pel asked.

'Just me,' Darcy said cheerfully. 'I knocked a glass over. I was in bed with a whisky and – er – a book.'

Pel didn't argue. Darcy was far too good a sergeant for him to question what he got up to in his spare time.

'Archavannes',' he said. 'Hauliers, at St Peuple. Check up on them.'

'Now?' Darcy sounded alarmed.

'Before I get back tomorrow. I wouldn't wish to take you from your book.'

Darcy laughed. 'Right, Patron! I'll do that. What have they been up to?'

'I don't know,' Pel said. 'Probably nothing. But it might be a good idea to pay them a visit.'

## seven

Pel wasn't sorry to be back in Burgundy. Paris gave him a bad stomach and pains in the head.

He had visited relations there as a boy, but that had been in the days when every corner was a famous picture that filled you with a warm flooding affection. The streets had still glowed in those days as Utrillo had painted them, and the misty water had shimmered as Corot had seen it, and he had thought then that he might like to work in Paris, feasting his eyes for the rest of his life on its steeples, domes and cupolas, on its centuries of life and architecture. It was different now. The crowded world demanded space and Paris, like everywhere else, had gone upwards. Skyscrapers spoiled the view from Sacré Coeur and vast new blocks lined the motorway out of the city to the south.

As he stepped off the train that brought him home, he drew a deep breath as though he had just returned to the surface after being at the bottom of the sea. This, he thought, despite the ancient Peugeot he drove, despite the badly painted house that looked as though it were about to fall down, despite Madame Routy and the television that drove him demented, despite the job he considered sadly underpaid and grossly over-demanding, was where he belonged. He could easily leave Paris to the Americans.

Darcy was sitting at his desk writing in his notebook when he arrived at the Hôtel de Police. He looked up and grinned.

'Enjoy yourself, Patron?' he asked.

'I didn't go for a holiday,' Pel said stiffly.

'There's still no need to waste the place, Patron. Seen the paper?' He tossed across *France Soir.* There was a picture of Pel looking as if he'd been struck by lightning, and a great deal of the usual speculation. The hints of a great love affair between Miollis and his wife made Pel want to vomit.

GILLES ET ERNESTINE: LE TERRIBLE SILENCE.

Judging by the headlines and the heavily-posed picture of Madame Miollis gazing sadly but with little regard for the truth at a photograph of her husband, they could have been Héloïse and Abelard, instead of a small-time crook and his moll.

Pel glared at the story and tossed the paper back. 'Did you find out about Archavannes'?' he asked sourly.

Darcy nodded. 'Yes, Patron. Run by a guy called Louis-Arnold Archavanne. He's in his forties. His father started it in a small way after the war but he died eight years ago, and this Archavanne started to expand about three years ago. New lorries. New buildings. More staff. It's a thriving concern.'

Pel took out a cigarette, eyed it warily, hesitated, then shoved it between his lips with a despairing gesture. Lighting it, he dragged the smoke down to his socks, coughed a few times, and looked up with a flushed face.

'Let's go and see him,' he said.

'We can't, Patron,' Darcy pointed out. 'He's away today. I enquired. In case you hadn't noticed, it's Saturday.'

'*I* work on Saturday.'

'*He* doesn't. I fixed it for Monday. At his home. It's just down the road from the business.'

'Right. Send Nosjean in.'

Nosjean appeared cheerfully. He was in good form. He'd spent the evening before at Odile Chenandier's flat. It always did Nosjean good to see Odile Chenandier because to

Nosjean she seemed the only person in the world more retiring than he was.

'That enquiry you're on,' Pel said. 'How's it going?'

'Not much so far, Patron,' Nosjean admitted. 'But it's moving ahead. I picked up three names: Lorre, Hertot and Ramou. All students. All different faculties. All different subjects. They were friends of Cortot's. They've used drugs. I brought them in and questioned them.'

Pel frowned. 'We could pull in a dozen a day if we tried,' he said. 'There's not much future in that. The man we want's the man who's pushing it. Do they still use drugs?'

'They say not and they say they were soft drugs, anyway.'

'Soft or hard, they're all drugs. One leads to another. Did they know Cortot was on heroin?'

'They thought so. They didn't know who was supplying him, but they mentioned a man called Nino.'

'Italian?'

'They didn't know. They say they've never seen him and never spoken to him. They got their stuff – mostly pot – from other students. No heroin. They swore no heroin. They only knew Cortot because they went to the parties he went to.'

'Drug parties?'

'Yes.'

'Did they know anything else about this Nino?'

'They thought he came from Auxonne. I went back to Mortier. He said he often lent Cortot money. He supposed he used it to buy drugs.'

'Can Professor Foussier help? He's supposed to head this anti-drug committee at the University.'

Nosjean pulled a face. 'Patron, he talks a lot and likes to think he's living dangerously, and he's always on the telephone with new information. But it always seems to be information we've already got. I don't think he's even penetrated the fringe.'

Pel frowned. He'd had occasion to contact Professor Foussier himself. A fussy, handsome forty-year-old with long stork-like legs, he was too overblown for Pel and far too fond of himself. Every woman in the city seemed to belong to his fan club and many of them would happily have climbed into bed with him. The committees he served on always had a plethora of women from the expensive avenues of the city and he'd noticed there were a few more from Paris, even a few titles. Not just Second Empire titles, either, which didn't even impress the servants.

'How about that rope trick of Cortot's?' he asked. 'Was it a student lark? Because if it was, we'll want to know who did it. Did these students you mention have anything to do with it?'

'They say they never saw him at all that day. They attended all their classes and in the evening they drank together in the Bar Mistral, ate in a restaurant near the University, then went to Hertot's rooms. They were all a little drunk and they spent the night there together. They each confirm for the others.'

'They could all be lying. I'll want to know who this Nino is. Find out. And we'll have this lot in and talk to them. Send Misset in as you go out.'

Misset's first words were to ask for the night off.

Pel glared. 'Why?'

'My wife needs me.'

'I expect Krauss' wife needs *him*,' Pel snapped. 'And . Lagé's needs him. Why do *you* expect special treatment?'

'I've got more children than they have.'

'You can hardly make that an excuse. Because they're more careful, *you* can hardly expect to collect the rewards.'

Misset's face went stiff. 'The Church's views on birth control are well known, Patron.'

Pel waved his objections aside. 'What about this Baranquin character?' he asked. 'The break-ins.'

71

'He *must* have had an accomplice, Patron. I've worked it out.'

Pel glared. 'Is that *all* you've worked out?'

'We've been occupied with this Miollis thing, Patron.'

Pel grunted. 'Bend your mind to it, Misset,' he said. He spoke softly but he managed to inject a great deal of menace into his words. 'And as you go out, send Lagé in.'

Lagé was cheerful. He was snowed under with reports and his fingers ached with typing. He wasn't the brightest of detectives but he was willing.

'Your hit-and-run?' Pel said.

'Progressing, Patron. I think that's how it's going to turn out. Not murder. Judge Brisard's handling it.'

'Stay with it,' Pel said. 'Let's see Krauss now.'

I might as well make myself thoroughly depressed, he thought, and Krauss ought to provide the grande finale.

At midday Pel went to see Judge Polverari, who was still in a glow of pleasure after his visit to Paris and in no mood to worry. He insisted on taking Pel out for a beer at the Bar du Destin.

'Archavanne will wait,' he said.

Pel went home gloomily, wondering what sort of horror the weekend would produce. Madame Routy was growing more indifferent to his wishes with every week that passed. Food was bad, the house was not much cared for, and Pel felt as if he'd been orphaned. What he needed, as Darcy had told him many times, was a good woman to love and cherish him, to iron his shirts, to provide good food, to get up when he was called out in the middle of the night so as to offer a cup of hot coffee before he plunged into the bitter air, and to welcome him back with more coffee, perhaps even a brandy, and above all a warm bed.

Somewhere in his life, Pel felt, he had missed out. There had been a time when he'd thought he might marry a girl from Vieilly, the village where he'd lived as a boy. She'd been slim and laughing and in her way elegant. Hardly a Madame Faivre-Perret, who looked so well dressed she seemed to have just been taken out of a box for display, but prettily clothed in a rustic sort of way. He had spent half his youth gazing at her, trying to decide whether he was suffering from love or just plain lust, and devising schemes to get her in dark corners that had never seemed to come to anything. Once, when he'd made sergeant, he had gone back full of nostalgia to look her up, but she'd married a butcher, had four children and grown fat. Life was full of nasty knocks.

When he opened the door, the television was going full blast and sounded like a pile-up on the N74. There was, however, a vast bonus in the presence of Didier Darras. Didier Darras was twelve years old and Madame Routy's nephew; and from time to time, when Madame Routy's sister had to disappear to look after her sick father-in-law, Didier Darras came to stay with Madame Routy. Pel could think of nothing more likely to make the evening worth while.

The meal was a veal stew, so bland it was tasteless, and the wine was leftovers from the previous day, sour enough, Pel decided, to give him indigestion for a week. But afterwards, they played boules in the lane behind the house and on the Sunday went fishing at St Broing.

'Why didn't you ever get married, Monsieur Pel?' Didier asked as they sat watching their rods.

'Nobody ever asked me,' Pel said.

'I thought the man asked the woman.'

'Just a joke,' Pel said feebly.

'I'm going to marry Louise Blay. She lives next door. I used to pull the legs off her dolls.'

'And now?'

'She doesn't want to play with dolls any more. She's different.'

'It's surprising,' Pel agreed. 'But this, I hope, isn't the only reason why you intend to marry her.'

'Oh, no. I like her. There's only one trouble. She sends letters to me. She's always writing letters. Not love letters you understand – '

'I trust not, mon brave.'

' – but letters, all the same. Telling me what she's doing, where she's going. I don't write back. I don't like letters. They give too much away, don't they? My father laughs. He says "Say it with flowers, say it with drink, say it with chocolates, but never with ink." What does he mean?'

Pel smiled. 'The same as you, I imagine, mon brave. Never put it in writing. He's probably wise.'

They found a restaurant at Dinot. It was nothing to write home about, but the soup was good and they served trout. When they got home, Madame Routy, who had prepared a casserole, was speechless with fury. It fell off Pel like water off a duck's back.

The following morning while he was eating his breakfast Nosjean telephoned. 'I've found out who Nino is, Patron,' he said. 'He's a chap called Fran Nincic. I got the name from a girl friend of that student, Ramou. Ramou swears he doesn't know him, but I'm not sure I believe him. I've checked the telephone directory but there's nobody of that name.

Pel wrote the name down on a piece of paper and went back to his breakfast. Didier was sitting alongside him and he glanced at what Pel had written down.

'What's that?' he asked.

'It's a name,' Pel said.

Didier stared at it. 'I've never heard anybody called that before,' he said. 'Fran Nincic. That's a funny name.'

Pel stared at what he'd written. Since you mentioned it, he thought, it *was* a funny name.

It was funny enough, in fact, to try on Darcy when he got to the office.

'It isn't French,' Darcy said. 'But what *is* these days? Nege-
bauer. Niekreszewicz. Mamedoff, Abu Alir, Han Sung. I've
come across them all in the last year or so. The country's full
of the fag-ends of pogroms, the old colonial empire and
everybody else's cast-offs.'

'Let's find out, shall we?' Pel suggested. 'Who's the
expert?'

'How about the University, Patron? There must be a
faculty that deals with ethnics.'

'Right,' Pel said. 'Get Misset on it. He doesn't seem very
busy. Then organise a car. I want to see this Archavanne.'

Archavanne's business seemed to consist of several new
corrugated iron sheds like hangars in a field just outside St
Peuple. St Peuple was only a small place, with one bar, one
café and a few houses, a typical Côte d'Or village of ancient
farm buildings just beyond St Seine l'Abbaye. You could see
it as you descended the hill from Cestres, a grey sprawl of old
stones and weathered timbers so thick and hard the ravages
of hundreds of years of woodworm had barely touched them.
Archavanne's garage lay in the bottom of a valley with steep
fields on either side at a point where the road flattened out
to give ample space for a row of yellow-painted lorries,
trucks and vans. Further along, hidden by a row of trees, was
a new house, red-brick, ugly and big for the area, with wide
windows and terraced gardens made from the slopes of a
field. They looked new, cheap and nasty, with rows of
yellow-painted pots full of geraniums.

Louis-Arnold Archavanne was a squarely-built man who
gave the impression that he had once been a lorry driver
himself.

'But, of course,' he admitted. 'I did my time at it. I worked
for my father. Eighteen years. All over the Continent. Spain,
Italy, Austria, Switzerland, Germany, Holland, Belgium.
Everywhere you could send a lorry I took one.'

He was bald-headed, with eyes heavily wrinkled as though he had peered through too many windscreens into too many suns, and thick forearms strengthened by wrestling for hours at a time with heavy steering wheels.

He also laughed a lot, as though he enjoyed himself and enjoyed enjoying himself. His voice was loud and he spoke most of the time in a shout, as if he'd spent his life trying to talk over the roar of a truck engine.

'We're not big yet,' he said. 'But we'll get bigger.'

He seemed to revel in his growing wealth and importance, and Pel caught his eye more than once dwelling lovingly on the appalling room they were in. His wife, who brought the drinks in, went with it. She looked like Archavanne, and Pel reflected that men's wives often began to look like them after twenty years of marriage. Like Archavanne, she was square and solid, with too much make-up, and like Archavanne she laughed a lot as though she, too, enjoyed what his hard work had brought them. Judging by the spotless nature of the room, she spent all her days cleaning and tidying it.

They were both tremendously enthusiastic and the house was luxurious in the manner of the house of a peasant who had come to wealth. The things in it were valuable, but the taste was atrocious, with too much that was bright and too much that was metallic, as though Archavanne had suddenly found his firm very profitable and was eager to let it be seen in his home.

'It was my father's wish,' he said, 'to be as big as some of the big boys, and now it's *my* wish. My father ran it from a yard behind the bar at St Seine l'Abbaye. We hadn't half enough room and had lorries parked all over the place. One in a farmyard. Two by the crossroads on some land we rented. Another was always parked behind the Old Man's house and when you looked out of the salon – if you could call it a salon! – you found yourself looking straight up the exhaust pipe of a damn great Creusot. Talk about spoiling the view.'

Pel let him run on and he didn't need encouraging. 'I built this place,' he said. 'I couldn't stand the overcrowding. I heard the garage here was going, so I snapped it up. It had plenty of land and the farmer sold us a bit of his field. After all, in this line, you don't have to be in the middle of the city. What you need is space. If you've got the lorries, people'll come to you.'

Pel fished in his pocket and brought out the paper he had taken from Miollis' flat. Laying it on the table, he rested his finger end on the number, 80-35-01-601. 'That's your number,' he said.

Archavanne frowned. 'Where did you get this?' he asked.

'It came from the flat of one, Gilles Miollis, of St Denis, Paris. Know him?'

Archavanne rose. 'I think we'd better have a drink first,' he said. 'How about a coup de blanc?'

He busied himself finding a bottle of white wine and brought glasses which he set in front of them. He took a long time pouring them.

'Miollis,' he said, frowning. 'Gilles Miollis. I don't know anybody of that name. Who is he, anyway?'

'He was found in a car in the Rue du Chapeau Rouge, in the city, four days ago,' Pel said.

'Dead?'

'They usually are,' Darcy said drily, 'when they've been murdered.'

Archavanne smiled. 'I didn't know. Is he the man they mentioned in the paper?'

'You read it?'

'It didn't mean a thing to me, of course. What do you want from me?'

'Did you know Gilles Miollis?'

'Never met him in my life.'

'I didn't ask that. I said, do you know him?'

'No. Should I?'

'Your telephone number was found on this paper, which was found in his flat in the St Denis district of Paris.'

Archavanne smiled again. With relief. 'You know,' he said, 'when you first arrived I thought you were after me.'

'Would there be any reason for us to be after you?'

Archavanne lifted his glass. 'There's always a reason when you're in business,' he said. 'I thought you were after me for contravening traffic regulations.'

'The Police Judiciaire don't deal with traffic.'

'No, I suppose not. But you know what lorry drivers are like. They fail to fill in log books. They don't do what they're told. They don't use the tachographs. Those are the things they have in the cab to prove they've been where they say they've been, instead of fifty miles off their route, carrying a wardrobe to their grandmother's new house, or helping their girl friend to set up home in a different village.'

Pel's finger was still resting on the telephone number on the sheet of paper. 'The number, Monsieur,' he said quietly. 'How could he have got hold of your number?'

Archavanne shrugged. 'The same way everybody else gets hold of it,' he said. 'Advertising. We use the trade journals.' He rose and fished in a drawer to produce a fistful of yellow pamphlets, all bearing the name of his firm. 'You'd better keep one. We stick them in letters and they get passed round. You'd be surprised. I expect he got hold of it that way.'

'As far away as Paris?'

Archavanne smiled. 'We had someone enquiring not long ago from as far away as Dunkirk. One even from Bayonne, which is close to the Spanish border. He was probably up to something.'

'He was a small-time crook.'

'Very probably.' Archavanne was not perturbed. 'Dishonest people like to rent vehicles from established firms.

When they get up to something the name of a reliable firm on the vehicle they're using can be quite an asset. One of our vans was used in a bank raid in Amiens last year.'

'Could he have been smuggling?'

Archavanne shrugged. 'It's not unknown. One of our drivers was caught bringing watches in from Switzerland two years ago. It'll be in your files.'

'Do your drivers take pep pills?'

'I expect so. You sometimes need them, believe me.'

'Benzedrine, for instance?'

'I wouldn't know. Why?'

'Benzedrine tablets have been found. Did Miollis ever contact you?'

'Not to my knowledge.'

'You ever been hired by people from Paris?'

Archavanne gestured. 'Often.'

'Ever heard of Pépé le Cornet?'

'Who's he?'

'He's one of the top villains in Paris. *He* could be interested in hiring vans.'

Archavanne shrugged. 'If he was, he didn't give that name. But there's nothing to stop them giving a false one, is there? And if they guarantee the cash and they seem straightforward, who are we to argue?'

'What about Marseilles? Ever had requests from there?'

'From time to time.'

'Recently?'

'No. But – ' Archavanne shrugged again ' – what's to stop them coming through somebody a bit nearer. We wouldn't know. If you're thinking of crooks, I've known it to happen.'

Pel *had* been thinking of crooks. Big crooks. The suspicion was growing in his mind that the big boys were moving into his area.

'Ever hear of a man by the name of Nincic?' he asked. 'Fran Nincic.'

'That doesn't sound French.'

'It probably isn't.'

'I'd better check.'

Archavanne picked up a telephone on the window ledge and pressed a button. 'Géraldine,' he said. 'Have we ever had an enquiry from anybody called Miollis or Nincic? N-I-N-C-I-C.' He looked at Pel. 'Géraldine's my secretary. We always keep a list of people who enquire. If we hear no more from them, we send them a letter and a pamphlet. You'd be surprised how many of them are just hesitating and change their mind when they hear from us.' He turned to the telephone. 'What's that? Right. Thanks, ma chérie.' He looked at Pel and smiled. 'No Miollis,' he said. 'And no Nincic.'

# eight

It was Nosjean who turned up Fran Nincic, but it was Didier who put them on the right path.

'We have a boy at school,' he told Pel over dinner, 'who's called Zupancic. I've just remembered him. His mother speaks French in a funny way.'

Pel's ears pricked up. 'In a funny way?' he asked. 'What sort of funny way. Is he a foreigner?'

'No.' Didier was busy with the pommes frites and didn't bother to lift his head. 'He's French. But I think his father came from somewhere else.'

'Where? Do you know?'

'No. It's a funny name. I can't pronounce it. Full of Js. Lub-something.'

Pel leaned forward. 'Ljubljana? Could that be it?'

'It might.' Didier shrugged and dug again at the pommes frites. 'I'm not much good on names. Where is it?'

Pel wasn't much good on names either and he wasn't sure. Somewhere in the Balkans, he thought, and when he got to the office he dropped it for safety into Nosjean's lap. Misset was still trying in vain to get an interview with Professor Foussier – chiefly, Darcy suspected, because he wished to meet the legendary Mademoiselle Chahu, his personal assistant – but Nosjean, suspecting, after what Pel had told him of Didier's comment, that the name was East European, took the problem to the library, which sent him to see a

Hungarian professor of physics called Pazstor who had fled
to France during the revolution in Budapest in 1956.

'Slavic,' the professor said at once. 'The "ic" at the end is
equivalent to the Russian "itch" and the German "itz". They
all come from the same stem. Probably Balkan.'

'Can you be more precise?' Nosjean asked.

'Serbian. Slovene. Croat. The area known nowadays as
Yugoslavia. Perhaps Bulgarian, Romanian or Hungarian.
There was a lot of shifting about after the Second War among
the populations which fell along what is now the Iron
Curtain. A lot of them preferred not to live under Russian
domination and moved westwards. Some were also forced to
come to France after 1940 by the Germans to work and some
stayed. There were thousands of displaced persons in 1945.
Come to think of it, there's a Nincic who's a lab assistant in
the Department of Pathology. Probably the same family.
You'll be able to get the address at Biological Studies. Try
him. At least he'll know where the name comes from.'

'Serbian, eh?' Pel said thoughtfully as Nosjean reported to
him. 'Let's have his address.'

Fran Nincic lived at Auxonne. Pel knew the place well. It
was noted chiefly for the fact that there was born the man
who had promoted during the Revolution the system of
metric weights and measures used throughout Europe, an
innovation somewhat more intelligent than the renaming
during the same period of the months – Vendémiaire,
Brumaire, Frimaire – which had ended up translated by the
English as Wheezy, Sneezy, Freezy; Slippy, Drippy, Nippy;
Showery, Flowery, Bowery; Wheaty, Heaty and Sweety.

'Go and see him,' Pel said. 'Take Misset,' he added
maliciously. 'He was hoping for the afternoon off.'

Nincic's home was one of a group of small neat white
houses, all new, well built, substantial and expensive-

looking. Outside was a Mercedes, white, with splayed wheels and a streamlined roof.

'He seems to be making a lot more money than he ought to be,' Nosjean said. 'That wasn't paid for from the wages of a lab assistant.'

Nincic was a tall young man, handsome, dark and fiery-looking, and he made no bones about his background.

'Yes,' he agreed. 'I think my great-grandfather *was* a Serb, from Sarajevo. But my grandfather and father moved after the First War to France and became French citizens. I was born in Auxonne and I've lived here ever since.'

'And your father?'

'He married here. He trained as a chemist and runs a pharmacy at Longvic. He left Auxonne fifteen years ago. I sometimes help in the evenings.'

Nosjean studied him. 'Why didn't *you* go into the business?' he asked.

Nincic gestured. 'I didn't wish to. Not my line at all. You have too many worries these days.'

Misset cocked a thumb. 'That your car outside?'

'Yes.'

'Expensive.'

Nincic smiled. 'I like cars, and I save hard.'

'Insured?'

'Why?'

'We like to do Traffic's job,' Misset smiled. 'If they find any unwanted corpses about, they report them to us. If we find any uninsured cars we mention them to Traffic.'

Nincic gave Misset a cold look. 'It's insured. With Mutuelle.'

While they were talking, a girl appeared from the kitchen. Nincic didn't introduce her, so Nosjean asked her name.

'Duc,' she said. 'Madeleine Duc.'

'Girl friend?'

'You could call me that.'

'Address?'

'Why?'

'Because I'm asking.'

'I don't have to tell you.'

Nosjean knew the answer to that one. 'I think you do,' he said. 'We're from the Police Judiciaire and I can make you if I have to.'

She glanced at Nincic who shrugged. '*This* is my address,' she said.

'All the time?'

'Yes.'

'You a student?' It was a shot in the dark.

'Yes.'

'Long way from the University, isn't it?'

'We go in every day,' Nincic said. 'By car. If I'm not here, there's a train. It's not far.'

Nosjean smiled. 'How old are you?' he asked the girl.

'Twenty.'

'Parents alive?'

'Yes.'

'Do they write to you here?'

She hesitated, then glanced at Nincic. 'No,' she said. 'I share a room in the city with a girl in Applied Agronomy. Edith Roux. My letters go there. She brings them to class for me.'

'It's no business of the police,' Nincic pointed out.

Nosjean smiled. 'Who's making it their business? I'm asking questions because I have to, that's all.' He came to the point quickly, beaky-nosed, angular and as intense as a young Napoleon.

'Paul-Edouard Hertot, Achille Lorre, Jean-Pierre Ramou and Philippe Mortier,' he said. 'Know them?'

Nincic smiled. It was an engaging smile. 'Yes,' he said. 'I know them.'

'What do you have in common?'

The smile vanished again. 'What is this? An enquiry?'

'Yes,' Nosjean said bluntly. 'An enquiry.'

'And why are you asking *me* these questions?'

'Because they also knew a boy called Jean-Marc Cortot. And Cortot's dead. He was on heroin.'

'So? What has this to do with me?'

'Your name's been mentioned.'

'In connection with drugs?'

'You're a research assistant at Biological Studies.'

'Yes.' Nincic laughed. 'But *look* at me! Do I look like someone on drugs?'

'Lots of people on drugs don't look like people on drugs,' Nosjean said in a voice as flat as a smack across the chops. 'It depends what they're on.'

Nincic scowled. 'Are you accusing me – ?'

'I'm not doing anything except ask questions. Did you know Cortot?'

'Yes.'

'Do you know where he got his drugs?'

'Why should I?'

'Just answer the question.'

'No, I don't. Will that do?'

'Did he get it from your department?'

'We don't handle those kind of drugs.'

'But you use them from time to time. On rats and things.'

'Yes. And we have to sign for every gramme and milligramme we use. You can check the books.' Nincic's face darkened. 'Anyway, what's behind all this – ?'

'Behind all this is a dead man,' Nosjean said, feeling a little prim and self-important. 'The police have to find out how he came to meet his death.'

'And are you suggesting – ?'

'We're suggesting nothing,' Misset said sharply. 'We've told you several times we're merely asking questions. If students in the city are getting drugs, it's our job to find out where.'

'They're not getting them from me,' Nincic snapped.

'In that case,' Nosjean snapped back, 'you've nothing to worry about.'

Nincic calmed down a little and even tried to make amends. 'Look,' he said, 'I'm sorry I was short. I realise you have a job to do. But when this sort of thing is flung at you it shakes you a bit. Let's have a drink and forget it and I'll do my best to answer your questions.'

He produced a bottle of wine and poured four glasses. Misset sat near the girl. She wore an elusive perfume, was very attractive and had on a low-cut dress that showed a lot of cleavage. Misset found it disturbing.

'Now, go on,' Nincic said. 'Let's see what we can do to help. I knew Hertot, Ramou and Lorre.'

'How?' Nosjean asked.

'I met them at a party. They were always together.' Nincic hesitated. 'As a matter of fact,' he said, 'I guessed they were on soft drugs.'

'How about Cortot? He was on heroin.'

'I didn't know that. I thought he was like the others. After all, people don't go around telling you "Look, I'm sniffing dope." But you sometimes begin to suspect. Behaviour. That sort of thing. There are lots of kids trying dope these days. More than there ought to be. Personally, I think the university authorities ought to sling them out. They just get in the hair of the serious students and get them a bad name.' Nincic smiled. 'After all, some go to university to work, don't they? They want to go into the professions, and they'll not manage *that* on drugs, will they?'

'Hardly,' Nosjean said.

'Universities are the basis of France,' Nincic went on earnestly. 'They always have been. And if they get a bad name, the whole thing falls apart. There's enough Marxism,

Communism, Maoism and all the other isms, without druggism.'

'Ever heard the name Pépé le Cornet?'

'Never.'

'Maurice Tagliacci?'

'No.'

'Ever come across other students on drugs?'

'One or two.'

'Know where they get them?'

Nincic shrugged. 'No, I don't. Have you seen Professor Foussier? He says what we need is something like Alcoholics Anonymous. I try to talk to these kids when they come to the lab and start trying to wheedle stuff out of me. They get up to some pretty bad habits, I can tell you, because they're away from home for the first time. They get slovenly, then they start drinking and eventually trying drugs. I've pleaded with more than one of them to cut it out.'

Nosjean didn't believe a word of it.

Nincic's father lived with his wife over his shop in the Rue Georges Guynemer. There was a microphone and a loudspeaker by the door and Nosjean had to announce who they were before the *cordon* was pulled and they could enter.

The old man had the same fiery eyes as his son and the same aggressive spirit. 'I've been in business since the war,' he said. 'I started with money I'd saved. There's nothing wrong with that, I hope.'

'Nothing at all,' Nosjean agreed. 'Do you ever have trouble with students trying to get hold of drugs?'

'The shop's been burgled four times. Chiefly for tranquillisers or benzedrine – what they call pep pills.'

'Have they ever come in demanding harder drugs?'

The old man gestured. 'They have done. We always send them packing.'

'Who's "we"?'

'I have one assistant. My son helps occasionally in the evening.'

'Why didn't *he* join the business?'

The old man shrugged. There was a suggestion of disappointment in the gesture. 'He prefers the University. He studied there, of course. I sometimes wonder if it was a mistake. People who go to university sometimes get the bug and they can't live without it. Sometimes they don't ever grow up.'

It seemed to be time to go to the top. If anybody knew the drug scene at the University it had to be Foussier.

Taking out his notebook with all the telephone numbers of his contacts, Nosjean deliberately waited for Lagé to come into the office before he asked for the number.

'Is that Mademoiselle Chahu?' he asked. As he saw Lagé's eyebrows shoot up, he dropped his voice to a conspiratorial murmur. Lagé leaned to one side, straining his ears.

'This is Sergeant Nosjean. You told me I could contact you any time.'

The voice that answered was dark velvet in colour. 'That's correct,' it said. 'I remember.'

'I need to see Professor Foussier.'

'The Professor's always booked up two days or so ahead.'

'This is the police, Mademoiselle,' Nosjean pointed out. 'It's urgent.' He decided to inject a little drama into the discussion. 'Two days from now might be too late.'

There was a long pause. 'I'll see,' the voice said.

As he waited, Nosjean smiled at Lagé, who rose abruptly and left the room, frowning. But to Nosjean's disgust, when Marie-Anne Chahu came back on the line, it was not to say an appointment had been made but merely that Professor Foussier would speak to him on the telephone.

'Drugs,' Foussier said in a hurried eager voice as if he were headlining a lecture. 'They do, of course, pose a problem here and unfortunately it's already a *growing* problem. In this city – away from Paris and Marseilles – we haven't been very bothered with it up to now, but there have been cases.'

'Many, Monsieur le Professeur?' Nosjean asked.

'Not many,' Foussier admitted. 'One or two. Then it became three or four. Eventually it became five or six. Next year I expect it will be seven or eight. Which is why I agreed to head the committee we set up to look into it. After all, who's likely to know most about the students and what they get up to but the heads of departments?'

'What happens to the students if they're found out?'

'A few are sent home,' Foussier said. 'Or, if they need it, they have treatment. One or two are caught by the police – you people. The worse they're affected, the more careless they become, of course.'

The urgent voice went on, enthusiastic and full of concern. Foussier was a man who was highly publicity-conscious and liked at every opportunity to get in touch with anyone who might get his name in *Le Bien Public,* and his office sent out a stream of notes, advices and opinions on every subject under the sun to anyone who wanted to receive them – and a great many who didn't.

And since Foussier's interests seemed to cover the whole University spectrum and a few subjects outside such as flying, he had a pretty wide field for airing his opinions. Every society in the city had him as a patron or a benefactor – even Lagé's half-baked photographic society – and they were all proud to pass on information about his activities on their behalf. It was a threadbare edition of *Le Bien Public* that didn't include his name at least half a dozen times. Nosjean often wondered if he were fishing for a Légion d'honneur.

As Nosjean tried to pose a question he interrupted in his plummy arrogant voice. 'You must have the letter I wrote you on the subject,' he said.

Nosjean couldn't resist it. 'Which one, Monsieur le Professeur?' Up to now he had three, all carefully filed.

There was a moment's silence. Foussier clearly hadn't noticed the sarcasm. 'The one dated the 12th.'

'Yes. I have that.' Nosjean was reading it even as he listened. 'Mon cher Sergeant Nosjean,' it read. 'You have asked about the student Cortot. I knew the boy well. His was a weak character not strengthened by his military service. He was lonely and his tutor passed on to me the suspicion that he was on drugs, knowing I would be interested in helping him. I considered he needed clinical assistance and I advised this. He doesn't appear to have acted on the advice...'

Foussier was still rattling on. 'Everything's in that letter,' he said. 'All my thoughts on what happened. You may use it, of course, or you may pass it on to the Press. Just as you please.'

Nosjean managed to shove his voice through a chink in the diatribe. 'Have you come across instances of drug pushing, Professor?'

Foussier paused, as if he were startled that anyone should have the temerity to interrupt him while he was in full cry. 'Not yet, thank God,' he said.

'Could it be that someone's trying to expand the scene here?'

There was another pause. Nosjean repeated the question and Foussier came to life sharply. 'More than likely,' he said. 'Judging by the increase. It's only a marginal increase, but it is an increase. It started three years ago, I suppose. That's when we found our first suspect. It's quite new.'

'Somebody's noticed us, I think.'

'Yes, we've been discovered all right. Perhaps it comes from Marseilles. I don't know. I often wonder if it isn't a Russian plot to undermine the youth of the West.'

It was something that had crossed Nosjean's mind more than once. Get the whole population sloppy with drugs, then let the tanks roll.

'But why *here*?' he asked.

Foussier paused again. 'Because it's safe, perhaps. Well away from the usual places like Amsterdam, Marseilles and Hamburg. It would make a good picking, after all, wouldn't it? *And* a safe picking. Do you have a narcotics squad, sergeant?'

'All forces have a narcotics squad,' Nosjean said cautiously. He didn't add that sometimes the narcotics squad consisted of men taken off rapes, assaults and robberies with violence and that, at that moment, it consisted chiefly of him, Nosjean.

'Not as big as a Paris or Marseilles operation, I imagine,' Foussier said. 'After all, we're a bit out of the way here, aren't we, from the clever boys who're being watched by the police.'

'Do you think there *are* clever boys setting up in this city, Professor?'

Foussier gave a little laugh. 'There are clever boys everywhere these days, aren't there, sergeant? Everybody wants a quick return for their money. My father once said he considered a good profit was ten per cent. He was complaining of people who wanted fifty per cent. Nowadays they want a hundred – and even more. The media don't help. Every fifth programme's about some tycoon who uses his money for power. It's only television, it's true, but you'd be surprised how it influences young people. When they're young they get dreams and it's then that they're vulnerable.'

When Nosjean put what he had learned to Pel two days later, the corruption case at St Clément had come to a head and a sous-brigadier and two policemen had been suspended, and

Pel had had to sit in on the Chief's enquiry with Judge Polverari.

He listened quietly, while Darcy leaned on the door, a half-smile on his face.

'So Foussier thinks we're becoming a drugs centre, does he?' he said. 'Well, he may be right. We're nicely central, of course. At least for Eastern France, Switzerland and South-West Germany. No wonder Miollis was interested. How about Nincic? Is he a pusher?'

'Nothing's known, Patron. But I've a feeling he's involved.'

'Why?'

'Just a hunch.'

'Hunches are good things for a detective to have, mon brave,' Darcy said. 'Hunches are what make detectives. Krauss never had a hunch in his life, except that it's lunch hour or time for a beer.'

'We'd better go and see him.' Pel leaned forward. 'Even hunches are based on something,' he went on. 'What's yours based on?'

Nosjean shrugged. 'His set-up. It's not what a research assistant affords. He runs a Merc. It's insured with Mutuelle. I went to see them. I found out he took out a foreign travel insurance in February and another in May. There was one last winter, too.'

'Where did he take them out for?'

'Mutuelle said they covered "all countries", so they could be for anywhere. It's a lot of trips abroad for a research assistant, Patron.'

# nine

When Pel and Darcy reached Auxonne, Nincic wasn't there, though his girl friend, Madeleine Duc, was.

Pel came to the point quickly and placed on the table the photographs of the bone button that had been found with Gilles Miollis in the boot of the Renault in the Rue du Chapeau Rouge.

'That's edelweiss,' he said. 'They have it in countries where there are mountains. Serbia's mountainous.'

The girl looked interested.

'Your friend, Fran Nincic, is from Serbia.'

She smiled and shook her head. 'He's French,' she said. 'His grandfather came to France about 1919. His family have lived here ever since.

Pel pushed the photographs forward. 'Of course,' he admitted, 'it could be German. Or Swiss. Or Italian. It had a scrap of green cloth attached to it. And that probably makes it German.'

She looked puzzled.

'Your friend, Nincic,' Pel said. 'Does he have any clothing of that type?'

'With bone buttons?'

'Like this one.'

She smiled. 'Nino's a smarter dresser than that. That sort of thing's a bit out of date, anyway, isn't it? Even Germans don't wear it much these days, and lederhosen are definitely out. People these days prefer jeans.'

It was a point, Pel had to admit. There was no such thing as national dress any more. Only international dress, with everybody trying to look like Americans. Even countries tried to look like America; while children, whom teachers spent years trying to teach French or English or German, much preferred to sound as if they came from Texas.

'Where's Nincic at the moment?' he asked.

The girl's shoulders moved. 'Away. On business.'

'I thought he worked at the University?'

The shoulders twitched again. 'It doesn't stop him doing a little business on his own, does it?'

'What sort of business does he do?'

'He doesn't tell me. I don't ask.'

It was a funny world, Pel thought, when a girl would happily live with a man, cooking his food, darning his socks, warming his bed, without being interested in what he did for a living.

'Why is he in business?'

'Why?' She seemed puzzled.

'There must be a reason for a man to want to do two jobs at once.

The shrug came once more. 'To make money, I expect. Everybody wants their own set-up, don't they?'

'He told my sergeant that his own set-up was the one thing he didn't want.'

'Oh, he does.' She smiled pityingly. 'Believe me. And a better one than his father's, too.'

'What's wrong with his father's?'

She pulled a face. 'A small pharmacist. Pharmacists don't make the sort of money Nino wants.'

Pel guessed at the sort of money Nino was after. 'Where has he gone?' he asked.

'He said Dôle.'

'He went away in May and February, too. And last winter. Did he say he was going to Dôle then?'

'That's what he said.'

'Then why did he take out a foreign travel insurance for his car to cover those dates?'

Her smile died. 'Did he?'

'Yes.'

'He didn't tell me. Perhaps he changed his mind.' She was trying to appear indifferent but Pel could see she was troubled. She didn't like to think her boy friend had lied to her about where he'd been and was doubtless wondering if he'd been visiting another girl.

'When is he due back?' Pel asked.

'I don't know.' Again the casual attitude. 'It doesn't make any difference to me, anyway. I'm going home for a holiday this weekend. To Avallon. My father's a dentist there.'

Pel pondered. There was something about Fran Nincic that smelled and it seemed no coincidence that the car in which Miollis had been found had also come from Auxonne.

'The 13th,' he said. 'Remember it? Weekend before last. Was he here then?'

'No.'

Pel gave Darcy a quick glance. 'Where was he? Do you know?'

'Yes. I was with him. We went camping. In the Jura.'

'You were together the whole time?'

'Why?'

'Just answer the question.'

She stared at Pel, then gave a giggle of laughter. 'That was the weekend that man Miollis was murdered, wasn't it? You think Nino might have done it.' The giggle became a gurgle and she stared at Pel as if he'd suddenly grown two heads. 'Oh, no,' she laughed. 'Not Nino!'

Pel waited patiently until the laughter died down. 'Were you together the whole time?' he repeated coldly.

'Of course! Day *and* night. We went camping.'

Camping was a useful alibi. It was difficult to check campers. Doubtless Nincic was clever enough to be aware of it, too.

'Only we didn't bother to camp,' she went on. 'All that fuss about going to a site. Signing in. Putting your name on the fiche d'hôtel. Kids playing football. People playing radios. We just found a field and slept there.'

'How?'

She gazed at him with large, frank brown eyes. 'We just went into each other's arms.'

That wasn't what Pel had meant but he didn't argue. She had answered his question. It made it even more difficult to check on them.

'Where exactly did you go in the Jura?' he asked.

'Pontarlier way.'

'That's close to the Swiss frontier. That could account for the button. Go there often?'

'Not since last year.'

'Did you go last year, too?'

'Yes. We met some Austrian students who'd crossed the border. There's a café on this side.'

'Did you know their names?'

'No.' She shrugged. 'I'd never seen them before. They were from Innsbrück and were climbing in Switzerland, but they'd taken a day off to come into France.'

'It's not climbing country there.'

'It's *walking* country.' She smiled. 'I expect they were just collecting countries. You know how you do.'

Pel had never wanted to collect anywhere in the world but Burgundy. 'Go on,' he said.

'We got talking, because Nino's parents had lived in Innsbrück at one time and he recognised their accent. They asked us to post some letters for them to Austrian students in France. The café had no stamps. The season hadn't started. Nino said he'd do it and they gave him the money. It wasn't much. Just three letters and a small parcel.'

Pel's ears pricked up. 'What was in the parcel?'

'They said it was photographs. It was a small box, about the size you get photographs in.'

'Did you notice the names and addresses?'

'Yes. All in Paris. There was nothing on them. Just things like "Greetings" and "Grüss Gott". That's what the Austrians and the Swiss say to each other.'

'What about the parcel?'

'It was addressed to "Poste Restante" in Dijon.'

'And the name? Did you see it?'

The girl began to answer, then her eyes widened and she stared at them, her hand going slowly to her mouth.

'Oh, my God,' she said. 'It was Miollis. Gilles Miollis.'

While Pel was on his way back, Paris rang. Krauss took the message.

'They don't think any of *their* villains are working here, Patron,' he said as Pel appeared. 'They happen to be watching them because they've had a tip-off there's a consignment of drugs on the way. They also said that of the jewellery you took from Madame Miollis three of the pieces were stolen. Two of them belonged to a woman in the Sixth Arrondissement and the third came from Chartres. Nothing's known on the other pieces. They've also been in touch with the Police de l'Air et des Frontières and they think there's been trafficking in false passports.'

'They'd better bring in that heavy, Treguy,' Pel said. 'He was probably involved with Miollis.'

'Unfortunately, Chief,' Krauss said, 'that's not possible.'

'Why not?'

'They said he'd disappeared. Sunk without trace. Dodged their men and vanished.'

'Can't they find him through the Miollis woman?'

'No, Chief.' Krauss shrugged. 'She's vanished, too.'

The conference in Pel's office was subdued. Nosjean had just been to see an ex-naval petty officer called Mathieu who lived in the city.

'When I finished my time,' he had said, 'I came to live here. It's about as far as you can get from the sea in Western Europe.'

Nosjean had produced the photographs of Cortot. He looked very dead and very tied up.

'There's more rope on him than we used to tie up a cruiser,' Mathieu had commented.

'He was ex-Navy,' Nosjean pointed out

Mathieu had studied the pictures again. 'Well, *he* didn't tie those knots,' he said. 'Naval knots are designed so they'll not jam or stick. Those look like an old woman's knitting.'

'But *somebody* tied the knots, Patron,' Nosjean said.

'Could he have got his drugs from Nincic?' Pel asked.

Nosjean considered. 'Nincic's not on any list, Patron. But he seems to know a lot of people who use drugs.'

'Let's have a watch put on his place,' Pel said. 'Get Auxonne to cover it. I want to know immediately he comes back. Then contact the lab where he works. If he turns up, tell them I want to know at once.' He paused and extracted a cigarette from a packet on his desk. As he put it between his lips, Darcy leaned forward quickly with a lighter and the cigarette was glowing before Pel could have any doubts.

'The faster you go at it, Patron,' Darcy grinned, 'the more painless it is.'

Pel glared and turned back to Nosjean. 'What about this drugs committee of Foussier's? Do they know Nincic?'

'No,' Nosjean said. 'I saw one of the members. A·senior lecturer called Matille. I asked him what they'd discovered. He said nothing. He said they did a lot of talking but when it was all boiled down he didn't think they'd achieved much.'

'I'd better see Foussier myself.'

Nosjean smiled. 'I hope you're lucky, Patron. The Chahu dame seems to think he's made of uranium or something and somebody's out to steal him. But I have her telephone number in my file. She wrote a note about Cortot and told me to ring if I wanted any more. Foussier doesn't give interviews. He writes letters. He's a compulsive letter writer. I have several.'

'I've got one, too,' Lagé agreed enthusiastically. 'About the photographic society. He sent us a talk to read. He took a lot of trouble.' He shot a triumphant glance at Nosjean. 'It was all there: Lens. Shutter position. Light. Pose. Naturalism.'

'What's he mean by "naturalism"?' Darcy asked. 'Nudes? I've seen it outside the night spots in Paris. It's another word for striptease.'

'This isn't.' Lagé looked offended. 'He meant normality of pose. Normality of lighting. Normality of expression. That sort of thing. I read it myself. It went down well. I got it from La Chahu.'

Pel stared round at them. Lagé was glaring at Nosjean, who was looking faintly prim and self-important. Darcy was watching them, his eyes full of humour.

'Who is this damned Chahu woman, anyway?' Pel asked.

Darcy kissed the tips of his fingers. 'Half the sergeants' room's fallen for her, Patron,' he said. 'She's beautiful. She has secrets.'

'Perhaps I ought to know more about her.'

Darcy gestured. 'It shouldn't be hard, Patron. You've got as good a source of information as anyone. A woman as beautiful as she's said to be must go to a good hairdresser. The best in this district's Nanette's. You have a contact there.'

Pel sniffed to show that Madame Faivre-Perret wasn't a subject to be bandied round the sergeants' room. All the same, he thought, it was time somebody really got past this Chahu woman. He looked at Lagé. Lagé seemed besotted by Foussier, but Lagé wasn't one of the brightest acquisitions to

Pel's team. Nosjean? He was learning fast, but he was still a bit young – especially where women were concerned and to get to Foussier it seemed they had to get past La Chahu.

He sniffed again, rubbed his nose, and looked at Darcy. Darcy had a way with women and always had had. When other men couldn't get a thing out of them, Darcy had a gift for worming his way into their confidence – sometimes, Pel knew, even into their beds.

'*You'd* better have a go at her, Darcy,' he said.

# ten

The day Ramou, Hertot and Lorre appeared in Pel's office, the morning was so hot the tar was melting in the streets, and a young American had been arrested for holding up traffic by trying to fry an egg to prove it was as hot as New York. Even without jackets, the men in the Hôtel de Police wilted in their clothes.

The sky was like a bronze bowl and the girls looked heartbreakingly beautiful in their summer dresses, but by afternoon the heat had become oppressive enough to be wearisome and the air was charged with thunder. Walking became an effort and the three young men who were brought in by police car were hot, bored and inclined to try to be clever.

They gave their names none too willingly and with a wealth of snide remarks to each other that Pel allowed to wash over him without appearing to hear. He sensed they were nervous and allowed them to enjoy themselves.

'Home towns?' he asked briskly.

'Marseilles,' Ramou said. 'Notre Dame de la Garde area.'

'Paris,' Hertot added. 'Montparnasse district.'

'Orléans,' Lorre ended. 'The Tours road. My father keeps a bar on the outskirts of the city.'

They were all at the University on grants, but Ramou's grant appeared to be bigger than the grants of the other two because he was better dressed, had good shoes instead of down-at-heel sandals, and was full of self-importance.

'Are you on drugs?' Pel asked.

'I've smoked pot,' he admitted.

'I'd advise you not to,' Pel said.

Ramou gestured contemptuously. 'It's harmless. It's the law that's stupid.'

Pel sighed. Soft drugs led to medium drugs and medium drugs to hard drugs, but there were still a lot of enlightened people about who considered like Ramou that soft drugs were an asset to happiness. For the life of him, Pel could see no point in taking drugs at all – unless, like Evariste Clovis Désiré Pel with his cigarettes, you needed them for the maledictions and malfunctions of the body that were brought on by a job that was too demanding and far from overpaid.

He gestured at Nosjean who made the three boys roll their sleeves up. There was a lot of giggling and shoving and pretending to do a striptease.

'No signs of injections, Patron,' Nosjean said, his face stiff with disapproval.

'What were you looking for?' Hertot asked.

'Syringe marks,' Ramou explained. 'If you syringe hard enough you can blow up your arm like a football.'

'Why not use a bicycle pump?' Lorre asked.

'Or the air pipe at a garage?'

'As a matter of fact,' Ramou said, 'I always inject myself in the backside. Would you like me to take my trousers down?'

Pel found them stupid and rather silly, anxious to show off to indicate their courage, manhood and virility. They all professed to be anarchists but managed, nevertheless, to argue about what kind of anarchy it was, and they all complained that France was demanding too much of them, giving them too little, and even expecting them to go into the army to do their military service when they'd finished their studies, something they all intended to avoid if possible. Pel, who would have died to defend Burgundy, even if not necessarily Paris, waved them out of his office, saddened and faintly disgusted by them.

'They seem too half-baked to be murderers,' he said to Nosjean.

'They could be contacts, Patron,' Nosjean said earnestly. 'After all, Ramou comes from Marseilles. So does this guy, Tagliacci, whoever he is, and so did Treguy, that heavy you bumped into in Paris. Hertot comes from Paris, for that matter, and that's Pépé le Cornet's district. However we try to push it aside, it's a connection with the gangs, and obviously so was Miollis.'

Pel was well aware of it, but the day was stiflingly hot and he was inclined to be lazy.

'This Ramou one has money, too,' Nosjean went on eagerly. 'I've watched them. I've seen them in bars. He spends. The others don't spend half as much. So where does he get it? He's on a normal grant like the others, so he can't have wealthy parents.'

'He probably has a wealthy boss somewhere, though,' Pel admitted.

'Nincic, Patron?'

'Perhaps. But even Nincic – if it *is* Nincic – can't be operating alone. Drugs are too big a business and involve too many people.'

'Perhaps *he's* working for one of the Paris mobs or someone in Marseilles,' Nosjean said. 'Somebody's using him – Tagliacci or Pépé le Cornet.'

Pel shrugged. Sometime's Nosjean's eagerness wore him out.

'We'll wait,' he said. 'Perhaps Darcy'll bring something back.'

Certainly Darcy was trying hard.

The girl thundering away at the electric typewriter in the outer office of Professor Foussier's private suite wore a pale green dress that matched her eyes. Her figure was something to write home about and her legs were slender and shapely. Having listened to Nosjean and Lagé, not unnaturally Darcy jumped to the wrong conclusion.

'You Mademoiselle Chahu?' he asked.

The girl smiled. 'Not me,' she said. 'I'm Angélique Courtois. I'm the second string.' She saw the look of disappointment on his face and grinned. 'They always pull a face like that.'

She had an easy manner and her smile was unforced. Darcy leaned forward.

'You're *second* string?' he said. 'The first string must be good.'

She obviously enjoyed the flattery. Perhaps, Darcy reflected, La Chahu soaked up most of it and Angélique Courtois normally only got what was left over. She didn't seem to mind, however, and he suspected she had a forthright, realistic nature that was well aware of her own faults and her own virtues.

'I want to see Professor Foussier,' he said.

She grinned again. 'The Professor never sees anyone except by appointment. He's a busy man and insists people make arrangements ahead, so he can arrange his day.'

'Very well,' Darcy said. 'Let's make an appointment.'

She grinned once more. 'Unfortunately,' she said, 'he never allows anyone to make appointments for him but his personal assistant.'

Darcy frowned. 'All right,' he said, 'where's his personal assistant?'

Angélique Courtois giggled. 'I'm afraid she's not here today. She's owed a day or two off. She'll be at home, I expect. I would be if I weren't holding the fort. In bed.'

'I should think you don't look too bad in bed,' Darcy said.

She looked up. She was young but she wasn't all that innocent. She didn't say anything but she didn't blush either and her gaze didn't falter. To Darcy it was the old green light. For Darcy the green light in a girl's eye always shone as clear and bold and truthful as the light on the point at Cape Finisterre. His father had come from the north but his mother had come from Toulouse and, in spite of generations of northern Darcys standing in serried rows in the shadows behind him, his instincts had been most definitely inherited from his Gascon mother.

And he knew the signs because he'd grown up learning them. He had, in fact, spent most of his life making up for his cowardice at the age of thirteen when he'd fled in terror from the hot eyes of the girl next door one warm summer evening at a Bastille Day fireworks display. Once his heart had stopped skidding about under his shirt, he realised he'd passed up something no male with a drop of red blood in his veins ought ever to forswear and he'd never missed a chance since. Now when a girl looked at him in invitation, with interest, or simply with approval, it registered in his mind like the symbol on a cash register. Ding.

'Do you go out at nights?' he asked.

'Often,' Angélique Courtois said.

'Not just with girl friends, I hope.'

She smiled. 'Oh, no. Nothing unnatural about me. I'm engaged to be married, as a matter of fact.'

'Congratulations. What does he do?' Darcy always liked to know that. If they were all-in wrestlers, boxers, weight-lifters, anything that involved the use of muscles, Darcy moved with care.

'He's a librarian. He works for the Government.'

'Here?'

'No. He's in Mulhouse.'

Darcy smiled. Mulhouse was a long way away, and librarians weren't noted for being muscular.

'How do you manage?'

'He comes to see me once a month.'

'That's not enough to keep a girl happy,' Darcy said. 'How about coming out with me?'

She gave him her telephone number without hesitation. 'I'll pick you up,' he said. He glanced at the number. 'Is this home? With Mammy and Pappy?'

'Not likely. I'm a big girl. It's a flat. In the Rue de la Fontaine. The top floor of a house owned by some people called Roblet. They're friends of my parents. They're supposed to keep an eye on me to make sure I don't get up to mischief. I live on my own.'

Darcy smiled. 'Splendid,' he said. 'Now you'd better tell me where I can find La Chahu.'

Marie-Anne Chahu lived in an apartment in a block called the Maison Joliet in the Place Wilson area. Darcy's eyebrows lifted as he studied it. Foussier, he decided, must be paying his personal assistant a great deal of money, because this wasn't the sort of place that normally contained secretaries' apartments. This was a new building with a long green lawn, freshly planted trees and an underground garage and, instead of a concierge, a man in a plum-coloured suit sitting in an office just inside the main doorway who stopped Darcy as he pushed inside.

'Who are you looking for, Monsieur?' he asked.

'Mademoiselle Chahu,' Darcy said.

'Friend of hers, sir?' The man behind the glass had been told to be careful but discreet.

Darcy produced his badge. It had the effect of knocking the smile off the other man's face.

'I don't have to be,' Darcy said. 'Which is her apartment?'

The man behind the glass wore a different face now. His sly features changed. 'Number 27, Monsieur,' he said briskly. 'Second floor. But I'm afraid she's just gone out for lunch.'

And doubtless, Darcy thought, not to Le Snack, which was the bar across the road. People who lived in apartments such as these didn't eat standing up at the zinc.

'I'll wait,' he said, more and more intrigued.

'There's a chair over there, Monsieur.'

Darcy smiled. 'Outside,' he added. 'In my car. And don't tell her I'm here.'

Making himself comfortable outside, he lit a cigarette and opened a newspaper, sitting so he could watch everyone who came and went. The women who appeared through the door, he noticed, were all well dressed, in clothes that spoke not of the Nouvelles Galeries but of the small boutiques near the Place des Ducs, where the prices were twice as high and the goods twice as select.

The sun was hot and Darcy was nodding when he saw a British Triumph 1500 sports car, blue, hooded and sleek, disappear into the underground car park. It was driven by a woman and he knew at once that it could only be Marie-Anne Chahu.

Jumping from his car, he entered the building and took the lift to the second floor. As he left it, it slid silently down again and he saw it had gone to the basement. Walking quickly along the landing, he watched from the corner. After a while the lift returned. The woman who stepped out, he knew at once, was Marie-Anne Chahu. She wasn't a girl any more, he noticed to his surprise, and was in her early thirties, but she was quite as beautiful as everybody said and Darcy couldn't imagine why he hadn't bumped into her before. A man with an instinctive nose for attractive females, he couldn't understand how he'd missed her.

She wore her hair up and a neat grey dress with white cuffs and collars, which Darcy's practised eye told him was expensive. Since Angélique Courtois had also worn a neat dress, he assumed that Foussier liked his secretaries to be smart, efficient-looking and unobtrusive.

Deciding that Nosjean and Lagé had been right about Marie-Anne Chahu, for a moment he wondered if he'd made arrangements to meet the wrong girl. But then he realised there was a cool look about this one also that suggested she knew exactly what she wanted out of life and was determined to get it. The Triumph alone seemed to indicate that.

He watched her enter her apartment and gave her time to settle down before walking along the corridor and ringing the bell. The door was wrenched open at once and he was greeted by a smile that died at once as she saw Darcy. She had obviously been expecting someone.

She was tall, almost as tall as Darcy himself, with a superb figure, neat ankles and wrists, and a long slender neck. She was dark, with a cloud of brown hair about her face and the most enormous eyes Darcy had ever seen. Not brown, like so many people with dark hair, but blue, fringed with huge dark lashes that slanted upwards at the corners. They seemed to fill the whole doorway.

'Yes?' she said sharply. 'What can I do for you?'

There would have been a time once, Darcy thought, when she could have done a lot for him. But not now. Darcy was an easy-going, free-wheeling sort of policeman, modern as a flying saucer, taking his pleasures where he found them and never without a girl. But his girls were natural, as modern as Darcy and free with their favours, but still spontaneous, uncalculating and happy. There was something missing from Marie-Anne Chahu's lovely face, something that another man without Darcy's experience might have missed, something that Lagé and Nosjean *had* missed. She was very much a woman and she wore her sex like a badge of office, but her features had hardened to a mask he'd seen before on women who abused trust and love. Her innocence, even the very essence of her womanliness, had vanished.

He put on his best smile. He sometimes practised it in front of the mirror. It showed his strong white teeth.

'Detective-Sergeant Daniel Darcy,' he said. 'Police Judiciaire.'

Her eyebrows rose. 'Police? How can *I* help?'

'You're Professor Foussier's personal assistant, I believe?'

'Yes, I am.' She spoke brusquely, as if she wished to be rid of him. 'And I'm off-duty at the moment.'

Darcy didn't budge. 'I shan't take a second,' he said.

She studied him for a while, then she opened the door. 'You'd better come in.' She paused. 'I was just going to make a couple of telephone calls. Please sit down. I'll be with you in a moment.'

She gave him a sharp angry look and disappeared through a door, beyond which he caught a glimpse of an enormous bed and decorations in pink and white. The door shut and he heard the telephone tinkle, then her voice came, quiet and too low to catch.

While she was speaking, he took the opportunity to inspect his surroundings. The carpet was pale yellow, deep and expensive, and the furniture wasn't the usual mixture of Louis XVI, Second Empire, Between-the-Wars Gothic and Post-War Cubic that he saw in the homes of most of the people he visited. There was a great deal of *confort anglais* here, deep chairs and settees and subdued lights. There was a television on a trolley that was doubtless wheeled in front of the settee when Mademoiselle Chahu was entertaining friends, and an expensive hi-fi equipment which was doubtless used to provide sweet music to go with the soft lights. He wondered who paid for it all.

As she reappeared, Darcy got down to business. 'I'm really wanting to see Professor Foussier,' he explained.

'This is hardly the place to ask,' she said sharply.

He smiled. 'I went to his private office. The girl there said he permitted no one to make appointments but his personal assistant – you.'

'That's true, of course. But I'm off-duty. Didn't she tell you that? I'm owed a few days.'

'Is it impossible?'

'Without his diary, yes. You could try his home.'

'We have a drugs problem,' Darcy said. 'At the University.'

She shrugged. 'It happens all the time. We no sooner find one student than another starts. The Professor takes it very much to heart and watches the problem very carefully.'

'*Is* there a problem?'

'There is at most universities.'

'Foreign ones, too? Swiss? German?'

'I've heard the Professor say there is. Most have someone keeping an eye on it, and the Professor keeps in touch with them, because the same names keep cropping up.'

Darcy could well imagine.

'He's not only concerned with student welfare,' she went on. 'He's made an extensive study of the use of drugs. In fact, he started by writing a thesis on it while a student himself at the Sorbonne.'

'He must know a lot about it.'

'Yes. This is why he insists on appointments. He's so busy. He's not only concerned with student welfare, he's also interested in photography – '

As Lagé had mentioned, Darcy remembered.

' – botany, shooting, ornithology, the history of Burgundy, Germanic and East European languages, motor racing, flying, navigation, engineering, finance and electronics. He's an expert on electronics. In fact, he's devised a system for his lecture hall where he can turn off the lights at the back while he's standing at the front.'

'What's so special about an electronic device to switch the lights off?' Darcy asked. 'It's just a more expensive way of doing something you'd normally do by running an electric wire round the room.

She gave him a cold look. 'It also works the projector and moves the curtains.'

Darcy grinned. 'And doubtless makes the coffee for the interval.'

'It saves paying several men's wages.'

'Capitalist stooges,' Darcy said placidly. 'Robbing working men of their jobs. Everybody's at it these days.'

Again the cold look. 'Lyons University has one. There's one in Vichy and one or two even outside France. The Professor is also politically motivated. He's a committed Communist, believes in it and doesn't hesitate to make his views known.'

'No wish to become a deputy?' Darcy asked sarcastically.

'He's been asked to stand. He prefers not to.'

All the same, Darcy thought, he's quite a boy. He seemed to have spare time for everything. Darcy only seemed able to find spare time for girls.

As he rose to leave, he caught sight of a painting on the wall. She saw his eyes on it.

'It's the Golden Mount,' she said. 'It's a Buddhist temple. It's over a hundred metres high. I bought it in Bangkok.'

'On holiday?'

She shook her head. 'A Far East tour with the Professor. He was visiting universities there.'

She was obviously glad to see the back of him. As he rode down in the lift, he glanced at his watch. It was well into the afternoon now and, leaving the building, he decided that if Marie-Anne Chahu had the day off and had had to make hurried telephone calls when he arrived they were doubtless to warn someone she was expecting not to arrive for a while.

Wondering who it was, he went back to his car and parked further away where he couldn't be seen from Marie-Anne Chahu's window. Like Nosjean, Darcy sometimes had hunches.

After a short wait, he saw one of the city's leading citizens approaching. He was a man in his forties, fat and pale-faced, a man who sat on a committee that had been formed to watch the welfare of young people and make sure they didn't fall by the wayside. Darcy grinned.

'So that's him,' he said to himself. 'Léonard Durandot, by all that's wonderful!'

Durandot entered the building warily, glancing about him like a burglar bolting from the scene of a crime into a street full of policemen. Since he lived in a large house near Messigny with a wife and four children, perhaps it was as well. It didn't bother Darcy. He was just curious. A man had every right to have a mistress and, remembering Marie-Anne Chahu's figure, Darcy felt he could hardly blame him. He just liked to know who was bedding whom. It often helped.

Satisfied, he was just about to start his car when he noticed a girl approaching the building on a scooter. She was young, dressed in a skirt and striped blouse, and she had a pile of books strapped behind her on the pillion. She was so obviously a student, Darcy's hand hesitated over the ignition key. In the last few days to Darcy students had come to mean drugs and he found this interesting.

Perhaps he was mistaken and the man he'd just seen entering the block of flats had nothing to do with Marie-Anne Chahu. Perhaps his interests were elsewhere and quite innocent, and the building represented something else entirely. Was the man they were after in there somewhere? Was Marie-Anne Chahu – the thought struck him with startling force – was she some sort of go-between for one of the gangs? It would certainly explain the expensive tastes.

He watched the girl enter the building. She seemed remarkably in control of herself. She was pert, high-breasted, clean, dark-haired and almost danced along, and, acting on an impulse, Darcy left his car and went into the building and back to Marie-Anne Chahu's flat. This time when she opened the door, she frowned at him angrily.

'Thought I'd left my notebook here,' he said.

'No,' she said. 'You haven't.'

He smiled. 'Just thought.'

'Is it something policemen make a habit of doing?'

'Not all of them,' Darcy said. 'Just me.'

As he returned to his car, he was frowning. He had been half-expecting to see the young student in the flat, looking guilty with money in her fist. Or at the very least Léonard Durandot, just unbuttoning his jacket. The flat had been empty of anyone but its owner.

He was still frowning as he started his car. On the way back into the city, he stopped at the office of an estate agent he knew.

'I want to know who owns the Maison Joliet, the new block near the Place Wilson,' he said. 'There's only one.'

The estate agent gestured. 'That's the Charles Rolland Company, I think. Hang on, I'll check.'

He returned a moment or two later. 'Yes, it's Rollands'.'

'Rented or owned?'

'All rented. Unfurnished.'

'I'd like to know who pays the rent on one of them. Will Rollands' tell me?'

'Shouldn't think so. It's a very discreet place.'

'That's what I thought. Find out for me, will you? Number 27.'

'It'll take time.' The estate agent smiled. 'What are you after, you old ram?'

Darcy smiled and tapped his nose. 'Ring me at the office. I'll be back in an hour or so.'

Driving towards the city centre, he stopped again, this time in front of a car showroom. The space behind the glass was full of British cars, among them a Triumph 1500. For a while, he stood outside, staring at it, then he marched through the door and asked for the manager.

'Monsieur Bazin's in the bar next door, having a coffee,' he was told.

To Darcy's surprise, the first person he saw in the bar was Emile Escaut, who was sitting in front of the zinc with a whisky in front of him. This time his trousers were a bright jade green and he wore a checked pink shirt, though he didn't look any cleaner than when Darcy had first met him in the Rue du Chapeau Rouge near the body of Gilles Miollis. He was deep in conversation with the barman and didn't notice Darcy, who took up a position by the door so that Escaut couldn't reach the street without having to brush against him.

Bazin, the manager of the car showroom, was an old friend of Darcy's and the coffee he was supposed to be drinking turned out to be a large beer.

'Coffee's not much good,' he grinned. 'Not in this heat. What are you after?'

Darcy smiled. 'A Triumph 1500,' he said.

Bazin's eyebrows shot up. 'Want to buy one?'

'No. I want to know if you sell many.'

Bazin hoisted his face out of his beer and nodded enthusiastically. 'Oh, yes. Almost every day.' He grinned. 'Not many, mon brave. They're a little expensive for ordinary people.'

'Do you keep records?'

'But of course.'

'Who owns one with the registered number 2731-QT-21? Blue. White-walled tyres.'

'I can find out.'

'Do that. I'll call in after I've had a beer.'

As Bazin finished his drink and left, Darcy moved nearer to Escaut who saw him approach through the mirror behind the bar. He turned quickly, his face startled. Darcy smiled at him.

'Bonjour, mon brave.' He gestured at the whisky. 'Expensive drink for a man of your means.'

Escaut shrugged. 'I treat myself once in a while.'

'On Perdrix's money?'

'Whose?'

'You know who I mean, my friend. Your girlfriend's father.'

Escaut frowned. 'He doesn't give *me* money.'

'How about his daughter. Does she?'

Escaut shrugged. 'She has some.'

'How much of it are you hoping to get your hands on?' Escaut gave him a look of sheer hatred. 'None. It's hers. She does what she likes with it.'

'Then what are you hoping to get out of it?'

'Out of what?'

'Living with her.'

'Nothing.'

'No?' Darcy smiled, things beginning to click in his head. 'Haven't you ever hoped that Pappy would offer her hand in marriage?'

Escaut frowned. 'I expect we'll get round to that in time.'

'Unless, of course, Pappy pays up a substantial sum first to discourage you.' Darcy leaned forward. 'Didn't someone do something like that with Alexandrine Bétheot, daughter of the head of the Pigues Pottery Group. Limoges way.

'Did they?' Escaut was studying his whisky as if he'd suddenly spotted a goldfish in it. 'I don't know.'

Darcy gestured. '*He* had a daughter about the same age as your girl friend, who got herself caught up with some slob. He paid out quite a good sum to call him off.'

'Did he?'

'Yes. It's easy for people like that these days, of course. These wealthy chicks try to look as scruffy as the rest to show they're egalitarian and Marxist. It makes them easy pick-ups. We have a file on the Bétheot case. Full of names. Guy by the name of Patrice Bourges, I think. Looked a bit like you, come to mention it.' Darcy finished his beer and slapped Escaut on the shoulder. 'Be seeing you, mon brave.'

Outside, he halted in the doorway of the car showroom and stared back at the bar. Almost immediately, Escaut appeared, wiping his mouth with the back of his hand. Pausing in the doorway, he stared to right and left, then hurried off. He seemed alarmed and Darcy smiled. He enjoyed alarming people like Escaut.

Lighting a cigarette, he entered the showroom. Bazin met him.

'That was easy,' he said. 'It belongs to a Mademoiselle Marie-Anne Chahu.'

'Did she pay for it or did someone else?'

'Dieu, how would I know?'

'Can you find out?'

'I expect so. It'll be in the files in our accounts department.'

Darcy smiled. 'Show me the way to your accounts department.' he said.

Darcy was still smiling as he drove back past the University but, as he turned into the Boulevard Gabriel, he saw the young bright-eyed, high-breasted girl he'd seen entering the Maison Joliet an hour before. As she sailed past him he made a forbidden U-turn and followed the scooter past the University buildings standing like the white hip-bones of some huge dead monster on the bare slope. At the Faculté de Droit she parked and vanished inside. Following her, Darcy saw her wave to the porter.

'That girl,' he said. 'Is she a student?'

The porter smiled. 'Yes, Monsieur. A good one, too. Nadine Weyl. She works hard and enjoys university. She's the sort we need. She's from Metz. Poor but brainy.'

Darcy walked slowly back to his car. There seemed to be a lot of intriguing angles to the Marie-Anne Chahu business, he decided.

# eleven

Professor Foussier lived at Francheville, hard under the edge of the Plateau de Langres, where the fields run in long mellow folds and the villages have a lost look as if they've been dredged up from the seventeenth century.

It was a place of old houses, with an ancient church alongside the stream. Behind it lay the presbytery and to one side, just beyond the churchyard, was what had once been the home of the Seigneurs of Francheville. The Seigneurs of Francheville had never been wealthy and their home had not been a château, but it was large and it had the beauty of old age. Professor Foussier had bought it ten years before when the previous owners, beggared by their excesses, had had to sell.

As the car drove through the huge iron gates and crunched luxuriously up the gravelled drive, Pel looked about him enviously. As a boy in Vieilly he had worked as a gardener's assistant in just such a house as this. They were shown in by a girl in a grey dress that was discreet enough not to offend the girl by branding her a servant but let it be well and truly known that she wasn't a member of the family. The interior of the house was efficient and colourful, and Foussier's wife went with it. She was no longer young but was still full of beauty, and there seemed a formidable strength of character in the bright black eyes and strong chin. Pel had heard of her. She had one of the finest collections of pressed flowers in France, if not the whole world.

Foussier was not at home and Madame Foussier tried to explain. 'He's a very busy man, Inspector,' she said. 'He's obviously been delayed. He never normally misses appointments. He's surprisingly humble about that sort of thing.'

Pel struggled not to show his irritation, something he never found very easy. It was Saturday and Saturday was supposed to be a day of rest when half of them were off-duty. They never were, of course, and certainly not *that* Saturday, with all the enquiries that were pending. Only Misset, complaining that he was bringing up a clutch of children who never saw their father, had chivvied Pel into allowing him to be free.

Foussier's wife realised he was angry and tried to put things right. 'My husband finds the strain a little too much at times,' she said. 'And occasionally he goes into retreat. What I mean is he goes flying or sometimes disappears for a day or two. Sometimes from here. More often when he's on one of his trips abroad. In the early days, my husband's assistant, Marie-Anne Chahu, used to telephone me in alarm, wondering what had happened to him. But he was just recharging his batteries, that's all, going somewhere he wasn't known and walking – or reading, or merely thinking. Perhaps that's where he is now. He'll be here soon.'

It didn't please Pel to think that the man he'd come to see was probably floating about among the clouds. He managed to control his temper. 'I was hoping to ask your husband about a man called Nincic, Madame.'

'Fran Nincic?'

'Do you know him, Madame?' This seemed to be an unexpected bonus and helped to make up for the absence of Foussier himself.

'Isn't he the young man Marie-Anne Chahu took a fancy to?'

Darcy and Pel glanced at each other. Better and better.

'Did she?'

'I think so. She's rather a greedy young woman. She has plenty of men but always seems to like more. She met him here. My husband gave a party. Most heads of departments do from time to time, you know. For people who've helped them. Monsieur Nincic was among the guests and Marie-Anne had been a great help in organising everything. She's most efficient. I have to admit, of course, that there *was* something rather special about Monsieur Nincic.'

'There was, Madame? What sort of thing?'

Madame Foussier gestured. 'About the eyes. He was very male and very sure of it. Practical. Barbaric. I heard he was Hungarian.'

'Yugoslav,' Pel corrected. He paused. 'This affair between him and Mademoiselle Chahu – did it go any further?'

She shrugged. 'Probably. I don't delve into the private affairs of my husband's employees. I'm already too involved in his.'

'Of course, Madame. This work for students your husband does must sometimes be a great trial to you.'

'He was certainly quick to recruit me to give advice on drugs.'

'To students?'

'Good heavens, no! To the committee he heads. I'm not qualified to discuss cures. I can only advise on which drugs cause depression and which hallucinations. That sort of thing. I qualified as a doctor. I never practised, though, so I'm probably out of date. But my father was also a doctor and my brother works for Produits Pharmaceutiques de Lyon who, as you'll doubtless know, make drugs.' She gestured again. 'Still, it's not me they come to, it's my husband. They're always telephoning.'

'Does he ever tell you about them?'

'Never. He's very discreet. He ought to have been a doctor. In fact, he nearly was. His father was a doctor, too, in Alsace,

MARK HEBDEN

and at first his bent was in that direction and this was how
we became acquainted.' She gave a little laugh. 'I'm sorry,
Inspector. We were talking about your students and their
problems. My husband preserves the secrecy of their identity
most meticulously. He's very conscientious about it and it
worries him a lot. It even depresses him a little, I think. He
becomes preoccupied and distant and his thoughts are
sometimes far away. He has so many things on his mind, of
course, so many interests. He could have been a success at
any one of half a dozen professions. This, of course, is why
we have all this.' She gestured at the elegant room they were
sitting in. 'He happens also to be clever with the stock
market, too, you see.

'His sister was also brilliant,' she went on. 'They were very
much alike – even to look at. But in her case there was
something missing, something unstable, and she couldn't
cope with her own brains. She married beneath her – a man
who wasn't even honest.'

'Do other universities contact your husband?'

'But, of course. They all have committees on drugs these
days. My husband's in constant contact with Professor
Schutz, of Vienna, and Professor Liener, of Geneva. Von
Hoffbaur, of Heidelberg, too, and Etain, of the Sorbonne.'
She smiled. 'Perhaps I'd better write them down.'

She drew a piece of paper from a drawer. It was an old
letter, Pel noticed, carefully cut to a useful size and clipped
with others to make a jotting pad, and it occurred to him that
perhaps some of Foussier's wealth came from the hard-
headed Alsatian habit of wasting nothing.

She began to write. 'I'm sure my husband would be happy
to give you a complete list, but perhaps these will help for the
time being.'

Pel took the paper. Turning it over idly, he saw a name
on it.

120

'Ma chère Noëlle,' he saw. 'Je suis heureux de t'informer – ' then the paper had been cut.

'That's me, of course,' she said. 'My name was Noëlle Hérisson. My collection was known as the Hérisson collection originally. You've heard of my collection, I suppose. Would you like to see it?'

Pel couldn't tell a delphinium from a daisy. Geraniums were easy because they were so bright they leapt out and snapped at you, but the rest were just flowers.

He was looking for an excuse when they heard a car arrive and Foussier appeared at a rush. He was tall for a Frenchman, tall enough even, Pel thought, for an American. No Frenchman had a right to be that tall – especially when Evariste Clovis Désiré Pel was on the short side. However, there was some satisfaction to be gained from the fact that Foussier was also overweight and that his stomach bulged, though he was still too good-looking by a long chalk, with his smile, flashing eyes and long greying hair, something that also caused considerable resentment to Pel, who considered he personally looked as if his face had been trodden on. What was more Foussier was also immaculately dressed, which made Pel feel like a plumber who'd come about a blocked lavatory.

'I'm so sorry I'm late,' he said at once. 'I'm always so busy I lose touch with time.' He indicated chairs and began to empty his brief-case of maps, slide rules and dividers. 'I've been flying,' he went on. 'I have a Centre-Est DR 220. It's a two-seater trainer that can be used as a three-seater. I've been at it for fifteen years now. I love to get up there on my own. It rests my mind to do navigational problems.'

It exhausted Pel merely to work out how much he had left of his salary after he had deducted mortgage, insurance, pension, hire purchase, Madame Routy's salary and a few other things.

Foussier gestured and flung back a lock of long grey hair. 'I take it it's about the drugs problem you wish to talk,' the deep plummy voice said. 'Of course there is a problem. There's always a problem where there are young people but here it's nothing like it is in Paris, Marseilles, Amsterdam, London or the United States. There, it's become a menace.'

'It's growing here,' Pel pointed out.

Foussier gestured. 'But still hardly big enough yet to be important.

'It's always important when someone dies,' Pel said. 'And someone has.'

Foussier was nodding now, his expression concerned. 'Yes,' he said. 'The Cortot boy, of course. He wasn't exactly a tough character, though, was he?'

'Did you know him?' Darcy asked.

'He came to me for advice. I told him he should take treatment.'

'How much of a problem do you see exactly?'

Foussier toyed with a pen. 'I know they experiment, of course. All young people experiment. In politics, in ideologies, in religion – ' he paused ' – in sex. And nowadays, with more freedom, it's much easier.'

'Did you know the ones who *were* experimenting?'

'I could guess. But I have no proof. And I can't accuse them. I might be wrong. One of the lecturers at the Sorbonne once did accuse one of his students. It landed him in a slander action. The pupil just had unnaturally bright eyes. I have to wait for them to come to me.'

'Do they?'

'Not often. But the excuse's always the same. They want to live. As if they *aren't* living? Here! At a university in one of the most beautiful cities in France! They don't realise how fortunate they are. However, it seems now that someone else as well as myself has realised this need they feel, and started to trade on it. Unhappily, there are plenty of people in the world today like that.'

'There are indeed,' Pel agreed. 'Have you ever heard, for instance, of a man called Tagliacci?'

'Tagliacci?' Foussier considered for a moment then shook his head. 'Never.'

'Pépé le Cornet?'

The heavy leonine head shook again. 'Who's he? He sounds like a gangster.'

'He *is* a gangster.'

'I thought he might be. The name has a ring. It seems to go with the sort of people I'm after. I'm already making enquiries.'

Pel sat up sharply. 'What sort of enquiries?'

Foussier smiled. 'I've been in contact with one or two – ah – disreputable people I've heard of in Marseilles. I'm hoping to find out where these drugs are coming from.'

Pel shot an alarmed look at Darcy. 'We'd prefer it if you didn't,' he said.

'Oh?' Foussier seemed offended. 'Why not?'

'It could tread on the toes of the police engaged in narcotics work. People making private enquiries have the habit of causing the pushers and the importers to lie low just when the police are wanting them in the open.'

Foussier gave him a look that was suddenly cold. 'I have to do my duty,' he said.

Pel returned the look with interest. He hated do-gooders who had to do their duty. Almost as much harm was done by them as was done by the do-badders.

'There is another point, of course,' he advised.

'And that is?'

'It could be highly dangerous.'

'For whom?'

'For you. Marseilles is a tricky place. There are always clashes there. Corsicans, Algerians, local heavies, the Foreign

Legion. They're always at each other's throats. It's like Chicago.'

Foussier shrugged. 'That's a risk I have to take. I've undertaken this work and I must carry it to its proper conclusion. I'm not afraid.'

He sounded pompous and Pel wasn't sure whether he was trying to impress them or himself.

'If I didn't take risks,' he was saying now, 'the whole thing would be quite pointless. I'm sure you see that.'

'No, Monsieur,' Pel snapped. 'I don't! Men involved with drugs are unemotional people. They must be or they wouldn't be able to make money out of the destruction of young lives.'

There was a distinct trace of hostility in the air as Foussier replied. 'I'm sure if I were to put to them the damage they're doing – '

Pel interrupted sharply. 'If you find out what they're doing and let them know you're aware of it,' he snapped, 'I can well imagine their next step would be to eliminate you.'

'I don't believe it.'

'Marseilles Bay,' Pel said, 'must he full of blocks of concrete containing people who thought they knew how to stop drug pedlars. The safest way's to leave it with us. We have the organisation and, if necessary, the weapons. Amateurs can only damage our prospects and put themselves in unbelievable danger.'

The interview came to an abrupt and unexpected end. What had promised to be a useful and informative interview had ended up in acrimony and bad feeling. As they were shown out and headed for the car, Darcy was scowling.

'The trouble with him,' he said, 'is that he's too clever by half and it would serve the bastard right if the boys from Marseilles did strap a bit of railway line to his feet and dropped him in the sea off Hyères.'

# twelve

When Pel told Polverari about Foussier's intentions, the judge sighed. 'It's always the same,' he said. 'Once they're hooked on doing good, they stay hooked. I suppose we'd better keep an eye on him, though, in case someone decides to do him in.'

'With those sort of friends,' Pel growled, 'we don't need enemies. We have enough on our slates without looking after people who persist in shoving their long snouts in where they're not wanted.'

Polverari shrugged. 'Nevertheless –' he gestured ' – I'll have a word with the Chief.'

Pel returned to his office, feeling overworked and martyred. It made his day, and for a while he sat thinking, scratching with his pencil at his blotter as his mind roved over the Miollis business. After a while he came to life and, to his disgust, he found all his doodles were of cigarettes.

He tossed the pencil aside, still brooding heavily on the witlessness of do-gooders and particularly Professor Foussier. Anybody who thought they could sort out the Marseilles gangs with good intentions had another think coming, he decided. You didn't go after that lot with appeals for mercy. You went after them with a gun. *Two* guns, in fact. More, if possible. A tank if you had one. Nobody dealing in drug trafficking ever took chances and anyone who thought he could start a conversation with them was likely to end up with a bullet in the head. Like Miollis.

Apart from himself, everybody else was out of the office stuffing themselves with beer and sandwiches at the Bar Transvaal. As the sun passed its zenith they began to return and he could hear Lagé and Misset talking next door and Krauss going on again about his retirement. He listened sourly. He was feeling exhausted. The Chief was in a bad temper and wasn't inclined to give Foussier the bodyguard that Polverari had suggested, considering like Pel that he was shoving his nose in where it wasn't wanted, and it had required all Pel's tact to bring him round. Depressed by the day and the heat, he was just about to light another cigarette to bolster up his despair about being unable to stop smoking when the telephone rang. To his surprise it was Madame Foussier.

'Inspector – ' she sounded agitated ' – I think you'd better come out here at once! A man telephoned a little while ago and asked for my husband. Fortunately he was out and I was suspicious because he didn't sound at all like the people he associates with.'

Pel was sitting up now, alert at once. Reaching for a cigarette, he stuck it in his mouth only to realise there was one already there. Disgusted at his weakness, he flung them both across the room. 'Did he give you a name, Madame?' he asked.

'Yes, he did, Inspector. Treguy.'

Treguy! So he'd turned up again! Pel slapped the desk in his anger, and, ignoring the two cigarettes on the floor, reached for another. And that fool, Foussier, had been so certain nobody would be interested in him!

'Madame,' he said quickly. 'I would advise you to lock the doors and, if you know where your husband is, to get in touch with him at once. I suspect this man might be dangerous. We've already been involved with him once.'

The voice at the other end of the line grew unexpectedly sharp. 'Then, if you knew of him, Inspector, and thought he was dangerous, why didn't you do something to stop him bothering my husband?'

Pel glared at the telephone. He got control of his anger. 'We did,' he said. 'I have already warned your husband.'

'I think you should have done more than that. What he needs is a bodyguard.'

'Madame, he's got one!'

'I've seen none.'

In a fury, Pel contacted the uniformed branch and was informed that the Chief had instructed that the bodyguard was to start that afternoon.

'It had better start at once,' Pel snapped. Slamming down the telephone, he ran to the Chief's office. The Chief's bad temper hadn't diminished.

'Damn this Foussier!' he snarled. 'If he's tangling with the Marseilles lot he's handling a time bomb. Why did you tell the Quai des Orfèvres to let this Treguy go, anyway? I expect we'd better get them on to it. But I'm due to see Senator Forton. You fix it, Pel.'

Pel's authority wasn't quite as powerful as the Chief's and it was another hour before anything started happening. And another hour after that when the telephone rang in Pel's office to tell him they were just too late.

'Foussier's just telephoned in,' he was told. 'He's found a bomb attached to his car.'

'What! Where?'

'He's at the University.'

'Hold him! Who's handling the bomb?'

'Inspector Goriot. It's at the Faculté des Langues Modernes. They've cleared the place and called in the army. There's also a Madame Foussier on the telephone, she'd like a word with you. She says her husband's been on to her and insists on keeping it quiet.

'Tell her from me – ' Pel's voice rose angrily ' – that we can't keep it quiet! We asked him to be careful and he refused! I shall arrive eventually with my cohorts of minions and I'm afraid her husband will just have to lump it!'

When Pel reached the Faculty of Modern Languages the army bomb-disposal unit from the barracks had already made the bomb safe.

There were crowds on the sidewalks, marshalled by the police, and hundreds of cars piling up, honking madly, the traffic police gesturing furiously at them, their faces savage. Students, many of them regarding the affair as a great joke, were watching from the opposite side of the road, resisting as hard as they could the efforts to move them on. There were police trucks and cars everywhere and more arriving all the time, together with two or three army trucks from the barracks in the Avenue du Drapeau, which at least was handy and had despatched its representatives at once.

A young sous-lieutenant, who didn't look old enough to have left school, was talking with Inspector Goriot.

'Bit crude,' he was saying. 'Looked as if it had been hurriedly put together.'

'Everybody's at it these days,' Goriot said gloomily. 'Kids blowing up their girl friends because they won't come across; husbands blowing up their mothers-in-law because they nag. It's not surprising though, is it? After all, everybody knows how to do it and you can buy the stuff at any gardening shop. Even the kids' comics tell them the ingredients.'

'This isn't kids' comic stuff,' Pel snarled. 'Nor someone blowing up his mother-in-law. Where was it fixed?'

'Connected to the exhaust. With a detonating device that would set it off when the engine started. It would have exploded the petrol tank and at the very least given him some nasty burns. I think it was activated here. It wouldn't be a minute's job to get under a car and connect it.'

'*Here?*' Pel glared. 'Where everybody can see?'

Goriot sighed. 'There's a garage down the road,' he said. 'The officials of the University are always having them look at their cars if they've given trouble on the way in. There are always people in overalls looking into engines. Nobody would take any notice.'

They found Foussier waiting inside the entrance hall. He was surrounded by students and university officials, all looking a little scared and excited. Foussier seemed calm but a little nervous.

'My wife telephoned to tell me about this Treguy character,' he said. 'I decided it was just someone who was trying to be funny.'

'Treguy worked for a Paris mob, Monsieur,' Pel growled. 'The Paris mobs don't go in for jokes.'

Foussier gave a little shudder and ran his hand through his hair.

'I'm still a bit unnerved. I suppose I ought to make a point in future of checking my car.'

'I think that would be a good idea, Monsieur. How did you come to spot the bomb?'

Foussier gestured. 'I had just reached my car when I remembered something and took out my pen to make a note of it. My hands were full –' he gestured at a number of books and a briefcase that stood on a table near the door ' – and I dropped the pen. It rolled half-under the car and it was as I was on my hands and knees trying to reach it that I remembered my wife's telephone call. I looked under the car and there it was.'

'I hope you'll bear my warnings in mind in future, Monsieur. The Paris and Marseilles mobs aren't to be tampered with. I'd advise you *always* to check your car. I've arranged for a police watch to be placed on you.'

Foussier looked angry. 'I don't want a bodyguard!'

Pel was growing angry, too, now. 'Imagine what would happen if anything happened to you,' he snapped. 'A man engaged in all the activities you're engaged in. A man working for the young. You're well known, Monsieur. The newspapers would crucify us if we permitted anything to happen to you.'

Foussier frowned. 'Of course, of course! I realise. Nevertheless I have my duty to do.'

As Pel opened his mouth to protest further, Foussier held up his hand and managed a twisted smile. 'My lectures, I meant, Inspector. No more. I still have those. We can't let assassins stop the world from turning, can we?'

Grudgingly, Pel admitted that he was right and equally grudgingly Foussier agreed to a bodyguard for the time being, so that for a change they parted on slightly better terms.

During the afternoon, Pel went out to Francheville to see Madame Foussier. It was an unsatisfactory interview because she clearly suspected the police of falling down on their job in not providing immediate protection for her husband, and was inclined to be hostile, while her talk with Treguy had been so brief as to provide no clues whatsoever to his whereabouts.

By the time he returned to the city, Pel's ill-temper had increased. Foussier, he decided, was becoming a pest. He couldn't possibly be aware of the man-hours his stupidity was costing them. A man had been on and off the telephone to the Quai des Orfèvres ever since, and half the Paris force had been trying to contact Treguy's boss, Pépé le Cornet, who had finally been tracked down near Etables in Brittany buying cattle for a farm he maintained near Chartres. He had been driving a Cadillac and had with him a girl of unparalleled beauty. Pel had listened sourly. All he had was a garden twelve metres long, a clapped-out Peugeot and Madame Routy.

Pépé le Cornet's reaction to the news that they were seeking Treguy had been that if Treguy was in Burgundy then he had better return to Paris – quick! Treguy had no business branching out on his own and if he were doing any threatening, he wasn't doing it on behalf of Pépé le Cornet.

'If he's gone over to that lot in Marseilles – ' he had announced. He had left the sentence unfinished, because it looked very much as though Treguy *had* gone over to that lot in Marseilles.

Another part of the Paris force was hunting through all the small hotels and boarding houses to find Madame Miollis, and the only thing that gave anybody any satisfaction at all was that at last they had a bodyguard on Foussier.

It was as Pel brooded on the injustices of life that Krauss brought in a special edition of *Le Bien Public*.

'They've got it in about Foussier,' he said.

He held out the paper to Pel. 'BOMB ATTEMPT ON PROFESSOR,' it announced. 'RAYMOND FOUSSIER'S ESCAPE.'

Pel waved the paper aside. Doubtless, he thought bitterly, *France Soir* and *France Dimanche* would produce a woman from somewhere before long, perhaps even a scandal. He almost hoped they would.

As the door closed, he sat brooding again, staring at his blotter with its doodles of cigarettes. It seemed, he decided, that his neck of the woods was suddenly growing dangerous. Despite his job, he had always thought of Burgundy as a peaceful province. Even the ancient Gauls had professed a liking for its suave countryside and life-giving beverage, and the place had a continuing vitality all its own.

'Je suis fier-e d'être Bourguignon.' As the tune entered his head, Pel almost stood and saluted. After all, why not be proud? Molière had praised the place and its wines, and a certain Colonel Bisson, marching his men north after Napoleon's Italian campaign, had even drawn them up outside the gates of Clos Vougeot and presented arms.

Burgundy was something special and he didn't like the idea of Marseilles or Paris gangsters muscling in. Burgundy was for Burgundians. They ought to be living happily in the old way with good honest crimes committed by good honest Burgundian criminals. They needed gangsters, do-gooders and gang feuds as they needed a hole in the head. It was already occupying three men eight hours a day to keep watch on Foussier's house. One false move by him and the whole thing would fall apart just when it was beginning to knit together.

His runaway thoughts slowed and he gave a sigh heavy enough to shift a windjammer. Nothing was knitting together, he realised. Nothing at all. It was just easy to blame somebody else.

Heading home that evening in a state of depression, he had just taken off his jacket and lit what he tried to imagine was – but knew very well wasn't – the last cigarette of the day, when Darcy phoned.

'Patron?' His voice sounded heavy with foreboding. 'They've found Treguy.'

'Already?' Pel's heart thumped. 'Where?'

'In a field near La Charité-sur-Brenne.' Darcy paused. He sounded tired. 'He's dead.'

# thirteen

Sighing, Pel reached for his jacket and headed for his car. 'What time will you be back?' Madame Routy screeched from the kitchen where she was sweating over the cooker.

'God knows,' Pel said. 'Probably never.' Didier was sitting on the terrasse with his fishing rod. 'Are we going fishing?' he asked.

Pel shook his head. 'Alas, no, mon brave. There's work to do.'

'The murder?'

'Not *the* murder. A murder. Another one.'

'Honest?' Didier's eyes gleamed. 'Can I come? Perhaps I could help.'

'I doubt it, mon brave. And I suspect it will be a long, hard and difficult night.'

'Who is it?'

'A Parisian gangster who's been shoving his nose into our business down here.'

'Is it a gang feud?'

'That's the way it looks.'

'Maybe they bumped him off because he knew too much.'

It hadn't been Pel's view but he had to admit it was a possibility.

'They're clever, you know, Monsieur Pel,' Didier said. 'It's the clever ones you have to look for. Look at Landru.'

'Exactly,' Pel agreed. 'Look at Landru. All those women he polished off.'

He drove into the city, scowling. The place was becoming stiff with corpses. First Miollis. Now Treguy, to herald the start of a gang feud. Pépé le Cornet had made no bones concerning his feelings about Treguy having gone over to Tagliacci. And where in the name of God was Nincic? He still hadn't turned up and the Path Lab where he worked was beginning to grow worried. Perhaps *he* was a corpse, too.

Darcy, Leguyader and Doc. Minet were all waiting when Pel arrived. Standing to one side was a man in blue cotton trousers and a red checked shirt. He was smoking a pipe, carried a heavy dogwood stick and had the placid look of a countryman who knows he's not involved.

'Who's he?' Pel asked.

'Robert Morvan, of La Charité. He found the body.'

'Where is it?'

Darcy gestured towards an old Peugeot, as grey, ugly and ancient as Pel's own, that stood behind the hedge, just inside the field. Watching them, a herd of black and white Friesian cows mooed a soft welcome.

'They must have driven in there where they couldn't be seen,' Darcy said. 'That's where it happened.'

Treguy was crouched in the rear seat, his face deep in the corner cushions, the wound in the back of the head.

'Shot,' Minet said. 'Same gun as killed Miollis, I'd say.'

The big Parisian looked curiously shrunken in death and Pel studied him for a long time. It was a classic execution and Morvan, the farmer, could add nothing. He had walked across the fields from his house two kilometres away, checking fences and generally looking over his property, and had ended up by deciding to visit the cattle in case the heat was distressing them. Seeing the car in the field, he had decided it belonged to picnickers or to a young couple stirred to passion by the temperature, and had headed towards it to throw them out.

'I found him instead,' he said in a flat voice.

'Better get a statement,' Pel said to Darcy. 'Then he can go. I expect he's busy.' He turned to Doc. Minet. 'When was he killed?'

Minet shrugged. 'Hard to tell exactly in this heat. Twenty-four hours ago, I reckon.'

'Soon after he telephoned Foussier's home.' Pel turned to Darcy. 'Have Pépé le Cornet brought in. Find him. He's somewhere. Have him arrested.' He turned back to Minet. 'Revenge motive, I imagine,' he growled. 'For transferring to Tagliacci and moving in on Pépé le Cornet's operation. Something of that sort.'

He lit a cigarette gloomily, wondering if the gangs had picked on the city because its airport was small and casual in its attitude to regulations. Pel had once flown to London and he had noticed there had been no security checks. The bar had been operated by the boy who weighed the baggage and the duty-free shop by the girl who handled the tickets, and there was nothing to stop passengers – or, for that matter, the people who'd come to see them off – buying duty-free goods and passing them into the city. There was doubtless also no one to check what was inside suitcases either, because customs vigilance was as casual as everything else and Tagliacci or Pépé le Cornet had probably noticed it too. Whatever else, the gangs were efficient. They had too much to lose.

'Let's have a watch kept on the airport,' he said briskly. 'The stuff might be coming in that way. What about fingerprints?'

'Plenty on the car,' Prélat, the fingerprint expert, said. 'Mostly the dead man's.'

'No others?'

Prélat shrugged. 'There'll be a few, I suppose. I'll let you know if we identify them.'

By the following Wednesday, Pel's mood was murderous. The newspapers were having a ball. Two murders were enough to start them sending up rockets. *France Soir* was beginning to grow hysterical and even the normally staid *Bien Public* announced 'Encore Un Cadavre! Une Exécution?' as if they were stumbling across corpses all over the area.

Pel gazed at the words, wishing he could consign Henriot, who covered the district, to everlasting torment. Alongside the story was the news that Foussier was being guarded, which brought to Pel's mood the sweetness and light of a cat in a sack. The newspapers, he decided, were getting their perspectives all wrong because it was surely Foussier's self-important interfering that had been the cause of both the bomb and Treguy's death.

There were pictures, too, of course. A new one of Foussier, dark-eyed, good-looking and romantic enough to set his female admirers swooning in droves. The one of Pel was *not* new. He obviously didn't rate so highly and it had been taken at an enquiry in the uplands the winter before when he'd been half-frozen. He looked as if he were on his last legs and he wondered gloomily if Madame Faivre-Perret had noticed it. Since she didn't ring up enquiring despairingly about his health, he could only assume she hadn't. Or couldn't have cared less.

The attitude of the Quai des Orfèvres in Paris seemed one of indifference. They appeared to take the view that they were well rid of Treguy and the moves to apprehend the murderer at their end seemed to be mere formalities, as if they considered whoever had removed him had done the world a good turn. Just to cheer them all up a little more, they passed on the information that Treguy's boss, Pépé le Cornet, had also now disappeared.

'We think he might have come your way,' they said.

The news sent Pel's spirits lower than ever.

'Where are they hiding?' he growled.

'Well,' Darcy said, 'they won't be staying at the Hôtel Central, Patron. That's for sure.'

'Warn everybody to keep their eyes open. Every town and village in the area. Especially the hill villages. They're probably holed up in some old house. They're like rats. They've got hideaways in every province in the Republic.' Pel stared at his desk for a moment, his hands automatically fiddling with a pack of Gauloises. 'And while you're at it, contact Marseilles. Find out if any of *their* people have disappeared, too.'

It didn't take Leguyader long to decide with certainty that the weapon that had killed Treguy was the same one that had killed Miollis, but the search for it revealed no more than Prélat's search for fingerprints. There were one or two dabs belonging to Madame Miollis but, since she'd been sleeping with Treguy, it was not hard to believe she could also have been in his car at some time. There were also one or two of Miollis', which seemed to indicate that Treguy had been keeping on the right side of both halves of the family, and it was obvious that Miollis, being already dead, could hardly have killed Treguy.

All the usual things had happened, of course. The staff of the civil half of the airport was strengthened and regulations were tightened to the extent that passengers started to complain. It was typical of the public, of course. Try to protect their lives and they immediately objected to having their comfort interfered with. Nevertheless, for the moment, the airport seemed to be airtight – including that part occupied by the Armée de l'Air.

An appeal had also gone out for anyone in the district where Treguy had been found who might have seen someone acting strangely to come forward (since the area was almost as barren of life as the Sahara, nobody had); dozens of policemen had searched around the cow pats on hands and knees for clues (as usual, there was nothing to be found but those objects that indicated picnickers, tramps and lovers); and the Chief remained in a bad temper (most of which he directed at Pel). With the heat, the ground had been too hard to provide imprints either of car tyres or shoes while, just to improve matters, the cattle which had tramped the area had effectively destroyed anything that could have given an indication of what might have happened, and into the bargain had left evidence of their presence in the flat, brown, drying, fly-encrusted cakes which not only impeded the search but also added to the distaste and ill-temper of the policemen making it.

Darcy's request to Marseilles about their mobsters came back to them within a few hours and he appeared in Pel's office with a grim expression.

'Marseilles reports that everybody's present and correct – ' he began.

'That's something,' Pel said, relieved.

' – except Maurice Tagliacci.'

'What's his line? Do we know?'

'Anything that brings in money. Prostitution, extortion – '

'Drugs?'

'And drugs. They *think*. They're not certain, but they feel he's in that racket, too.'

'And he's disappeared? Which way?'

Darcy sighed. 'This way, Patron. Again – they *think*. He runs a supermarket down there. It's a cover-up, of course, for other things and enables him to get around the country, ostensibly buying for it. They think he's in this area after wine.'

'Contact all the warehouses and vineyards. See if he's been seen around. And broadcast his name with Pépé le Cornet's, in case *he's* big enough to have a hideaway as well.'

The conference in Pel's office was gloomy. The leads seemed to have dried up and only Darcy still seemed ebullient. He was convinced somehow that the drugs Miollis had been working had some sort of source in the Joliet Building where Marie-Anne Chahu lived.

The thought that Marie-Anne Chahu was Foussier's mistress also intrigued Darcy. He was a man who didn't like to let things alone, so when he went off duty the following evening, despite having worked a matter of eighteen hours without stopping, he snatched a beer and sandwich, and borrowed overalls and a box of tools from the carpenter who did odd jobs about the Hôtel de Police. Hanging about outside the Maison Joliet during the next few days, he was surprised at the number of students who appeared. Moving upstairs, deeply concerned with the carpet on the second floor, he noticed that they all seemed to be visiting Marie-Anne Chahu. Without fail, however, they stayed no more than a moment or two then headed back round the corner to the lift out of his vision.

It puzzled him and, with the promise that there were pretty girls and even the legendary Chahu to be seen, he managed to rope Misset into the scheme. He couldn't use Lagé or Nosjean because La Chahu appeared to know them both and Misset was by no means averse to being included.

'You're not studying *her*,' Darcy warned him sharply. 'You're studying what goes on in the flat.'

Misset was given a large wrench and a key for the radiators and the next time Marie-Anne Chahu received a visit, Misset knocked on the door and asked to see the central heating. His report was depressingly devoid of drama.

'They just talked in the doorway for five minutes,' he said. 'I heard a bit of chat about examinations, then the kid collected a list which the Chahu dame took off a pile in the hall and handed to her.'

'Get a look at it?'

'I got a look at the pile. Examination dates and lists of questions. That's all. I helped myself to one.' Misset handed it over to Darcy. 'Seems to be mostly in Russian.'

'Old examination questions in Slav languages,' Darcy said disgustedly. 'Did you see any money change hands, or anything that might have been drugs?'

Misset grinned. 'Nothing. I was by the radiator in the corridor when the kid came out and I managed to crash into her. Sent her flying. Even managed to uptip her handbag. It was one of those open canvas things and the whole lot came out.'

'Whole lot of what?'

'Make-up. Handkerchief. A few coins. Eight one-hundred-franc notes – '

'That's a lot of money for a student,' Darcy said.

Misset shrugged. 'Some of them aren't badly off, and some are careful with their grants, and it *is* the beginning of the month. There was a lipstick, a pair of specs not in a case, one of those things they do their nails with, a notebook – '

'Anything that might have *contained* drugs?'

'Nothing.'

'Could she have stuck them in her pocket?'

Misset grinned. 'This one, mon brave, didn't have a pocket. She had one of those sheath dresses on. Fitted like a skin. I managed to get my hands on her for a second.' Misset grinned. 'Not bad either.'

'What about the books? Anything between the leaves?'

'Couldn't have been. I sent them skating down the corridor. It would have fallen out.'

Darcy frowned. 'What happened?'

'She gave me a dirty look, picked her stuff up and headed for the lift. That's all. Disappeared round the corner. I heard the doors go. When I got there, the light had gone out.'

Darcy was worried. Was Marie-Anne Chahu running something? It didn't seem possible. Women as poised as she was didn't go in for drugs. Sex, yes, but not drugs. And why so many students?

It all seemed depressingly normal. Students were always seeking questions from previous papers to guide them in their studies, and the obvious place to pick them up was from their professor's assistant. But why not at the University or Foussier's private office? Why at La Chahu's flat?

With his shrewd eye, Darcy had not failed to notice also that the girls all seemed cheerfully normal. Working on the carpet with his bag of tools, he watched them appear round the corner from the lift, disappear into La Chahu's apartment, reappear two minutes later and vanish round the corner back to the lift. It seemed perfectly straightforward behaviour and what was more they all seemed bright young creatures, well endowed with busts, behinds and legs. For the life of him he couldn't imagine why girls like that, in the full flush of youth, desirable, ripe for love and obviously of a type to attract males like wasps round a jar of jam, should go in for drugs.

He decided to rope in the doorman. His name was Joachim Salengro and he was as mealy-mouthed an old rogue as Darcy had thought on first meeting him.

He winked and placed a finger alongside his nose. 'Sure, I'll keep my eyes open,' he said, standing in the doorway of his office to brush his plum-coloured suit. 'There isn't much goes on round here that I don't know about.'

Darcy gave him a cold look. 'You didn't know about this,' he said.

# fourteen

What, Pel wondered, should he do about Madame Faivre-Perret? Darcy was right of course. She was a source of information that ought never to be neglected. Burgundy was wine, and wine made the city wealthy. In addition, there was the railway, metallurgy, farm produce, printing, glass, chemical and other industries. Even mustard. The city's mustard was famous and, Pel suspected, it added its mite to the place's prosperity.

And with the wealth and prosperity came the need to spend. There were shops in the city that catered for expensive tastes and, situated midway between Paris and the South, it was a splendid centre for women's fashions. And with women's fashions went hair, and, so Pel had been told, women talked under hair-driers.

But surely not about gangsters! He could hardly expect to pick up tips about Tagliacci or Pépé le Cornet or anyone who was being used by them. Nevertheless, Darcy seemed to feel that in the apartment of Marie-Anne Chahu there were secrets that could be of help to them, but since they had no good reason to demand a search warrant from Judge Polverari, it seemed to leave him no option. It was worth trying, he decided. They could lose nothing.

For a long time he continued to hesitate then, quite deliberately, he lit a cigarette and, drawing in the smoke, allowed it to drift round his lungs and sinuses and the various other tubes in his chest and head. It was like running a flue brush through them. Feeling better and more confident, he took out his list of telephone numbers, staring at the names, his finger on that of Madame Faivre-Perret. To an outsider it was just a name. To anyone who knew her, it meant a woman no longer young who was running a hairdressing business because she was a widow. To Pel it meant all the delights of civilised living after Madame Routy's more homely ministrations.

Madame Faivre-Perret had an office decorated in pink, green and white that seemed to suggest luxury and the sort of exotic delight that Pel, a bachelor attended only by a disgruntled housekeeper – who, he suspected, resembled the harpies knitting round the guillotine during the Reign of Terror – had never in his life experienced. Of course, he told himself firmly, he was going to see her only on police business. Nothing else. Certainly not because he *wanted* to go and see her.

But would she see him? There had been only one previous occasion and then she'd provided information that Pel had wanted, gleaned from the chatterings of her customers as they submitted to the attentions of her assistants. After that, he'd decided he wasn't in the same league and had never telephoned again. He had often thought he might, but he had always put it off and by this time he hardly dared.

'Inspector *who*?'

He couldn't bear the thought of that reply in answer to his 'This is Inspector Pel.'

But there *was* information to be obtained. There *was* police business in front of him.

He picked up the telephone, demanded the number, brushed off a fatuous enquiry of the man on the switchboard who fancied himself as a joker and asked if he wanted a shampoo and set, and sat back to wait.

The voice in his ear came so unexpectedly it made him jump. 'Geneviève Faivre-Perret speaking.'

'This is Evariste Pel.' Pel's voice came out as a croak and he had to clear his throat to make himself heard. 'Inspector Pel, of the Police Judiciaire.'

He waited for the 'Inspector Who?' bit, but it didn't come.

'Oh, hello, Inspector!' There seemed to be genuine pleasure in the voice. 'Where on earth have you been?'

'Busy,' Pel mumbled. 'A lot of work. I'm having to crave your assistance once again. There's information I need.'

'I see. Why haven't you been to see us for so long?' Suddenly Pel was also wondering why.

'We don't get many enquiries of this kind,' he mumbled.

'Surely you don't have to be making an enquiry to call in to have a cup of tea?'

'I *don't*?' Pel's heart thumped.

'We make coffee or tea all day. Women under driers need to quench their thirsts. What can I do for you? I suppose you wish to be discreet, so please feel free to come and see me.'

Pel put the telephone down. He felt as if he'd just run from the Place Darcy to the Place des Ducs at full speed, dodging the buses all the way. He couldn't imagine what had been so exhausting.

He stood up, jerked his jacket straight and pushed his shoulders back. Why should he be so unnerved? His ancestors had marched with Philip the Bold. They had defied the Kings of France. They had probably even been with Vercingetorix at Alesia when he'd stood up to Caesar. His shoulders sagged. And they'd probably also been marched off as prisoners and slaves to Rome when Vercingetorix had been beaten. His shoulders came up again. But they'd probably also been freed because of their courage and intelligence, and made their name there. For all he knew he had Italian cousins.

'I'm going home,' he told Darcy as he left the office.

Reaching the house in the Rue Martin de Noinville, he braced his shoulders for Madame Routy's insults. She was sitting in a deckchair in the garden. He saw her eyes open for a fraction of a second as he appeared, then she closed them again hurriedly, feigning sleep. She obviously had no intention of dragging her fat backside out of the chair to do anything to help.

Going to his room, he took out his best suit. It was a dark charcoal colour, and was the one he kept for when they made him President of the Republic or something. With it he tried a new deep blue shirt he'd had sent for Christmas. His sister was married to a draper and sent him a shirt every winter. Being conservative in taste, he'd always assumed they were part of her husband's stock that they couldn't sell, but since the triumphant result of wearing the last one, he had changed his views.

He put on the shirt, and with it a deep wine-coloured tie. He decided he looked rather good.

'Monsieur Pel – ?'

Swinging round, flushing, he saw Didier standing in the doorway.

'Yes, yes?' In his embarrassment at being caught admiring himself, Pel's voice was sharp.

'I was wondering – ' Didier had a book in his fist that Pel saw was a history of the Napoleonic wars ' – what was the "mot de Cambronne"?'

'The word of Cambronne?'

'I've heard the older boys at school talking about it. They say "The word of Cambronne to you" to each other. I wondered what it was.'

'The word of Cambronne – ' Pel coughed and delivered up the polite fiction that had gone down in history ' – came when Cambronne was asked by the English at Waterloo to surrender. He said "Le Garde meurt mais ne se rend pas." '

'That's *eight* words.'

'Yes – well – ' What Cambronne was reputed actually to have said was 'Merde', but Pel felt he could hardly pass that on to a small boy. He was just trying to find a way out of it when Didier noticed the dark suit and blue shirt and began to grin.

'You're going to see *her?*' he asked.

'See who?'

'The one you went to see last time I was here. You got yourself dressed up as if you were going to a party at the Elysée Palace.'

Pel flushed. 'I'm on police business,' he said firmly. 'Sometimes it's necessary to be dressed up. It depends who you're going to see.'

Didier stared at him for a moment, still smiling. 'Does she like you?' he asked.

'Who?'

'Her. The one you're going to see.'

'I don't know,' Pel said stiffly. 'Probably not.'

'I'll bet she does.'

'You speak from experience, no doubt.'

'Yes. You get to know that sort of thing. They always pretend not to be interested, but they are really.'

'They are?'

'Oh, yes. I've found it with Louise Blay, anyway. You don't have to mess about. You have to tell them what you think and they usually go along with you.'

'They do?'

'Oh, always.'

Pel studied the boy solemnly. 'I wish, mon brave,' he said, 'that I had your experience.'

Leaving the house, he drove back into the city, careful not to get oil from the car door on his sleeve. Pel's car shed oil as a road sprinkler sheds water. Parking at the Hôtel de Police, he walked to the Rue de la Liberté where the hairdressing salon was situated. The girl who met him at the door didn't ask his name and he could only assume she'd been warned to expect him.

Madame Faivre-Perret was in her office. It was up two flights of stairs and to Pel it seemed almost as if he were going to bed. The windows looked over the old roofs towards the Palais des Ducs. Madame Faivre-Perret raised her head as he appeared.

'Inspector, how smart you look!'

Pel bridled with pleasure.

'I think you've dressed specially to see me.'

'No, no!' he protested. 'Not at all!'

But he'd rather have died than appear in the suit he normally wore for work. Pel's working suits all looked as if they'd been run up by a man with one arm during the dark period of a thunderstorm, and, since he considered he was grossly underpaid and couldn't afford new ones, they all had baggy knees, saggy behinds and curling lapels.

She listened to his explanation, smiling. 'The first time I saw you, I remember,' she said, 'you were trying to roll cigarettes in the Relais St Armand. Do you still roll your own?'

It had been a period when Pel was making one of his determined efforts to cut down his smoking. Since then he'd decided to let his vices wash over him, even if it meant an early demise, and as she pushed a box of cigarettes forward, he selected a Gauloise. Drawing the smoke down gave him confidence. It also made him cough violently.

The tea tray arrived and she poured for him. After Madame Routy's slapdash methods and the thick crockery she insisted on using in case she broke it, it was the height of luxury.

'Now,' she said. 'What's your problem?'

'Do you know a Mademoiselle Marie-Anne Chahu?' he asked. 'She appears to be not without money –'

'And you thought she might be one of my clients and you wish to know more about her?'

'I know quite a lot already,' Pel said. 'She's a personal assistant to Professor Foussier.'

Well-shaped eyebrows rose. 'She's a lucky woman. He's an attractive man.'

Pel felt gnawings of jealousy. Nobody had ever called *him* an attractive man.

'She has a flat,' he said. 'In the new block near the Place Wilson. I wish to know who pays for it.'

She smiled knowingly. 'Doesn't *she*?'

'I doubt it,' Pel said. 'Not on the wages she must get.'

That night Darcy was also involved with enquiries with a female. His attentions however, were rather more earthy and the fact that he was still working an eighteen-hour day didn't put him off in the slightest

The breeze was heavy and warm, and the mosquitoes seemed to have come out in millions, so that it occurred to him he could have picked a better place to park his car than close to the lake at St Philibert. He had chosen a spot well shaded by trees, but unfortunately there was a stagnant pond close by and they were homing in, in squadrons, brigades and phalanxes.

'Daniel.'

'Yes?' As Darcy moved Angélique Courtois moved with him.

'No girl can give her mind to a thing like this when she's being eaten alive.'

'I can't shut the window,' Darcy pointed out. 'It's too hot.'

She pushed his hand away and scratched a growing puff of flesh on her knee where she'd been bitten. The linen dress she wore had ridden up more than a shade.

'Actually,' she said, 'I'm supposed to be engaged. I told you.'

'Why don't you wear your ring then?'

Her shoulders moved. 'It's inclined to be a bit inhibiting.'

'I don't suppose you've got a thing in common with him,' Darcy said.

'Oh, I have. When you get to the point of getting engaged you've usually talked about it.'

Darcy was silent for a while. 'You'll need a lover,' he said briskly.

She giggled. 'I will? Why?'

'Every wife needs a lover. I mean – your husband dozing in front of the television wearing yesterday's socks and last week's beard. You'll need someone to fill the gaps, if only to massage your ego.

'Won't my husband?'

'All he'll want is a quick tumble to help him sleep after a hard day, and there you'll be, warm, pulsating flesh, reeking of perfume. You don't choose a lover, you know, for his sense of humour or his IQ, and he won't ask you to nurse him through a dose of flu. Any woman who can manage on a husband alone has rigor mortis coursing through her veins.'

She was shaking with laughter. 'He's jealous. As hell. And he's a farmer's son.'

'Un moujik.'

'He'll probably shoot you. I know he's got a gun.'

'Come to that,' Darcy said, 'so have I. Only I don't use mine on birds and rabbits that can't shoot back.'

There was a long silence and she shifted uncomfortably. 'We ought to go somewhere else,' she murmured.

'Cars aren't very comfortable,' Darcy agreed.

'We could go to my flat.'

'Talking about flats,' Darcy said, 'how is it that Marie-Anne Chahu has such a big and expensive one?'

'Are you still going on about that?'

'It's my job to go on about things like that.'

'Can't somebody do it for you?'

Darcy smiled. 'About five days ago, I suggested to my chief *he* might. But he doesn't move very fast with women. How *does* she do it?'

'Well, I don't suppose her family pays for it. Her father runs a furniture shop in Brittany. They couldn't afford that sort of money and he's careful, I understand.'

'Does she earn a good wage?'

'Better than me. But not enough for that.'

'Is there a man?'

'If there is, she keeps it pretty dark. I've never seen anyone there.'

'Could it be Foussier?'

'The way he dashes about, I should think he never has time. I've often been to her apartment to collect things or take files and I've never seen any sign of him. Perhaps she just likes wealth.'

'Perhaps she needs it,' Darcy said. 'For reassurance. When you talk about Bretons being careful, you mean they're mean.'

'Well, she had to work hard. She told me. She got herself a place here at the University when she was quite old – at least twenty-four.' Angélique spoke with the assurance of youth.

'That's when Foussier spotted her. He told her she could do better than study to be a teacher of East European languages so he brought her in to help him.'

'*Does* she speak East European languages?'

'Yes. Three. It's useful in her job. The Prof was dead right. She does make more money than she would as a teacher.'

'But not enough to pay for a flat in the Maison Joliet.' Darcy frowned. 'Or to put down the cash for a Triumph. Certainly not both. Is she on the game?'

'What game?'

'The game women always get on to when they need money badly. Some go on to it to feed their kids. Some because they can't get a job. Some simply because they enjoy luxury.'

Angélique paused. 'I never thought of her that way.'

'I should start,' Darcy said.

There was a long silence then Darcy spoke again. 'This flat of yours. What about the people downstairs?'

She giggled. 'They'll be in bed by this time. They go early. They watch television in the bedroom.'

Darcy paused. 'What are *we* going to do in *your* room?' he asked.

She stared back at him, her eyes expressionless. 'What did you expect?'

Darcy grinned. 'It's far too easy to die a virgin,' he said. He switched on the engine as she began to push her hair straight and pull her dress down. 'Actually,' she said thoughtfully, 'I think it's a good idea being engaged. It keeps men at arm's length.'

Darcy's head turned. 'Don't you ever cheat a bit?'

'No, never.' She paused, then giggled again. 'But I'll not fight you off if you do.'

# fifteen

As Darcy put his head round Pel's door the following morning, Pel stared at him and frowned.

'You look like something the cat dragged in,' he said severely. 'Une gueule de bois, Patron.' Darcy shrugged. 'But I recover quickly.'

'You'll end up with no hair and a worn-out prostate. You're on the downhill slope already.'

Darcy grinned. 'I know. Heading like mad for the abyss. But what a way to go, Patron! And what's the point of a halo? – just something else to polish.' He paused, still smiling. 'We've picked up Tagliacci.'

Pel sat up with a jerk. 'What!'

'Uniformed branch brought him in. He was buying wine near Beaune. Will you see him?'

'Of course.'

'Here?'

'No. Downstairs in the interview room. I'm not laying out the red carpet for anybody dealing in what he deals in.'

Tagliacci was a young man in his early thirties, dark, Italianate and immaculately dressed in a way that made Pel feel like the man who'd come about the drains.

'Why have I been brought here?' he wanted to know.

'We're interested in what you're doing in this area,' Pel growled.

Tagliacci was not put out. 'Minding my own business,' he said.

'Out with it. What is it?'

Tagliacci's eyes flashed. 'I'm buying wine,' he snapped. 'And that's all.'

'Where are you staying?'

'I have a house at Dorsay-la-Rivière. It's a small place. Somewhere to get cool when it's too hot in the south. It's high up.'

'And lonely?'

Tagliacci smiled. 'And lonely. Do you have a place like that, Inspector?'

Pel glared. He couldn't afford a chicken house, on top of the mortgage he was paying for the house in the Rue Martin de Noinville. And doubtless, while he ran his old Peugeot, this crook had a Cadillac or a Merc – maybe even a gold-plated Rolls Royce.

The interview was an unsatisfactory one. Tagliacci was more than a match for them and they had nothing on him whatsoever. To all intents and purposes he was buying wine. He had the bills and the invoices and they were able to obtain by telephone proof from the vineyards – most of them small – who had sold it. There was no reason to imagine he'd done the buying himself, of course. He had henchmen to provide that sort of proof while he attended to the darker side of his business, but in fact he *had* put in an appearance at most of the places where he said he'd been.

They had to let him go in the end, frustrated at being able to do no more. As he went, he laid a couple of cigars on the desk for Pel and Darcy.

'Just to show there's no ill feeling,' he said smoothly. 'We all have our jobs to do and without our excellent police the country would descend into anarchy. And I'd vote Communist any time rather than have that.'

Pel glared at the closed door, his eyes almost red with his rage. 'Get hold of the Chief!' he snapped.

'We can't ban the man,' the Chief pointed out sharply. 'I understand your concern, Pel, but as far as we're concerned he's committing no offence buying wine.'

'The Cornet gang's moved in, too!'

'We don't know that. Not yet. We've only heard that they've left Paris. They may even be in Marseilles trying to take over Tagliacci's beat while he's away.'

'They might be here, too,' Pel said.

'On the other hand,' Polverari pointed out, 'I do agree that, in view of all the rubbish the newspapers have been printing, they've probably spotted an opportunity here and are about to move in to take advantage of it.'

It was Pel's feeling that the gangs had *already* moved in. In view of what had happened to Miollis and Treguy, they even seemed to be well established.

The Chief sighed. 'Do you need extra men, Pel?' he asked. 'We can always let you have more help. We can beg, borrow or steal a few from other places.'

Pel drew a deep breath. 'Not yet,' he said. 'If we can't ban the man, let's have a directive to everybody to keep on their toes. Even the men on traffic duty. Let's keep track of them, for God's sake.'

The Chief nodded and made a note on a pad. 'What's been done about Foussier?' he asked.

'We've got him guarded,' Pel said, warily because the question sounded vaguely like an accusation. 'I have no men to spare, but Inspector Goriot's agreed to lend us three of his to watch his house. They'll go with him wherever he goes.' He drew a deep breath, feeling a protest was necessary.

The Chief listened carefully to him then he sighed. 'The world can't stop because Marseilles and Paris have decided to move in on us,' he said. 'Foussier's every right to go on behaving normally.' He looked at Pel's narrow intense face. 'I suspect, you've already made it more than clear what the risks are.'

Pel became silent and the Chief frowned. 'There's nothing we can do more than we have done,' he said. 'It seems to me that the best way to protect Foussier is to clear the matter up, and the best way to start doing that is to find this man, Nincic.'

And that was that. A rejection, a calming down of ruffled tempers, and a ticking-off all in the same breath. Pel was seething enough when he went back to his own office to take it out of Darcy, who responded by snapping at Misset, who promptly turned on Krauss.

'What did I do?' Krauss asked.

In fact, news of Fran Nincic was nearer than they realised. As Pel reached his office, the telephone in the sergeants' room went. Darcy snatched it up and Pel heard his voice rise.

'When?' he said, and there was sufficient urgency in his tone for Pel to start reaching for spare cigarettes, notebooks and pencils. He knew the signs. He had just risen to his feet when Darcy appeared in the doorway.

'Nincic's been seen, Chief. The police in Auxonne have come up with somebody who saw him leave his house.'

'When?'

'Fourteen days ago. About that.'

'Fourteen days ago! Name of God, why not last year? Who is it?'

'An old dear who delivers church literature. She's only just mentioned it. She didn't know we wanted him, of course. He left carrying letters and papers, got into his car and drove off.'

When they reached Auxonne, there was no sign of Nincic and while they were sitting in Darcy's car looking at the house, a man leaning against a wall folded up the newspaper he was reading and strolled across to them. Reaching into the car window, he pushed forward a cigarette. 'Got a light?' he asked.

As Darcy offered him a box of matches, he spoke quietly.

'Merouac,' he said. 'Detective sergeant. You're Inspector Pel, aren't you?'

'Yes. Are you watching this place?'

'That's right. For Nincic. It's a slow job. I'm growing sick of it.'

'Do you know him?' Pel asked.

'I know *of* him. I know his car. I wish I could afford one like it.'

'Has he been back?'

'No sign of him. Not while I've been on the job. I heard he turned up some time ago though. An old dear said so.'

Pel and Darcy exchanged glances and, leaving the Auxonne man to watch, they drove into the town to see the old woman who had seen Nincic leave. She could add nothing to what they already knew. She had seen him leave. And that was all. Full stop. He had looked quite normal. She didn't know him, though he had accepted the pamphlet she had been about to push through his door, and had left in his car, after exchanging no more than a 'Good morning.'

During the afternoon, they relieved Merouac to get something to eat and waited in the hope that Nincic would come back. By late evening they were bored and frustrated and had drunk so many beers and smoked so many cigarettes Pel was wondering if police pensions covered stomachs ruined in the line of duty. He had long since come to the conclusion that Nincic had given them the slip.

'Think he knew he was being watched?' he asked. 'Perhaps that girl of his has been in touch with him.' He looked at Merouac. 'Has she been here?'

'I've seen no one at all.'

Pel made up his mind. 'All right, Darcy. We'll put out a general request. We want him finding.'

They returned in gloomy silence. Had Nincic got wind of what they were up to? And, if so, how? Who could have tipped him off? And who was behind him?

It was late when they reached the city and they turned off near the Cimitière de Pejoces to eat in a small restaurant Darcy knew, that was frequented by the men who worked in the abbatoirs. The meal was indifferent. The wine tasted as if it were suffering from metal fatigue, the knives were blunt and the steaks bullet-proof. Outside the window, a dog lifted its leg against a lamp-post. It seemed to symbolise their lack of success.

They had half-expected Nincic to turn up and even let something drop that would give them a lead, something that would tell them where the investigations into the deaths of Miollis and Treguy might lead. At least he'd have been someone to arrest so the newspapers and the Chief would quieten down for a while.

'I reckon he's skipped over the border,' Darcy said. 'I doubt if we'll ever find him now.'

Pel said nothing, and Darcy went on, enthusiastic as ever, full of energy and new ideas, always willing to give a little more than the job demanded. It made him a good policeman and an excellent second-in-command. It also sometimes made him a pain in the neck. Especially when Pel was in the mood he was in at that moment.

'We could get a search warrant and go over his place, Patron,' he was suggesting.

They were still discussing the possibilities, when Krauss came in for a beer on his way home. He looked his usual placid, indifferent self, eyes blank, brain in neutral.

'There was a telephone call for you, Patron,' he said cheerfully.

Pel lifted his head. 'Who from?' he asked. 'The Chief?'

'No. She didn't give her name.'

Pel's heart started to skate about under his shirt like aspic on a hot plate. 'Any message?'

'She asked if you'd ring. She left her number.'

'I know her number,' Pel said coldly.

Krauss grinned. 'She said you wouldn't know this one, Patron. This is her home.'

'Where is it?'

'I left it on your desk.'

'Can't you remember it?'

'Patron, for a brain I don't have a computer.'

Pel's gaze pierced him like an assegai. 'For *your* brain,' he snapped, 'you have a block of concrete. Go and ring the office and get someone to go upstairs and find it.'

Krauss looked indignant. 'I was just going home, Patron.'

'You could always go back to the Hôtel de Police instead,' Pel snarled. 'I'm an inspector and entitled to exquisite courtesies such as this.'

Krauss stared at him, wondering, in view of his impending retirement, whether to be defiant. He decided in the end that Pel looked so hot under the collar he could well end up with a nasty comment in his file that wouldn't help him get a job when he finally decided to look round for one. He sighed, asked for a jeton, and disappeared round the corner to the telephone. When he returned to lay a slip of paper bearing the number on the table, Pel was stuffing his food away so fast he was almost choking. He was also maliciously contemplating ordering Krauss to run him round to the Hôtel de Police where he'd left his car, but Darcy grinned and took pity on the older man.

'I'll run you to the office, Patron,' he said. 'It's on my way.'

'On your way where?' Pel snapped.

'On my way to where I'm going, Patron.' It took a lot to put Darcy off his stride.

At the Hôtel de Police, Pel was halfway inside when he decided to make the call from home. Ten to one, he thought, the man on the switchboard would try to listen in. In any case, his office, spartan, utilitarian and about as comfortable as the inside of a tank, was no place to talk to Madame Faivre-Perret.

He drove home as if the hounds of hell were after him. Madame Routy was watching the television as usual and the house was shuddering under the sound.

'Turn that thing off,' Pel yelled. Madame Routy took no notice, and Pel stalked across the room and pressed the switch. Madame Routy half-started to her feet, loud indignation on her lips at the invasion, then she saw Pel's face, thought better of it and instead sat in a seething fury as he picked up the telephone and dialled his number.

He stumbled over his apologies. 'I'm sorry I'm so late, Madame. I've been in Auxonne all day on a case. I've just this minute reached home. You must have been thinking of going to bed.' In Pel's mind were visions of filmy lace and soft lights. It almost gave him heart failure.

'Inspector –' the voice in his ear was chiding ' – please don't worry. I'm happy to be of assistance. I think I've found out something for you. I know of *one* person who contributes to the flat you're interested in. I know the wife of Charles Rolland. He knows everything and he talks to her.'

'I'm eternally grateful. Who would it be?'

'Professor Foussier.'

'Foussier!' Recalling Madame Foussier, Pel had assumed that even if Foussier was a pompous ass, shoving his nose in where it wasn't wanted and poisonous in the extreme, at least he appeared to have a happy married life. Most people – himself included – seemed to exist in a vacuum of dislike, deceit, immorality and disbelief, fostered by his own personal enemy, the television. It came as a blow. Happy homes, it seemed – even those occupied by pompous busybodies – weren't all they appeared.

'You sound shocked.' The voice in his ear was concerned.

'It takes a lot to shock a policeman, Madame.' Pel was boasting a little. 'It's just that the Professor has a reputation for good work. It doesn't seem to go with him. What about his wife? Does she know?'

'Perhaps she isn't interested. I gather there's a surgeon in Paris.'

Pel was frowning. The institution of marriage no longer seemed to have much meaning.

'Do you know her well?'

'Yes. She comes in here.' The voice in his ear was helpful. 'She talks to me a lot. She works for deprived children and so do I.' Pel was charmed at the thought. It showed kindness, and a loving nature.

'She has no children of her own, of course. There was even a time when she considered returning to her work as a doctor because of it, but she never did.' There was a little chuckle. 'I think perhaps, in spite of everything, she prefers simply to be a wife. Women are like that, Inspector.'

'They are?' Pel's mind was immediately full of thoughts of showing Madame Routy the door. 'This Marie-Anne Chahu,' he went on. 'Her apartment's a very expensive one. One of the best in the Maison Joliet. And I gather it's very expensively furnished. Supposing Professor Foussier *were* contributing to it, it would still take a great deal of money. Do you think she's playing false with him?'

There was a slight pause. 'There may be others, of course.'

'Does the name, Nincic, mean anything to you?'

'Nothing at all. I've never heard of it.'

She seemed quite happy to go on talking but he suddenly decided that if she appeared in front of her mirror the next morning with bags under her eyes, she'd surely blame it on him for keeping her up too late, and he hastened to terminate the interview.

'Madame,' he said, 'I'm most grateful.' He wondered what else he could say to show his appreciation, then he thought

160

with a shudder of Madame Routy and the television and wondered if he dared push his luck to arrange an evening out. You didn't have to mess about, Didier had said. Perhaps he was right. He took the plunge. 'Perhaps you'll permit me to repay you for your trouble by asking if you'd – ah! – if you'd dine with me one evening.'

He felt sure she'd find an excuse but to his surprise she laughed. 'Inspector, how charming! I'd be delighted.'

Pel couldn't believe his ears. She even sounded enthusiastic. 'Shall we say the coming Saturday?' he suggested.

There was a long pause and Pel's heart sank. Here it comes, he thought – the excuse he'd been expecting. Sorry, I'm already engaged. I've got to wash my hair. I shall probably have a headache. Don't ring me, I'll ring you.

'Of course,' he said lamely, 'if it's difficult – '

'No, no! Not at all!' His heart thumped again because she clearly didn't wish to put him off. 'It's just a little difficult because that day I have to go to Paris.'

'Perhaps the following Saturday?'

'Oh, no! That's much too far away!'

'*It is?*'

'But, of course! I'll manage somehow. I must make sure I get back in good time.'

As Pel put the telephone down, Madame Routy waited. For some reason she couldn't explain she'd let him ride rough-shod over her, something it had always been her proud boast could never happen. She half-expected him, even, to snarl at her again. But instead he took out the bottle of Scotch whisky he kept for special occasions and poured himself a good measure and even one for her. She decided he must have been promoted or something, because normally he considered whisky so expensive it was only kept to be looked at, not drunk, which was why Madame Routy left it carefully alone and went for the brandy instead.

Pel glanced at his watch, surprised to see how late it was. He wasn't sure they'd gained much – just the discovery of an alliance between two people, and there were plenty of those. Perhaps, however, he could use it, if he had to, to persuade Foussier to keep his nose out of police affairs. Apart from that, it didn't seem to offer much. But nosey-parkering was always police business and tomorrow he'd see Judge Polverari for a warrant to search Nincic's house. They were probably making progress. And, if nothing else, he'd got a dinner date with an attractive woman out of it.

It was so long since he'd taken a female out to dinner he wondered if he'd know what to do.

'I'm going to bed,' he announced cheerfully.

'I'll just finish watching my programme,' Madame Routy suggested warily.

'Do,' Pel said.

'I'll keep the volume down!'

Pel shrugged. 'It doesn't matter,' he said.

As he vanished – to her astonishment whistling 'Les Artilleurs de Metz' – she stared after him, her eyes like the twin barrels of a shotgun. It took all the pleasure out of turning the volume control to its peak when he didn't complain.

# sixteen

The following day was a Saint's Day and most people were on holiday. Shops were closed, bars were full and people were enjoying the weather. And near St Miriam, two small boys, Jean-Paul Jarry and Pierre Blot, came over the hill from Premières, where they had been fishing in a dam built by a farmer. They had taken out of it half a dozen fat perch and they had a pretty shrewd idea that the farmer wouldn't have wished them to, and they were in a hurry to get away with their spoil before he appeared.

They were taking a short cut across country towards the road to St Miriam where they lived, and they entered a belt of breast-high bracken which led down the slope to the road that ran along the valley where they had hidden their bicycles in the undergrowth.

'They're over here,' Jean-Paul said.

'No.' Pierre shook his head and pointed. 'This way.'

They stared about them. The road looked very much as it had before, yet somehow it looked different, and it dawned on them they'd returned to it at some point other than that from which they'd left it. And, unfortunately, in their eagerness to get at the farmer's perch, they'd not taken sufficient notice of their whereabouts. They'd not counted the telegraph poles or noticed the curve of the land or the kilometre sign.

'That bunch of trees was right in front of us,' Pierre said.

'No, it wasn't. It was on our left.'

Putting down their rods and their fish, they plunged back into the bracken alongside the road and began to search. A quarter of an hour later they'd also lost their rods *and* their fish.

'Why didn't you notice where we put them?' Pierre demanded.

'Why didn't you?' Jean-Paul retorted. 'What good are they, anyway, without the bikes?'

'Let's just have one more look. You go up there. I'll go down here.'

As they moved their separate ways, Pierre Blot was growing worried. If the bicycles failed to turn up it would mean a long walk home and an admission that they'd been to Premières, where he'd been told more than once not to go. He was still pondering the problem when he heard a shout.

'I've got the bikes!'

He turned and began to hurry back to where the other boy was, pushing as fast as he could through the bracken. The ground underfoot was uneven and several times he stumbled. Recovering, he pressed on. Finally he fell and a twig slashed him across the face as he went down. Rising, his eyes full of tears, exhausted now and a little overcome by the heat, he looked round to see what had tripped him. Whatever it was, it wasn't a root. It seemed to be black and appeared to be made of plastic. Curious, he pushed the bracken aside.

For a long time, he stared silently, then he began to back away. His foot caught in the foliage and, though he sat down heavily, he hardly noticed. Scrambling to his feet, he ran to the edge of the road, shouting. The other boy appeared, holding a bicycle.

'Have you found the rods?'

'No!'

'What's all the fuss about then?'

'We'd better get back to St Miriam.'

'Without the rods? Don't be silly.'

'I'm not being silly. I've just found a man in the bushes up there.'

The holiday everybody was enjoying didn't affect the police, of course. Holidays never did.

In the sergeants' room, Misset was still studying the map of the city, certain now that the shopbreaker, Hyacinthe Baranquin, had an accomplice waiting with a car. Lagé, still heavily enmeshed in paperwork, was sorting out the hit-and-run at Gévrey. Krauss, his passage of arms with Pel the previous evening long since forgotten, was as usual enjoying the papers and waiting for his retirement. His pension was drawing nearer and with every day he spent a little more of his time dreaming of what he'd do with it. His house was paid for and he'd been careful to buy a new car so that it would see him safely through the next few years until he decided what to do. Sometimes he thought of being a keeper on one of the estates outside the city. Walking through the trees with a gun sounded fine. But he had an idea there was more to it than that and felt he'd better find out more before he made up his mind.

They were all busy following their own particular enquiries because, despite the additional work that had sprung from the Miollis and Treguy cases, the other minor events couldn't ever be thrust aside. Despite the sorting out of facts and statements that involved Miollis and Treguy, in their spare time there were still the shopbreakers, the hit-and-runs, even Krauss' newspapers.

Nosjean, looking a little tired, was holding a piece of wood round which he had tied a piece of string. He had set it on his desk and sat staring at it, frowning deeply.

If Jean-Marc Cortot hadn't tied himself up, he thought, then who had? Cortot was an ex-seaman and no ex-seaman, according to Petty Officer Mathieu, would have tied the knots that had been found on his body. For a long time, it had been in Nosjean's mind that perhaps Cortot, in a drug-inflamed ecstasy, had scourged himself – which would account for the scars on his back and arms – and had *then* tied himself up. There was no knowing what fantasies drugs worked on people. Perhaps he saw himself as a martyr. Perhaps even as the suffering Christ. Unfortunately, after several years in the Navy, it would still be instinctive for him to tie a seaman-like knot. Unless he wished it to be believed that he *hadn't* tied the knots, and if that were the case, *why* should he wish such a thing?

The telephone went. Nosjean picked it up.

'Inspector Pel?'

'He's still at home. He hasn't come in yet.'

'Then you'd better get him in, my friend. Fast. This is Auxonne. We were asked to keep an eye on the house of a guy called Fran Nincic.'

Nosjean sat up. 'He's turned up?' he said.

'Yes, he has. But not at the flat.'

Pel was just dipping his croissant into his coffee. He had been tired when he had gone to bed and full of wine and beer after the wait at Auxonne, but for once he had been happy enough to be unconcerned with the effect it might have on the ulcer he was convinced was developing in his stomach. Nor had he heard the television, because Madame Routy had decided it might be safer to keep the volume down, and he had slept like a log. Coming to the surface as if emerging from a well of treacle, the first thing he had remembered had been his dinner date.

Sitting with his croissant in his hand, his thoughts were so far away he swallowed without even noticing it the mixture of chicory and liquorice Madame Routy managed to distil from the most expensive coffee beans on the market. He had decided on the Hôtel de la Poste at St Seine l'Abbaye. It would probably cost him his spending money for a month, but it would be worth it. It was a pleasant drive for a summer evening, with an attractive courtyard where they could take their aperitifs if it was still hot. The only time Pel had been there previously was when Polverari had taken him.

He wondered if he should hire a car. After all, his own might shed a wheel going down the hill from Darois. On the other hand, a hired car might seem too ostentatious, and if he were seen driving the old dropout Peugeot afterwards it would require some explaining away. For a moment he wondered if he could borrow Darcy's, which was a handsome new Citroën, but he decided against it. The look he knew he'd see in Darcy's eyes was enough to put him off. It would have to be the old car, he decided. Perhaps he could pay Didier something to give it a good clean up.

He had just put the last of the croissant into his mouth when the telephone rang. Didier answered it. He listened for a moment then handed it to Pel.

'It's them,' he said in a conspiratorial whisper.

'Who?'

'The police. He said it was urgent.' Didier looked almost as if he were conducting the enquiry himself.

His mouth full, Pel took the telephone.

'This is Nosjean, Patron,' the voice came. 'They've found Nincic.'

'What?' Pieces of croissant flew as the word burst out. 'Where?'

'Near St Miriam.'

'What was he doing there?'

'He wasn't doing anything, Patron. He was dead. They found him under some bracken at the side of the road.'

When Pel and Darcy arrived, the whole tribe were there – photographers, Doctor Minet, and Leguyader and his lab experts. They had erected a screen round the body and there were half a dozen cars pulled up by the side of the road. Two small boys, their rods still undiscovered, sat in one of the cars talking to a police sergeant.

'Shot,' Minet said. 'Back of the head. By the look of it, the same gun that did for Treguy and Miollis.'

'When?'

'Hard to say exactly. He's been here a long time. Fortnight ago, I reckon. Before Treguy, anyway.'

Pel sighed and went to talk to the small boys. Pierre Blot was still white-faced but thoroughly enjoying the attention. His mother was with him now, concerned that her child should be involved with murder. Pel didn't consider himself very good at interrogating children but he did his best.

'How did you come to find him?' he asked.

Pierre Blot looked at his mother who gave him a little nudge. 'I fell over him,' he said.

'You didn't see him?'

'Not at first.'

'They'd been fishing in Monsieur Naudot's dam,' his mother explained. 'They'd been told not to and they were afraid of what would happen.'

'I thought at first he was asleep,' the boy said. 'Then I saw all the flies.'

'You didn't touch him? You didn't disturb anything?'

'No. I just ran to Jean-Paul and we got on the bikes and went to St Miriam. I told Mammy and she rang the police. I expect Pappy will give me a hiding when he finds out.'

His mother put her arms round him and pulled him to her. 'I don't think so, Pierrot,' she said. 'Not this time.'

Pel nodded his thanks. Darcy was waiting by the car.

'There's nothing much we can do here,' Pel said. 'Not until Minet's finished and the Lab people have gone over the ground.' He offered his cigarettes and went on slowly. 'There's one thing that's clear,' he said. 'Whatever was going on, Nincic wasn't the top man. Let's get Nosjean searching the house. You and I'll go and see that girl friend of Nincic's.'

It didn't take long to establish that Madeleine Duc wasn't at the flat she was supposed to share with Edith Roux and they decided she must still be with her parents in Avallon.

'We'll find her,' Pel said. 'She said her father was a dentist and there can't be all that many there called Duc.'

In the verdant valley of the Cure, Avallon, with its two beautiful churches with their pointed barrel arches, contained the coaching inn from which Napoleon, on his way back to Paris after his escape from Elba, had gone to meet Marshal Ney at Auxerre and so turned his head he had changed sides with scarcely a second thought. That day it looked full of browns and sienas in the sunshine.

Madeleine Duc's home lay on the outskirts near the river. On one end of it, an addition had been built which they realised was a surgery. On the gate was a sign, Jean-Louis Duc, *Chirurgien Dentiste*.

The girl was surprised to see them, then fearful, knowing they could give away to her parents the fact that she was sharing a home not with a girl called Edith Roux, as they believed, but with a man called Fran Nincic. Clearly suspecting something, her mother insisted on sitting in the room as they questioned her and even sent a maid to fetch her husband.

Madeleine Duc looked a little like Pierre Blot, no longer poised and full of self-assurance, but frightened and, like Pierre Blot, a little worried about what would happen afterwards. Judging by the expression on the face of her father, she couldn't expect half the understanding Pierre Blot had received. It didn't take long to get out of her that, contrary to what she had first told them, she had *not* been with Nincic on the weekend of the 13th, when Miollis had been shot.

Her mother stared at her. 'Were you in the habit of going away with him, Madie?'

The girl frowned. 'Sometimes.'

'You never told us.'

'I didn't have to.'

'Nice girls of your age don't go off on holiday with men of thirty. There's only one thing they want.'

'For the love of God – ' the tormented girl burst out ' – he'd got it already. I'd been living with him, hadn't I? There was no reason why I shouldn't go off with him.'

'Did you go as his wife?'

'Of course I did! It didn't matter. People don't fuss about that sort of thing these days.'

'*We* do.'

Pel waited until the quarrel simmered down before continuing.

The girl sighed. 'I went to Edith's. She's the girl I was sharing with.'

'Was *supposed* to be sharing with,' her mother interrupted.

The girl ignored her, and kept her eyes fixed on Pel. 'Nino wanted to go off on his own,' she said. 'On business or something. He often had to. I didn't argue. He always came back.'

'More's the pity,' her mother commented.

The girl whirled round. 'Stop saying things like that! What do *you* know about love?'

'I've been married to your father for twenty-five years.'

'That doesn't mean a thing!'

They were glaring at each other and Pel had to slip his next words through a gap in the bitterness.

'That story you told me,' he persisted gently. 'About meeting a group of Austrians. What did he do with the parcel he was given? Did he post it?'

'I suppose so.'

170

'When?'

'Later, I suppose.'

'Not that day?'

'No. Perhaps the next day. I don't know.'

'Where did he keep it?'

'In the boot of the car. That's where he put it.'

'Locked?'

'I think so.'

'A parcel of photos? Why not on the seat?' Pel paused. 'You know why I came to see you, don't you?' he said quietly. 'I have good reason to believe that your friend, Fran Nincic, was involved in drug-peddling.'

The girl said nothing and her father jumped in quickly.

'You pick up with some funny types, I must say,' he growled. 'I never did think much of you going to university. It was your mother's idea, not mine.

'Blame me, of course,' the mother snapped.

Pel caught Darcy's eye on him. It was easy to see what the girl meant when she'd said there had been no love.

'Did *you* know he was involved with drugs?' he asked.

The girl nodded, not lifting her eyes.

'Madeleine!' Her mother looked horrified.

'Was he on drugs himself?' Pel asked.

'No. Never. He hated them. He said they were too dangerous.'

'But not too dangerous to sell to youngsters.' The cynicism of drug pedlars was something that always shocked Pel. 'When did he acquire that house of his?'

She shrugged. 'I don't know. About two to three years ago, I think.'

'That's when Foussier says drugs first started appearing in the area,' Darcy put in. 'Did you know his friends?'

She sighed and a tear trickled down her cheek. 'No. He kept them apart. He said our life was separate and private.'

'Did he have a gun?'

171

'Yes. He kept it in the glove pocket of his car. It was a Belgian automatic. It was only a small one.'

'Even small guns can kill,' Pel snapped. 'Did you ever hear his friends on the telephone?'

'No. Well, once. Just before he left the last time. Perhaps it was business.'

'What was being said?'

'I don't know. I heard him say "I did the job. I want a bigger share if I'm going to do jobs like that." I think he was selling a car for someone. He said something about getting rid of one.'

While Pel and Darcy were interrogating Madeleine Duc in Avallon, Nosjean and Krauss were going through Nincic's flat in Auxonne. The source of the bone button found alongside Miollis in the boot of the car in the Rue du Chapeau Rouge turned up at once – a mud-stained grey jacket with jaeger green collar, cuffs and pocket flaps.

'Austrian,' Nosjean said. 'Minus one button.'

'It must have been Nincic then who did for Miollis,' Krauss said. 'He lost the button as he hoisted him into the car. At least, that's settled.'

'But not the drugs,' Nosjean said. 'That's what we're looking for.'

They searched all the usual places – all the drawers and cupboards and under the mattresses. They also checked the pillows to make sure there was nothing there and had the tracker dogs in, but they provided no lead.

'He obviously didn't keep it here,' Krauss said.

They turned the carpets back and checked all the floorboards for loose ones or for new nails that would indicate a board had recently been hammered down. They checked the curtains to see if anything lay between the lining. They took out every book in the place and checked there was nothing in it or that the middle had not been cut out to provide a hiding place. They checked every tin in the kitchen and pantry. They checked every item of clothing.

Krauss particularly enjoyed himself going through Madeleine Duc's underwear. Nosjean stared at him coldly as he made his comments. Nosjean was young, idealistic, and in his way very moral, and it offended him that fat, middle-aged Krauss should hold up pairs of lacy pants and grin at him over the top of them.

Krauss talked a lot too. All the time. 'When I retire,' he said, 'there'll be no more of this. I'm going to fish. We've got plenty of rivers.'

'Can't you think of anything better to do?' Nosjean asked.

'Who wants anything better to do than sit on a bank in the sun with a bottle of wine, some sausage sandwiches, and a rod.'

'Why bother with the rod?' Nosjean asked coldly.

There wasn't much to find, but in the wastepaper basket there was a crumpled cigarette packet labelled 'Adler Cigaretten', with a picture of a double-headed eagle, and in the ashtray several cigarette stubs also marked 'Adler'. There was a passport, which had recently been stamped in Munich, which was unusual because these days under the European Economic Grouping, passports weren't often stamped. Together they seemed to add up to the fact that Fran Nincic's recent absence had been due to a visit he'd made to Munich where he'd bought a packet of cigarettes. Nosjean had recently been to Munich himself and he'd noticed that at the airport duty-free shop it was possible to buy, not only drinks from every country in the world, but also cigarettes and cigars. Nincic seemed to have spent his last weekend alive visiting Germany and, judging by the cigarettes and the passport, had returned quietly to his house just before Pel had put a watch on it.

When they'd finished searching, Nosjean sat down at the kitchen table and began to go through all the letters and papers Krauss kept dumping in front of him. They included bills, paid and unpaid, insurances, business letters concerned with Nincic's job, circulars from drug manufacturers and pamphlets from antivivisectionist societies.

'Keep them,' Nosjean said.

'What? The lot?'

'His Highness likes things kept.'

Among the papers was one that puzzled Nosjean. It had been torn into small pieces and Nosjean laboriously sorted them all out and played jigsaws with them until he had it all worked out. Then he slipped out to a shop down the street and bought a tube of glue and began to stick all the pieces down. When he'd finished he had a message.

'Pick up 27th. Usual distribution.' It was unsigned and not addressed, though in the wastepaper basket there was an envelope in the same handwriting, addressed to Fran Nincic at the address they were searching. Nincic had clearly not considered it worth tearing up what appeared to be an innocent envelope.

Krauss leaned over. 'What's it say?'

'It could be telling him to pick up a packet of drugs.'

'You've got drugs on the brain.'

So would you have, Nosjean thought, if you'd seen Cortot. He paused, staring at the piece of paper he'd been writing his notes on. He'd taken it from the wastepaper basket, a quarter sheet torn from some sort of pamphlet. Studying it, he held it against the light, then he laid his pencil sideways and began to scribble lightly. What was emerging from the scribbling was an address. The piece of paper he held was yellow and of a soft cheap type which absorbed pressure easily. He turned it over and saw there was printing on the back, but not enough to tell him what it had been announcing. He looked at his scribbles again and carefully moved his pencil backwards and forwards again until the whole address emerged.

It had quite obviously been written on another sheet which had rested on the piece Nosjean held. It had been done with a hard pencil or, more likely, a ball-point pen, and, though the top sheet – which was probably the other half of the pamphlet he held – had gone, the writing had left its imprint on the paper beneath:

*Alois Hofer, Nedergasse, 17.*

'Sounds German,' Krauss said.

'It's written on French paper,' Nosjean said.

'How do you know?'

'Because I've seen it before. Stick at it. I've got to see Leguyader.'

# seventeen

It took some doing to persuade Leguyader.

'Look, mon petit,' he said, warily examining the scrap of yellow paper as if it might bite him. 'I'm a busy man.'

'Yes, I know you are,' Nosjean said, as humbly as he could manage. 'But this is important.'

'Why can't it wait until tomorrow?' Leguyader demanded. 'I'm supposed to have finished for the day. My wife's at home waiting for me with my children. Two boys and two girls. They're doubtless standing at the door at this moment with my slippers in their hands and the newspaper resting alongside my chair, with a long cold pernod and a small piece of mild cheese – I like mild cheese with pernod. They're waiting to go into the ritual of the evening homage to Pappy, who has just returned home from a hard day at work, having earned a little more towards the meagre pittance the Government allows him. They don't expect much, as he doesn't. Just a smile and to be left alone.'

Leguyader liked to wax sarcastic. He was good at it, too, but for once it left Nosjean quite unmoved.

'It'll take you about five minutes,' he said earnestly. 'I've got it here. And I've also got a sample I want you to compare it with.'

Leguyader scowled. 'You're an irritating and opinionated young man,' he said. 'I expect you learn it all from that narrow-minded bigot you work with, Pel.'

Nosjean said nothing. He was half-way there, he knew. He laid on the table alongside Leguyader another piece of yellow paper that he'd lifted from Pel's files.

'This is it,' he said. 'I just want to know if they're the same.'

When Pel and Darcy returned from Avallon, Nosjean was waiting for them. He was quivering like a terrier at a rathole.

Waiting for Pel had meant giving up his night off and since Odile Chenandier had suggested that he might like to go round to her apartment for a meal, it had taken a lot of willpower.

'Please,' he had begged into the telephone. 'Not tonight.'

'But I've got it all prepared,' she had said, obviously close to tears.

'Can you save it? Something's come up. It's important. I've got to be here when the Old Man gets back.'

There was a long silence then a very tiny 'Very well.'

It sounded so miserable Nosjean hastened to explain. 'Look,' he said. 'It's not another girl I'm going to see. I promise.'

She was well aware of Nosjean's tendency to fall in love and she sounded much happier. 'It isn't? Not that nurse you met? The one who looked like Catherine Deneuve.'

'No. And it isn't my great Aunt Francine or my Uncle Edouard either. I'm not going to anybody's funeral or anybody's party. I've just got to stay here. In this office. If you're not sure, ring back in an hour. In two hours. Every hour if you like. I'll answer the telephone.'

There was a silence for a while then her voice came back, firmly.

'I'll not do that. I believe you, of course. I'll save it until tomorrow.'

Nosjean felt constrained to warn her. 'It's only fair to say,' he pointed out. 'I might not make it tomorrow either. This is important. It's something I've found. It might keep me busy.'

When Pel arrived he was in a bad temper and tired. The car had been hot and the road dusty. His shirt was sticking to his back and his underwear seemed to be wedged in a solid ball between his legs. There was a message waiting for him, telling him to see the Chief. The Chief was almost apoplectic.

'What in the name of God's happening?' he demanded. 'Has your department lost its wits? Or is it just behaving in its usual incompetent manner?'

He tossed a newspaper across the desk. *France Soir* was not merely hysterical. It had become accusatory. 'NUMERO 3,' it announced. 'OU SONT LES FLICS?' It set Pel's indigestion on fire.

'We're being pilloried,' the Chief said.

'Something will break,' Pel insisted.

'It had better. Would you prefer me to divide the enquiry into three and put a different man on each?'

'No,' Pel insisted. 'They're all connected.'

'How do you know?'

'Everything indicates it.'

'Well, you'd better do something about it soon or I shall have to. And ring Judge Polverari. He wants to know what progress is being made.'

Judge Polverari, an old friend of Pel's, was just as worried but a little kinder.

'There are a lot of insinuations flying about, Pel,' he explained. 'Judge Brisard made some comment.'

'He would,' Pel said. He had been conducting a running battle with Judge Brisard as long as he could remember. Once Brisard had been young and inexperienced and Pel had always got the better of him, but he was beginning to learn now and finding out how to hit back. Mostly below the belt.

Putting the telephone down, Pel sighed and stretched his legs. He needed a long cool beer, a bath, perhaps an aperitif and then a long leisurely meal, preferably with a beautiful woman. Since the last, which would have made it perfect, was most unlikely for the moment, when Nosjean appeared and asked if he had a minute, he had to listen.

As he gestured to him to go ahead, Nosjean laid a small strip of yellow paper on the desk. Darcy joined them and peered at it.

'This address,' Nosjean pointed out. 'I realised I was getting an imprint, so I scribbled it over and that's what I got: "Alois Hofer, Nedergasse, 17." '

'The German connection,' Darcy said. 'Here it is again.'

'But not unexpectedly,' Nosjean said. 'We found the jacket the button belonged to. And these.' He laid the cigarette stubs and the cigarette packet and the passport he'd found in front of them. 'That weekend Nincic was away,' he said. 'He went to Germany. His passport's marked Munich and I happen to know you can buy these cigarettes at Munich airport.'

Pel was listening quietly, ferreting about down the back of his collar with his handkerchief to wipe away the sweat.

'That's not all,' Nosjean went on. 'Notice the colour of the paper?'

'I have done,' Pel said. 'I've noticed it well. I've seen it before.'

'So have I, Chief. I took it along to Leguyader. He wasn't keen.'

'Of course not,' Pel said. 'Leguyader's a narrow-minded opinionated bigot who wouldn't do anything for anyone.'

Nosjean pushed the paper nearer. 'It took some doing,' he said, 'but I finally got him to put it under the microscope. Together with a yellow pamphlet you brought in. He said they were the same paper.'

Archavanne was sitting with his feet up, watching the television. It stood on a small trolley, flanked by two repulsive-looking chairs which had probably cost a fortune.

His wife showed them in then returned to the kitchen from which they could smell tomatoes and garlic cooking.

'Sit down, sit down,' Archavanne said cheerfully without bothering to get to his feet. He had to shout to make himself heard and Pel suspected that most conversations in that house were conducted against the fire-firing of the television. 'Have a drink?'

'Not just now,' Pel said.

Archavanne gestured. 'What's it all about?' he said. 'You still checking up on that case?'

Pel said nothing but fished in his brief-case and placed on the table first of all the yellow piece of paper Nosjean had found, still bearing Nosjean's scribbles and the faint imprint of the name and address of Alois Hofer, whoever he was. Then, still without speaking, he took out the yellow pamphlet Archavanne had given him when they'd last seen him, the pamphlet he claimed he sent out to customers.

'Same paper,' Pel said.

Archavanne's smile had died abruptly.

'Where did you get it?' he asked.

'That one,' Pel said, jabbing with his finger. 'From you. The last time I saw you. That one – ' he jabbed again ' – from the home of a man who was found murdered early this morning. A man by the name of Fran Nincic.'

Darcy moved across to the television and switched it off, Archavanne made no comment.

'Fran Nincic,' Pel said, 'seems to have been involved in smuggling drugs over the border. Probably from Germany. Did you know him?'

'No.'

'Never heard of him?'

'No.'

'He was found shot near St Miriam. I have reason to believe he was pushing drugs at the University. According to Professor Foussier and his committee, there's a growing problem there. Nincic worked in the research lab in Biological Studies. He knew many of the students who were on drugs. We think he helped to supply them. Why would he have a pamphlet of yours in his possession?'

Archavanne had recovered a little. 'How do you know it's a pamphlet of ours?'

'Same colour,' Darcy said.

'That sort of paper and colour's always used by printers for pamphlets.'

'True,' Pel agreed. 'It may be a coincidence. But it seems to be rather more of a coincidence, don't you think, that we should find it in the flat of a man suspected of drug-peddling, when we also found your telephone number in the flat in Paris of a man also suspected of drug-peddling – Gilles Miollis, the man who was murdered on the weekend of the 13th. Can you explain the coincidence?'

'I told you – ' Archavanne sounded desperate suddenly ' – we place these pamphlets in all our correspondence. Even if it *is* from one of our pamphlets, it could have come from anywhere.'

'This man, Nincic, is believed to have just been to Germany. Your lorries go to Germany, don't they?'

'Yes, but – '

'Did your lorries bring back drugs for Nincic?'

'I've never met Nincic.'

'That's not what I asked. This sort of thing's done by remote control, isn't it?'

'There's a note,' Darcy said. 'Saying that there's a parcel to be picked up on the 27th. Did you have a lorry returning from Germany on that date?'

'No.' Archavanne sounded triumphant. Too triumphant, and it made Pel immediately suspect he was on the wrong track.

'Switzerland, then?' he said.

'No.'

181

'I take it you sign your lorries in and out?'

'Yes.'

'You know when they leave and when to expect them back.'

'Not exactly.'

'You must keep some sort of record?' Darcy snapped. 'Or you wouldn't be able to do business. How can you hire a lorry to transport goods when you don't know when it'll be back?'

'We always have spare vehicles.'

Pel became brisk. 'I'd like to see your books,' he said.

Archavanne's voice grew harsh. 'You'll find nothing in them.'

'Nevertheless – '

Archavanne's voice rose. 'Look, I built this business up from nothing! Do you think I'd risk – ?'

'How did you build it up?' Pel asked quietly.

Archavanne stopped dead. 'What do you mean?'

'Where did you get the money? A loan from the bank?'

'Yes.'

'We can check.'

Archavanne had gone red in the face. 'Well – no, it wasn't a loan from the bank exactly.'

'Then why say it was?'

'Everybody thinks it was.' Archavanne gestured. 'People like to think you're well in with the bank. In fact, I raised it myself.'

'How?'

'I sold things. A bit of property.'

'About two – three years ago?'

'Yes.'

'Funny,' Darcy observed. 'That was just about the time Nincic started coming into money – just about the time drugs were first noticed at the University here. Where was this

182

property? And what was the date exactly? We'd like to check.'

Archavanne began to gesture again. 'It wasn't that sort of property,' he said, changing direction quickly. 'It was jewels. Old stuff. Family stuff.' He smiled as if he'd had a brainwave. 'Also we ploughed back every bit of profit we made into the business. I did it all myself. My father knew about lorries but he knew nothing about how to run a business.'

'We'd better have your books,' Darcy said. 'And your bank statements. You'd better also let us know where you sold this jewellery. It can't be all that long ago. They'll remember. Jewellers do. They keep accounts of everything they buy and sell.'

Archavanne's jaw hung open. 'They do?'

'In case we have occasion to enquire.' It was a blatant lie, because jewellers were as inefficient as any other businessmen at times, but it sounded good. Pel didn't comment and it was enough to make Archavanne turn from red to white.

'I'd like to know where all this is leading?' he blustered.

'Probably to prison,' Darcy observed in a flat voice.

'You've no proof.'

'We could soon find it. Sniffer dogs round your premises would soon indicate whether the stuff had been here.'

'They'd never – ' Archavanne stopped dead.

'Never what?' Darcy asked. 'Smell the stuff? Because it comes in sealed plastic packages? How did you know that?'

'I've read about it. I've seen it on the television.'

'Have no fear,' Darcy said. 'No matter how well they seal it, there are always a few grains that fail to go inside the bag. And that's enough for the dogs. They'd find it. Then we'd turn the place upside down.'

'My wife – ' Archavanne started to say something then stopped.

'Your wife knows nothing, of course?' Pel said.

Archavanne shook his head, and Darcy shrugged.

'She's going to get a shock, my friend,' he observed. 'You could make it easier for her by coming clean.'

Archavanne's face twisted, then he gave a vast shrug.

'*Did* your lorries transport drugs?'

Archavanne's hearty manner had vanished. 'Sometimes,' he said.

'You'd better tell us.'

Archavanne indicated the door. His wife was singing in the kitchen.

'Shut the door,' he appealed. Darcy shut it quietly.

'It's easy to slip a packet in a marked crate,' he went on. 'I supervised the warehouse when they were due and I worked late after everyone had gone. I took the packet out and resealed the crate.'

'Where did they come from?'

'Austria.'

Pel's eyebrows rose. 'Not Germany? Not Munich?'

'Chief,' Darcy said quickly. 'Munich's the nearest airport to the Austrian border. The nearest to Innsbrück.'

Pel stared at Archavanne. His bounce had gone and he seemed to have shrunk. It was easy to see why he'd seemed so agitated when they'd first been to see him. He'd suspected at once that they were on to him and it was after they'd mentioned that Miollis was dead, Pel remembered, that he'd recovered his aplomb.

'So you did know Nincic?' he said.

Archavanne nodded heavily.

'*And* Miollis?'

Archavanne nodded again, silently. 'The drugs came from Austria,' he said. 'When I took them out of the crate, I wrapped them up with scented soap or disinfectant to kill any smell, then I sent them to the Central Post Office to be collected.'

'When did this start?'

'Two or three years ago. I posted them here. Or in the city. Anywhere. I was always moving about and always passing post offices. I sent them addressed "Poste Restante".'

'Who to? Miollis?'

'Yes.'

'How did you get into this?'

'I met Nincic in a bar. He got talking. You know how it is.'

'Tell me.'

'I seemed to bump into him several times. We became friendly. He asked me to accept a parcel from Germany in one of my lorries. I agreed. He said it was a watch for a friend. It probably was. But there were others later and I got suspicious and guessed it was drugs. But when I tackled him with it, he told me I was as deeply in it as he was and that if I backed out, he'd tell the police.'

'Was *he* running it?'

'No. There was someone else. He said he got his instructions like I did.'

'Who from? One of the gangs?'

'I don't know. I expect so.'

'Which one? Tagliacci or Pépé le Cornet?'

'I don't know. The money always came in an unmarked envelope. I always knew what it was because there was always a blue cross on the corner and it was registered and marked "personal". It always seemed to be posted in the Central Post Office.'

'Did you never try to check who sent it?'

'Yes.' Archavanne was almost weeping now. 'I even waited outside but I never saw anybody I knew who could have done it. I soon learned about Miollis. I wondered who was picking up what I left, so I put it in a brightly coloured paper. One time it was green. Then yellow. Then a sort of orange. And one day I saw this little fat guy come out with the packet under his arm. I followed him to where he was staying. It was the Lion d'Or. It's a small hotel near the airport. I followed him and told him who I was. At first I thought he was going to go for me, but in the end, he saw I was bigger than he was, and we talked – chiefly about who was running it. He didn't know either. We became quite friendly. We even trusted each other. We had to, you see, because neither of us knew who was behind it all. We didn't think it was Nincic and we felt if we could ever find out, we should have a lever, too, as Nincic had a lever on us. So we could pull out. At least, that's what *I* thought. I don't think Miollis was so fussy. He didn't look like a man who was fussy.'

'Have you ever heard of a man called Alois Hofer?'

'Yes. But I don't know who he is. Nincic mentioned him. He's the contact at the other end of the line.'

'Why was Miollis used?'

'He thought it was because he came from Paris and wasn't known down here. When something was coming, he got a message, drove down, took a room at the Lion d'Or and kept going to the Post Office until the parcel turned up. He passed it on to Nincic and left again for Paris. He was paid like me, by post. Always a bundle of used notes.'

'Did *you* kill him?'

'No. Mon Dieu, no! I couldn't kill anyone.'

'You've probably done it already, between you,' Darcy snapped. 'There's at least one student, by the name of Cortot, who's dead. Probably others.'

'I didn't think of that.'

'People like you never do. If you didn't kill Miollis, who did?'

'I don't know.'

'Was it Nincic?'

'Perhaps. He struck me as the sort of man who could.' Archavanne was crying openly now. 'I think Miollis was growing greedy. He'd been doing it for two years and he said he was only the bottom of the pyramid and, since he was taking the risks, he felt he ought to be higher. Perhaps that's why.'

'He was also helping himself,' Pel said. 'Taking a little for himself and selling it privately. I expect Nincic noticed.'

Archavanne moaned. 'Well, whoever was behind it,' he said, 'they were making sure they were keeping *their* fingers clean. Nobody knew them, unless Nincic did.'

'And *he* can't tell us, can he?' Darcy said. 'Not now.'

Pel sighed and handed the slip of yellow paper to Darcy. 'File it,' he said. 'And take him away.'

Archavanne choked on his sobs as he stared round the room. 'All this,' he said. 'It'll all go.'

'You should have thought of that,' Darcy said.

'I *was* doing; all the time. What about my wife?'

'You should have thought about that, too.'

Archavanne was a wreck now with streaming eyes. 'But I built it all up. It was going so well.' His chief worry seemed to be less that he was guilty than that he wouldn't be able to carry out his life's ambition.

'Can I say something to my wife?' he begged. 'Tell her you're wanting my help or something. It won't be a lie.'

'You can tell her what you like,' Darcy said in a flat voice. 'So long as I'm there when you say it.'

As Pel left the house, he could hear Archavanne explaining loudly.

'But your meal's almost ready,' his wife was saying.

'It can't wait, chérie. These gentlemen say there's something they want me to look at.'

'Well, hurry back! Are you all right? You don't look well.'

'Indigestion. I had a beer too many tonight.'

As Archavanne appeared, he gave Pel a twisted smile. 'Thanks,' he said. 'She won't worry now.'

Pel grunted. 'She will, though,' he said. 'When you go away for a few years.'

# eighteen

With Archavanne safely lodged at 72 Rue d'Auxonne, better known to its inhabitants as the jail, the pressure lifted a little. Polverari was quick to offer his congratulations and even the Chief rang to say he was pleased.

They weren't much nearer to finding out who had despatched three dead men, however, and Pépé le Cornet and Tagliacci were still around somewhere. The fact that they appeared to have vanished into thin air by no means indicated that they'd left the district. Nevertheless, with his dinner date just over the horizon, Pel decided he could safely take half an hour off to get his hair cut, and, since he had to see Polverari he appeared at the office in his second-best suit, to try himself out on everybody.

Nobody noticed him.

Only Darcy.

'Patron!' he said. 'Turn round. Let me drink you in!'

Pel glared but he hadn't the heart that morning to snap at anyone. His best suit was hanging in the wardrobe, pressed unwillingly by Madame Routy who had felt she was pressing herself out of a job. His blue shirt was ironed and his wine-red tie handy. He had even got around to imagining himself selling his house and buying a new one in Plombières. He could already see himself domesticated, walking a dog down the lane, digging the garden.

Didier had watched him leave, smiling his secret smile, as if he knew everything Pel was thinking and convinced, Pel was sure, that it was entirely due to him that everybody was in such a good mood. Perhaps, Pel thought, they might have him to stay with them. He could mow the lawn and water the flowers. It would undoubtedly be better than Aunt Routy and the television.

He took out a cigarette. If it caused him to drop dead, he decided, at least he would die a happy man with the prospect of a date with an attractive woman shining in his eyes.

Returning from the Palais de Justice after reporting to Polverari, he found Darcy waiting for him. He'd had another go at Archavanne who was now like a limp rag. His wife was telephoning every half hour and it was finally beginning to dawn on her that the thing the police were wanting to investigate was Archavanne himself.

'It hangs together, Patron,' Darcy said. 'Nincic was Jugoslav in origin, and Jugoslavia – at least Serbia – used to be part of the old Austrian Empire. It gives meaning to the bone button. Nosjean's trying to find out if this Nedergasse he found's Austrian, too.' He put a file on the desk. 'I think, in fact, that our luck's beginning to change. While I was on to Marseilles about Tagliacci I started a few enquiries of my own going. This Escaut, for instance – '

'Which Escaut?'

'The one who found Miollis. His name's not Escaut. It's Bourges. Patrice Bourges. Marseilles has come up with his picture and record. He was going to marry the Bétheot girl but agreed to back off on receipt of twenty thousand francs. There's a case in Hyères too, and they think another in Toulon. He's been working the racket for some time.'

Pel nodded. 'That was a bit of luck.'

'Not luck, Patron,' Darcy corrected. 'Mark I eyeballs.'

What Darcy said about their luck changing suddenly seemed to be right because soon afterwards Nosjean turned up the information that there was a Nedergasse in the old town of Innsbrück. Nosjean had then got on to the library there and with the aid of Krauss, who spoke Alsatian German, had discovered there was a Number 17 and, that, according to the directory, the occupant of the address was one Alois Hofer, a bookseller.

'Get me the police in Innsbrück,' Pel said. 'Then get Krauss here.'

Krauss sat smugly in Pel's office as he waited for his call. 'Wonder if I could get a job as a translator when I retire,' he said.

Pel sniffed. 'You'd never stay awake long enough,' he growled.

The telephone rang. It was the Innsbrück police, and Pel went to the point at once.

'Ja, ja.' The man on the other end spoke French with a strong German accent that was barely understandable and the conversation was punctuated with interruptions from Krauss who was hanging on to the extension. 'We have the problem here also. We feel we have even become a distribution centre. After all, we, too, are very central and very handy for Eastern Europe.'

'Where does it come from?'

'Hungary. The Black Sea ports. Before that, Turkey and even farther afield.'

'Do you know a man called Alois Hofer, of Nedergasse, 17?'

'Oh, ja! Most certainly. He is a small-time crook. He calls himself a bookseller. What he sells are valuable books. Stolen ones.'

'Is he in the drugs game?'

There was a long silence as the Austrian at the other end of the telephone thought it out. 'He could be,' he said slowly. 'He's known to have a brother-in-law in Hungary. His sister married a Hungarian who came here after the Hungarian revolution. They came in hundreds and we all dug in our pockets to help them, you remember. Then they all decided to go back.'

'I remember.' Pel had been caught with that one, too. 'Go on about the brother-in-law.'

'Perhaps *he* has a brother-in-law, too,' the Austrian said. 'In Romania. It's possible.'

It's also possible, Pel thought, that *that* brother-in-law had contacts in Black Sea ports close to Turkey and the Middle East, and right back to the poppy fields.

'Can you get hold of this Hofer?' he asked. 'We're pursuing an enquiry here and his name has come up.'

'No,' the Austrian said. 'Is impossible.'

Pel thought he had misheard him. 'We want to interview him,' he persisted. 'Can you get hold of him for us?'

The Austrian laughed. 'No,' he said.

Pel glared at the telephone. 'Why not?'

The Austrian laughed again. 'Because he's disappeared,' he said. 'With his wife and all his family.'

Dismissing Krauss, Pel stared at his blotter for a while, then he rang his bell. It was Nosjean who answered.

'Bring in Mortier,' Pel said. 'Cortot's pal. We've run up against a brick wall.'

When Nosjean arrived at Mortier's flat, there was no answer to his knock but as he continued to thunder on the door, there was a blurred call from inside and, after scuffling sounds and what seemed ages of waiting, the door opened. Mortier's hair was dishevelled and he looked half asleep.

'You all right?' Nosjean said.

Mortier struggled to keep his eyes open. 'Yes, I'm all right.'

For once Mortier's brisk manner was absent. He seemed dazed and, suddenly, Nosjean realised that he wasn't the strong breezy young man he had thought he was. His chin was weak, and there was a looseness about his mouth. As Nosjean stepped inside the apartment, he sniffed.

'Something wrong?' Mortier asked.

'No.' Nosjean shook his head and peered again at Mortier. 'Are you on drugs, too?'

Mortier managed an indignant expression. 'No, I'm not.'

'I think you're a liar!'

'What!'

'Are you an addict?'

'No.'

Nosjean turned away and headed for the bedroom. There was a syringe on the dressing table. Swinging round, he reached out, grabbed Mortier's sleeve and pushed it up. The tell-tale pricks were there in the soft flesh on the inside of the elbow.

Nosjean stared at the student, disgusted with himself. He hadn't thought of Mortier. His briskness had put him off. Either he was more able to control himself or – because he had plenty of money – he managed to get hold of more of the stuff than most. In his anger, he pushed Mortier from him so that he reeled and fell into a chair.

'Salaud,' he said quietly. 'You're on it as well.'

Mortier's expression changed to one of defiance. 'So what?' he said. 'I just have a bit of fun.'

'Fun? You're on the hard stuff. How did it start?'

Mortier gave a huge shrug. 'Same way as everybody else, I suppose. At a party. Someone was trying marijuana. I started like that – over-the-counter stuff and LSD. Then mescalin and hashish.'

'Then cocaine,' Nosjean said. 'And finally heroin. You've had it, mon vieux.'

'Look, cop – '

'Never mind "cop",' Nosjean snapped. 'Where did you get it?'

'Here and there.'

'Did you get it from Nincic?'

'Well – yes.'

'Did you know he'd been murdered?'

Mortier's face fell. 'I didn't know – '

'Don't you read the papers?'

'They don't interest me.'

'Nothing interests you lot,' Nosjean snapped, 'except your own half-baked ideas. You should wake up. It might be you next. You told me you didn't know Cortot was on it.'

'Well, what if I did? Who cares?'

Nosjean stared at him for a moment, his eyes narrowed with dislike. 'Take your shirt off,' he said.

'What? What for?'

'Take it off!' Nosjean yelled. 'Or I'll tear it off.'

Unwillingly, Mortier unbuttoned his shirt. Nosjean couldn't wait and wrenched at it before he'd finished. A button shot off and rattled in a corner. On Mortier's back were the same whiplash scars he'd seen on Cortot's.

'*You* did it?' he said. '*You* tied him up.'

'Look, I – '

'You two bastards! You whipped each other! You scourged each other! Did he ever tie *you* up?'

'Yes.' Mortier's eyes were shifty. 'Occasionally.'

'Why? Because it gave you pleasure? Because you're twisted? Was he a homosexual?'

'Look – '

'Was he?'

'Yes.'

'You, too?'

'We can't help it if we're born with something missing.'

It was all quite clear suddenly. The two of them had been in the habit of indulging in erotic practices, beating, whipping, scourging, tying each other up. And this time it had gone wrong. The knots wouldn't come undone and Cortot had died.

'I couldn't unfasten the damned things!' Mortier's eyes were suddenly full of tears. 'He was choking! He wanted to get free, and I couldn't get him free! I panicked. The more I tried the more he struggled. Then I saw he was dead. I was frightened! I went out and locked the door! I knew my parents were in Paris so I went to see them. This was Friday. I came back on Sunday and rang the Police and told them I'd found him.'

Nosjean stared at him bitterly. 'Get your shirt on,' he said. 'We have questions to ask you and this time you'd better answer them truthfully.'

But they didn't get that far.

When Nosjean sat Mortier in the sergeants' room, he was weeping. 'What'll my people say when they find out?' he wailed.

'You should have thought of that one,' Nosjean snapped.

He had a suspicion that Mortier was in need of a fix and that he'd probably talk if he got one. But it would require the Chief's permission for him to have one from the police surgeon.

'It'll kill my mother,' Mortier was moaning.

Nosjean didn't answer and Mortier began to sob. 'Look, can't we arrange something?' he begged. 'I'm not short of money.'

Nosjean's eyes narrowed. 'You trying to bribe me?' he asked.

'Oh, God!' Mortier's sobs were racking his body now. 'I never thought it would end like this.'

Nosjean stared at him unfeelingly, then he telephoned for a uniformed man to sit with Mortier while he reported to Pel. 'Stay with him,' he said. 'And don't take your eyes off him. Got it?'

'Right.' The uniformed man grinned. 'I've got it.'

But he hadn't.

Nosjean was just explaining what he'd discovered to Pel when there was a scream outside. It came from the Bar Transvaal opposite and, as they hurried to the window, they saw a woman standing at one of the outside tables with her hands to her throat, her eyes wide and full of horror. They couldn't see what had happened, only the sun on the roofs of the cars in the car park. It was while they were trying to lean out far enough to see that the uniformed man appeared in the doorway, his face white. He didn't have to tell them what had happened.

'He jumped!' Nosjean said.

# nineteen

Pel was brooding.

The office was empty, with everybody across the road at the Bar Transvaal, and he sat alone, his spectacles on his forehead, turning over the papers in his file. Leguyader's people had removed the bloody mash that was all that remained of Philippe Mortier, and his parents had been informed and were already on their way to collect his body.

Nosjean was still clearing up. The Chief had come down on them all like a clap of thunder. Pel hadn't really been involved but, after the failure to provide a murderer for Miollis, Treguy and Nincic, he hadn't entirely escaped either, while poor young Nosjean had found himself standing rigidly, his face taut, his eyes flinching, as the Chief weighed into him. Pel had been obliged to watch.

What Nosjean had suffered was nothing to what Frachot, the uniformed man, had gone through. Despite everything, Nosjean had not really been wrong. He had told Frachot not to take his eyes off Mortier and Frachot had, and Mortier had dived through the open window.

'Just as if he was going into a swimming pool,' the policeman had bleated. 'Straight through without touching it.'

'Four floors up,' Darcy had commented. 'The poor bastard probably thought he could fly.'

It had been a wearing morning and Pel felt exhausted, and vaguely guilty.

The week had been spoiled. He had been looking forward to his dinner date but this business right outside his own office had cast a blight over it. It would require an effort now to be breezy over the aperitifs and chatty over the wine.

It depressed him also because it seemed to indicate they were no nearer the solution. They had Archavanne, and Miollis, Treguy and Nincic were dead. But someone else, someone more powerful, someone at the top of the pile, was clearly still around and still active. Without Miollis and Nincic, the thing would probably lie dormant for a while, but it would never be finished. It only needed a little time to set the thing up again, and the gangs were always greedy.

For a long time, he turned the papers, deep in thought. The file had grown bulky. In it was everything they'd collected, everything that had been written down – everything from Archavanne's pamphlets and the yellow slip imprinted with Hofer's address that Nosjean had found, to reminders they'd written to each other – even Krauss' note to him to ring Madame Faivre-Perret. Reminders sometimes had a habit of reminding – not only of what they were intended to remind about but other things, too. He moved them slowly, one after the other, smoking until his tongue felt like ashes and he was convinced his lungs were charred. He was under no delusions that his job had ended with the discovery of Nincic's body. Somewhere in the city there was still someone who could lead him to the source – whether it were Pépé le Cornet or Tagliacci – someone who knew the secrets. Was it the Chahu woman? Darcy seemed to think it might be. Or the doorman, Salengro? Darcy didn't trust him. Ramou? For a student he appeared to have more money than he ought to have. Madame Foussier? It was a startling thought, but not all that strange because she understood drugs and had a background of drugs. Foussier himself? That seemed crazy. And the link seemed to be Marseilles because Tagliacci had come from there, and Treguy had gone over to him. After leaving Paris and before he'd been killed, had he contacted Ramou, who also significantly came from Marseilles? The answer lay probably in someone's character and the most enigmatic character of the lot belonged to Marie-Anne Chahu.

The same view exactly was held by Darcy who was sufficiently intrigued by it to have decided that his lunch hour could be put to better use than merely for eating, and he was sitting in his car staring at the Maison Joliet, his mind occupied with the puzzle.

It wasn't a criminal offence for her to be Foussier's mistress, or anybody else's either. It wasn't a criminal offence for a man to pay for a love-nest and establish a woman in it. But what puzzled Darcy was why so many students went to see her. The number, he had noticed, had dropped recently, and he wondered if somehow someone had got wind of his interest.

Somewhere in that flat up there, Darcy felt, were the answers to a lot of questions, and the previous evening a curious little incident had occurred which he had felt was a bonus for his hard work. There had been a scuffle in the Café Schehérezade, which operated a disco where the students gathered to work off their energy, there had been too much drinking, and half a dozen of the youngsters had been brought in. No charges had been preferred because no damage had been done and it had been considered sufficient to have a uniformed inspector dish out a warning. But Darcy had arrived at the Hôtel de Police just as they were leaving, most of them a little shame-faced and glad that it was no worse, and among them, Darcy was surprised to see, was Ramou, and the girl, Nadine Weyl, whom he'd last seen riding on a scooter away from Marie-Anne Chahu's apartment block. And, as an additional extra, waiting for them at the door was Joachim Salengro, the doorman with the plum suit who protected the inhabitants of the Maison Joliet from such importunate visitors as Darcy. It was too good an opportunity to miss and Darcy had swept them all back inside the Hôtel de Police, full of good humour and interest.

'Trouble?' he asked.

'It was nothing,' Salengro said quickly. 'Just a lot of kids arguing. No damage done.'

'Students?'

'That's it.' Salengro's shifty rubbery face moved into a wink. 'You know what they're like.'

'It was a birthday party,' Ramou said.

'Whose?'

Ramou indicated the girl. 'Nadine's.'

'And you're all friends?'

'We belong to the same societies. That sort of thing. Go to the same parties. It's usual.' Ramou was still a little tipsy and inclined to smile a lot. The girl, however, looked scared and was saying nothing, her pretty face pale, her large eyes worried.

'Who was paying?' Darcy asked her. 'You?'

She shook her head and Ramou interrupted.

'Me,' he said. 'Good old Jean-Pierre.'

'Where did you get the money? Student grants aren't that big.'

Ramou slapped Nadine Weyl's backside. 'I'm fond of Nadine. I wanted to give her a good party.' He put his finger alongside his nose and grinned. 'And we have sources, you know. Kind uncles. Rich aunts. That sort of thing.' He fished in his pocket and took out two or three large denomination notes. 'I write lots of letters. It pays to keep them sweet and I remind them how angelic I used to look in my surplice as an altar boy in Marseilles.'

As he stuffed away the money, Darcy turned to Salengro. 'Were you at the party, too?'

Salengro gestured awkwardly. 'Well – yes, I was.'

'How come?'

Again the vague gesture and Ramou joined in helpfully again. 'He's my uncle,' he said. 'I'm from Marseilles. He's from Toulon. We stick together down there.'

Darcy had watched them leave, frowning. The explanation seemed sound enough and, in fact, when he checked, what Ramou said seemed to be true. The university records showed that it *was* Nadine Weyl's birthday, and Salengro *did* come from Toulon, so he might well have been Ramou's uncle. But it smelled all the same. It was asking too much of a man like Darcy that he should accept the coincidence of all three of them being together at a party. Salengro's job didn't pay enough for him to help impecunious nephews – if they *were* nephews – and Darcy had a shrewd suspicion that there weren't any rich aunts either.

Intrigued enough to want to find out, he entered the Joliet Building and walked quietly up the stairs. Standing on the corner by the lift, he eyed Marie-Anne Chahu's door. It was an ordinary door, painted green, with gold studs in it to give it class. What was she doing behind there, he wondered. What went on?

For a long second he studied it, then he began to step out the distance to it from the lift. Her flat was at the end of the corridor so there was nowhere else the students could have gone except back to the lift. Returning to the lift, on an impulse, he took it to the basement, then through all the floors, and finally back to the ground floor.

Salengro, the porter, was sitting in his office, smoking a cigar, his plum-coloured jacket hanging on the back of the chair, his sly ugly face watchful.

'You got a list of the people who rent these flats?' Darcy asked.

'Sure.' Salengro produced a plan of each floor, with all the names. None of them made any sense to Darcy. A few were known to him and, judging by the professions listed alongside them – as if they'd been chosen to preserve the tone of the place – they were all eminently respectable. Yet there had seemed to be more coming and going than there ought to be and it continued to puzzle Darcy. He knew the city well and most of the people in it, especially the wealthy and important into which class most of the names he'd gathered fell. There weren't many outsiders who visited the flats and they didn't look like drug addicts either. They were all successful people with clear heads, and it crossed Darcy's mind once more that Marie-Anne Chahu might be entertaining them in her bed. But he'd also noticed that they never took the lift to the second floor where she lived, but to the top floor, and on the top floor were people who might well be their associates and friends.

So far, with the Nincic-Miollis-Treguy business, he had devoted only the odd half-hour to the puzzle and he felt suddenly it needed more.

Returning to the lift, he rode to the top floor, and stood on the landing, staring about him. Trying various doors, he discovered linen cupboards and closets where the cleaning staff left their pails, brooms and vacuum cleaners. Eventually, he found a door marked 'Private'. It was locked, but that presented few problems to Darcy who opened it with a plastic banker's card.

There was a flight of stairs leading upwards to a flat high-walled roof area where there were several bed sheets hanging on lines in the sun. At one end of the roof space there was a small square brick construction. Moving closer, he peered through a window and saw it was a small furnished flat, complete with sitting room, bedroom, kitchen and bathroom. By pressing his face to the window, he saw a bottle of champagne and an ice bucket.

He stared at it a moment longer, then at the list of flat lessees, then he took the lift to the ground floor. Salengro was still in his office.

'What's that place at the top of the building?' Darcy asked.

'It's a flat,' Salengro said. 'What did you think it was? – a pigeon loft?'

Darcy gestured at the plan he held. 'Why isn't it on the list?' he asked.

'Because it's not for rent. It's mine. I live there. I'm relieved here at six until eight the next morning. We have a guy comes from an agency. When I go off duty, that's where I head for.'

Darcy frowned. 'And during the day?'

'It's unoccupied. Sometimes, when it's quiet, I slip up and do a bit of housework. Make the bed, vacuum, that sort of thing. It's not very big. It gets warm in weather like this.' A heavy hand gestured at a folding bed standing in the corner of his office. 'Then I sleep on that. There's a kitchen along the corridor. It's cool.'

Darcy studied the doorman. 'I noticed champagne up there,' he said. 'You have expensive tastes.'

Salengro gestured again. 'It's good for the stomach and I like it,' he pointed out. 'It's my only indulgence.'

Darcy eyed him. 'Apart from cigars,' he said.

When Darcy returned to the office, Pel was still staring at the file. In his bones he knew the answer was in the pile of papers somewhere. He was a great believer in details, feeling that, piled one on top of another, providing you got them in the right order, they made a whole.

The newspaper was alongside him, the front page containing a picture of the Perdrix girl with her parents. She looked sullen, and they had a firm grip on her arms, as if they thought she might bolt again at the first opportunity. Probably she would. It wouldn't help much, though, because Emile Escaut, né Patrice Bourges, was sitting in the cells until he was charged either with alienation of affection or demanding money with menaces. It was something Judge Brisard, in whose lap it had dropped, would have to decide.

As Pel brooded, the door opened and Darcy appeared. Sitting opposite Pel, he tossed across his cigarettes and described what he'd been up to.

'At first,' he said, 'I thought she was the mistress of Léonard Durandot, of Durandot Plastics. I even made a few enquiries round his works. They said he liked girls and was in the habit of pawing them in the office. But he wasn't in La Chahu's apartment that time when I went back. I thought he would be. She *must* be somebody's mistress, Patron.'

'She is,' Pel said. 'She's Foussier's.'

'Is she, by God?' Darcy grinned. 'I must admit, I wondered. After all, if I'd got as much money as he's got, *I'd* have a mistress.'

'Probably so would I,' Pel admitted. 'If I could afford one.'

'Don't get me wrong, Patron,' Darcy said. 'I've nothing against it. If it's there lying about loose, you might as well put it to good use. I'm just curious about who keeps who. It comes in useful sometimes. It certainly does in her case. You know who else have apartments in that block? Chaudordy, the surgeon, and Senator Forton, and old Gissey, of France Industrielle. They earn a bit more than she does, I'll bet. She also runs a Triumph 1500, too, and that's not chickenfeed. I run a Citroën.'

And I, Pel thought, run a Peugeot that looks as though it was made before World War I. Perhaps it was one of the Taxis of the Marne.

'Is she efficient?' he asked.

'That's my impression, Patron.'

'Perhaps she's also efficient at finance.' Pel spoke with the bitterness of someone who wasn't. 'Perhaps Foussier gives her tips across the pillow.'

'Perhaps.' Darcy frowned. 'But, you know, Patron. There's more, I think. Why does she hand out old exam papers to kids?'

'Why not?'

'She's not a tutor or a lecturer, Patron.'

Pel rubbed his nose and lit a cigarette from Darcy's packet.

'And there are a lot of people who visit that block,' Darcy went on. 'People who don't live there. Like Durandot.' He laid a list in front of Pel. 'I bet you recognise a few of those names, don't you?'

Pel did. His eyebrows rose. 'That one,' he said, placing a finger on one of the names. 'Sanctimony itself. And old Teeth and Trousers. What do they do there?'

'Well, Robert Volnay and his wife live on the top floor, Patron. So does René Walck. They're in business and very respectable. Perhaps this lot were just visiting friends.'

Pel sniffed. 'All the same, they'll probably turn out not to have been. How many flats are there?'

'Six on the top floor. One's a retired general who's a bachelor and eighty years old and another three are occupied by old women. Then there are Walck and the Volnays. And these people like Durandot and Teeth and Trousers *could* be visiting La Chahu. I did a bit of checking on her. She comes from Quimper and was a bit late in the day starting at university and I wondered what had happened to the years before. She worked in Rennes, it seemed, and there was a bit of scandal with one of the doctors there and she had to leave. So she's not exactly new to that sort of thing, is she?'

While they talked, Nosjean appeared. 'They said you were still here, Patron,' he said.

There were several bottles of beer on the desk and Pel pushed one across. 'Better have a drink,' he said. 'Was it painful with the Chief?'

'I expect I shall get over it, Patron.'

'Don't worry too much,' Pel said. 'The Chief's no fool and he knows your record. Frachot looks like getting a dirty mark on his file, perhaps even a transfer to one of the hill villages. There'll be nothing in yours. I'll see to that.'

'Thanks, Patron.' Nosjean cleared his throat. 'Mortier,' he said hesitantly.

Pel looked up, frowning. 'That's finished,' he said. 'The matter's closed.'

Nosjean blushed. 'I'm not sure it is, Patron.' He laid a slip of paper on Pel's desk. 'They just brought me the contents of his wallet. This was among them. It's a telephone number – one I've had for some time. I recognised it at once. It's the Chahu woman's. Why had Mortier got it in *his* pocket?'

Pel frowned, then he slapped the desk. 'Who are we looking for, Nosjean?'

'Whoever was responsible for what happened next door, Patron. The contact between people like Mortier and Cortot and Nincic – and the people in Paris or Marseilles.'

'Someone,' Pel said slowly, 'who has more money than they ought to have. Someone with access to information about students interested in drugs, someone with facilities to travel.'

'Marie-Anne Chahu!' Darcy said. 'She handles Foussier's files all the time! She knows as much as he does about drug-taking at universities!'

Pel pushed his chair back. 'Let's go and see this Mademoiselle Chahu,' he suggested.

Foussier hadn't been near the University all day and when they went to his private office, they found Angélique Courtois pulling the stamps off old envelopes.

'I save them for my young brother,' she said. 'We get mail from all over the world.'

Pel picked out one with an Austrian eagle on it. 'Do you get many from Austria?'

'Oh, yes. Quite a lot. Marie-Anne lets me have all the envelopes.'

'Does she handle the mail?'

'That's one of her jobs. Professor Foussier insists on it. He doesn't like his business going round the University. It's a hotbed of gossip.'

'Does she get private mail for herself in with it?'

She gave them a a beaming smile. It was mostly directed at Darcy. 'I expect so. The students fall heavily for her.' She smiled again at Darcy. 'They do even for me sometimes.'

'Ever heard of Alois Hofer?' Pel asked.

'Yes, I have.'

'Who from?'

'Marie-Anne.'

'Does she write to him?'

'She writes to a lot of people.'

'Is he one?'

'Yes. I've seen the letters. I post the mail.'

'Where is she now?'

'She's with the Professor.'

'And where's the Professor?'

'He's on his lecture programme. It's been arranged some time. Through the University. Slav languages. It's in Germany mostly.'

There was a dead silence. For a second no one spoke and no one moved. Then Pel glanced at Darcy and his brows came down.

'It's where?' he snapped.

'In Germany.'

'*What!*' Pel's face went red and he looked as if he were about to have a fit. 'In Germany? Who told him he could go?'

The girl looked startled. 'Nobody. He doesn't have to ask.'

'This time he does!' Pel snapped. 'He's supposed to be under police protection and that means he doesn't disappear into the blue without informing me first. Where is he?'

She looked flustered. 'I don't know the itinerary. I don't handle his appointments.'

'Who does? The Chahu woman? And she's with him! Name of God!' Pel cursed. 'Ring his home, Darcy. Ask his wife.'

Foussier's wife was away, too, but the girl who answered thought Foussier was at Munich University. A hurried call to Munich showed that he had indeed been there but had already moved on, and it was then that Angélique found a letter that showed he was due to lecture in Austria that night.

'It's one arranged by Professor Rosschnigg,' she said. 'In Innsbrück.'

'Innsbrück,' Pel said. 'Nedergasse!' His rage almost choked him, and he leaned over the desk, glaring at the girl. 'Why weren't we informed?'

She looked worried. 'I think you were. Marie-Anne rang up. They said it was all right.'

'Did they?' Pel's eyes gleamed as he saw the opportunity to get a bit of his own back for all he'd suffered from the accusations of incompetence. 'Did they indeed? Well, I want to know who, because there's probably a gang – probably *two* gangs – looking for him, with more joining in as they hear of the pickings here. Doubtless he thinks they won't follow him abroad. Well, he doesn't know men like Pépé le Cornet and Tagliacci! They have a long arm.' He swung to the girl again. 'When did they leave?'

'It must have been four days ago.' She looked startled and a little scared. 'They flew. He likes to pilot himself. They went to Dors – it's a small field just outside Innsbrück. He's been there before. He stays at the Tyrolerhof.'

Pel fished for a cigarette and began to head for the door. His face was grim. 'I think we'd better go and see the Chief,' he said.

# twenty

The Chief didn't argue. Since he had put the bodyguard on Foussier, he had to accept without protest Pel's charge that the bodyguard shouldn't have been removed without Pel being informed. Pel made as much of it as he could and the Chief was unable to put up too much of a resistance to his request to go to Innsbrück.

'Can't we leave it to the Austrians?' he asked.

'I think we ought to be there,' Pel said.

The Chief frowned. 'It should go through the Minister for the Interior. We should submit a file to the Director of Public Prosecutions so he can make the approach through diplomatic channels.'

'We'll lose her if we do,' Pel argued. 'The Austrians want to break this thing as much as we do. They'll cut corners.'

The Chief thought for a moment then capitulated abruptly. 'Right,' he said. 'I'll telephone ahead.'

'I'll supply the warrant,' Polverari added. 'It'll be up to you to make the formal application there. How are you going?'

Darcy was already looking through a guide. 'If we fly to Munich,' he said, 'you'll still have sixty or more kilometres to drive. By car from here, it's no further than to Marseilles or Le Havre. We could go by Belfort, then on to the autoway across Switzerland. We could be there in six or seven hours.'

'Tagliacci and Pépé le Cornet move faster than that,' Pel pointed out. 'This damned woman's probably putting the finger on Foussier already.' He drew a deep breath. 'If he can fly to this airfield at Dors,' he said, 'why can't we?'

Polverari and the Chief looked at each other. 'Very well,' the Chief said. 'We'll lay it on. I'll telephone Innsbrück and get them to meet you. The rest I'll sort out while you're on the way. Who're you taking?'

'Darcy, of course. And young Nosjean. He's done as much as anybody to crack this thing.'

But when they reached Pel's office, Nosjean had gone to meet Mortier's parents and only Krauss was there. 'Why not me, Patron?' he asked. 'I retire in a month's time. It'll be my last job. After this, the only travelling I'll be able to afford will be to Royan or the Jura with my grandchildren. And I speak German well.'

Pel was none too keen. Krauss had been loaded on to him when he had first set up his team and, while he'd never done anything very wrong, he also wasn't noted for brains or energy. However, if anything broke while he was away, he couldn't imagine leaving the office in the charge of Krauss, or Misset or Lagé either, for that matter. With Darcy away, only Nosjean had enough intelligence, despite his youth, to know how to act.

He looked at Krauss. He was sound on procedure and would know what to do in an emergency, and it might be a good idea to have a German-speaking officer with him.

'All right,' he said. 'Make sure we have all the documents we need.'

He turned away, wondering if he could get Nosjean to telephone Madame Faivre-Perret on his behalf. Nosjean was a polite young man, well brought up by a respectable mother and father and a set of adoring older sisters, and didn't make a habit of hanging about bars and chasing women. He would make sure the job was done properly. Pel was still wondering when Darcy stuck his head in the door.

'Car's ready, Chief,' he said. 'Krauss' down there.' He smiled. 'We ought to enjoy this. It isn't every day you get a trip to somewhere as pleasant as Innsbrück.'

Pel said nothing. Normally he would have welcomed the trip but for once, weighed down by the feeling that there couldn't possibly be time to go to Innsbrück, do what he wanted and return for his dinner date, he saw no future in it.

On an impulse, he snatched at the telephone and asked for the number of the hairdressing salon in the Rue de la Liberté. His voice was sharp and the man on the telephone didn't attempt to he funny.

'She's not here, Monsieur,' a female voice informed Pel. 'She's in Paris.'

Pel glanced at his watch, faintly alarmed. 'Isn't she back yet?'

'Well, she may be, Monsieur. But she told us she wouldn't be in today. If she is back, she'll have gone straight home.'

Frowning heavily, Pel dialled the number Krauss had given him. There was no reply.

Slamming the telephone down, he thought for a moment of sending Darcy to Innsbrück in his place, but that would have laid him open to charges of despatching a subordinate to do a job that required his own presence, and he began to wonder instead if he could send a note round or something and beg her to be patient. Then he realised, after all the fuss he'd made to the Chief about the urgency of the situation and with Darcy champing at the bit, there just wasn't time and he decided to let it go, hoping that the thing would be over quickly and he could get back. The fact that his life was probably ruined and the new house at Plombières had gone up in smoke was the sort of by-product you got from police work.

The journey to Innsbrück was murder. The mountains were full of air pockets and the pilot looked about sixteen. But he knew his job and they reached Dors without problems.

Krauss had brought everything. It was only as they left the aircraft that Pel noticed the suitcases he had with him. They all kept a bag handy in case they had to shoot off in a hurry somewhere, but Krauss' suitcases looked big enough to hold spare shirts, toothbrushes and toothpaste for everybody in the Hôtel de Police.

'In the name of God,' Pel said. 'What's in them?'

Krauss grinned. 'The documents, Patron. You said to bring them along with us.'

Pel sighed. Trust Krauss, with his thick head, to botch the thing. 'I meant the file off my desk,' he snapped. 'Not every damned piece of paper we've used.'

Krauss shrugged, unperturbed. He didn't perturb easily, which was probably why he'd gone through his whole career without ever getting too involved.

'They'll probably be useful, Patron,' he said.

The Innsbrück police had a car with an inspector and driver waiting for them and they entered the city along the Kranerbitterallee. Pel sat in the back, gloomily thinking of his dinner date. In his pessimistic fashion, by this time he was convinced that Madame Faivre-Perret had never had any intention of coming back from Paris, anyway. He didn't flatter himself that she would make a special effort for *him*, and he felt she had probably decided in the end she was better off without him.

The car swung into the Universitätstrasse then right by a set of yellow-painted barracks. Red-and-white sentry boxes stood in the dusty parade ground opposite the police building tucked among the trees. The word, *Bundespolizeidirektion*, in large black letters, hit them in the face.

The building was a new one, strangely out of place among the ancient buildings of the old Austro-Hungarian Empire and it had a Germanic look of efficiency about it. The Chief had done his work well and they were shown at once to the Director's office. The Director was a plump, pink-faced man with his hair cut en brosse. The telephone calls seemed to have satisfied him and he didn't argue.

'I think it's clear enough,' he said. 'You'll need help.' He indicated a lean Italian-looking man alongside him. 'Kommissar Bakt will be coming with you. He's been engaged on the problem here and he'll be as glad as you to see it cleared up.'

The Tyrolerhof Hotel was almost opposite the station at the end of the Sudtirolerplatz. It was well organised for tourists and full of every nationality under the sun. The reception desk was crowded but they pushed to the front and Bakt didn't bother to argue. 'Polizei,' he explained briskly and, as the clerk's frosty face melted, Pel nudged Krauss.

'Fräulein Chahu – Marie-Anne Chahu,' Krauss explained. 'French nationality. She's staying here.'

The clerk glanced at his book. 'That's right,' he said. 'Room 87.'

Marie-Anne Chahu was surprised to see them but she received them with a straight face. The room was clearly one of the best in the hotel. Immediately, Pel noticed a man's leather bedroom slippers in the open wardrobe.

'Whose are those?' he asked.

She frowned. 'I think that's my business,' she answered tartly.

'I think it's ours too. You'd better answer.'

She stared at them for a moment then she made a little gesture with her hand. 'They're Raymond's. Professor Foussier's.'

'What are they doing here?'

'We had breakfast together. We were organising his plans for the day. There's nothing wrong with that. We've done it before.'

'Is he sharing the room?'

She gave them a cold look. 'He has the room next door.'

'Where is he now?'

'I don't know. He likes to go off occasionally. Especially before a lecture. He's a man who lives at a tremendous pace and he likes to be alone. He could be at half a dozen places, all within easy reach of Innsbrück: Seefeld, Reith, Zir. They're all only an easy train ride and the station's only across the square. He'll be back in time for Professor Rosschnigg's lecture.'

'He's your lover, isn't he?' Darcy asked bluntly.

She made no bones about it. 'Yes,' she said simply. 'He has been for some time.'

'And you liked going abroad with him, didn't you?'

Her eyes blazed. 'What is this? Am I being accused of something?'

'Just answer the question.'

'Of course I like going abroad with him! The work's tiring because he has a fearsome energy, but he never fails to see that I eat well and have a good room.'

'We're not interested in morals,' Pel said. 'When you travel abroad with the Professor, there are periods when you're free to do as you wish, aren't there? – when you can conduct your own business.'

'I have no business.'

'Not even drugs?' Darcy asked.

She stared at them for a moment in silence, making a clear effort to control herself. 'Is this why you're here?'

'Yes, Fräulein.' Bakt spoke for the first time. 'It is.'

Darcy leaned forward, his hands on the back of a chair. 'You knew Fran Nincic, didn't you?'

'Yes.'

'How about Pépé le Cornet?'

'Who's Pépé le Cornet?'

'Never mind who he is. Do you know him?'

'No.'

'Maurice Tagliacci?'

'No!' She almost screamed the word.

213

'Did you know Nincic had been murdered?'

For a second she stared at them, then her hands went to her throat. 'Oh, God, no!' she said.

'He was another of your lovers, wasn't he?'

'Once.'

'He was trafficking in drugs. Did he use your apartment?'

She had recovered her spirits quickly. 'Of course not! He rarely came.'

'But students did, didn't they? Why?'

She laughed. It sounded strained and, after her shock over Nincic's death, quite unreal. 'Because I'm Professor Foussier's assistant. They come to me about his business.'

'Old examination papers!' Darcy said. 'Some of the students I saw visiting your apartment were hardly at the stage when they'd be thinking of examinations.'

'They're *always* thinking of examinations,' she said irritably. 'Examinations are something that brood over them from the moment they arrive.'

Darcy produced a sheet of paper. 'What about *these* students? They've been more than once: Renée Mazuy. Denise Monel. Nadine Weyl. Christianne Tisserand. Lionel Pépin – '

'Him!' she said.

'What do you mean – him?'

'Pépin's as queer as a straight corkscrew.'

Pel was frowning. He lit a cigarette quickly. 'Let's have a look at that list, Darcy,' he said.

Darcy handed over the paper. 'These are mostly girls,' Pel said.

'Girls take drugs, Patron.'

'Have you *seen* these girls? Do they look as if they're on drugs?'

'Of course they're not on drugs!' Marie-Anne Chahu interrupted.

'Then why do they come to your flat?' Darcy demanded.

Pel held out his hand. 'The other list, Darcy,' he said. 'The list of people who visit the building.'

As Darcy handed it over, Pel glanced down at it. 'All wealthy,' he mused. 'Including Teeth and Trousers.' He frowned and went on, half to himself. 'But *he's* not interested in girls. He's interested in – ' he stopped and looked at Marie-Anne Chahu. 'It wasn't drugs you were supplying,' he said. 'It was sex. You were procuring girls for these men!'

She was watching him closely, her eyes like stone.

'And for Teeth and Trousers, this kid – what's his name? – Lionel Pépin.'

There was a dead silence.

'Oh, mon Dieu,' Darcy muttered.

For a moment, she studied the four men, her mouth twisted in contempt. 'It's not a crime,' she pointed out.

'Don't be too sure of that, Mademoiselle,' Pel said.

She was still facing them angrily. 'They never used my apartment,' she fumed.

'No, by God!' Darcy's expression was full of bitterness and now he exploded. 'They didn't! Because you have *two* flats. Your own and the flat on the roof. The doorman's flat. It's perfect. "A bit warm in summer," he said, but who minds that when you're not wearing clothes? They picked up the money from you – eight hundred francs, a lot of money for a student – then they took the lift to the top floor. You made the appointments, and that mealy-mouthed bastard on the door rented it, provided bed linen and saw to the supply of champagne.'

She stared at him, her face transformed.

'You knew the kids who needed money and were willing,' Darcy went on. 'And you knew the men who were eager.'

'Name of God!' she said. 'Nobody worries these days about morals! The kids were the last people to argue. Their parents couldn't supply them with money and their grants

215

were small. I did no more than introduce them. What they got up to afterwards wasn't my affair.'

'How did you learn the names of the willing ones? Was it Ramou?'

'Of course it was! He knew them because he slept with them himself. It was Ramou who approached Salengro and got him to rent his flat.'

Her eyes glowed with hatred. 'I merely passed on what was wanted.'

'And got paid for it!'

'No!'

'What about the flat? And the Triumph? Were you blackmailing these men?'

'No! Never!' Her face was suddenly ugly. 'They were always pestering *me*! They were always after *me*! I didn't want their fat, bloated bodies! I did it to keep them away! I told them I'd find someone to take my place! There were always kids who were desperate for money!'

As she became silent, Pel looked at her in wonderment. There was a long pause. 'I thought I'd seen the lot,' he said slowly. 'But this is a new one.'

'And not, I think,' Bakt said, looking far from happy, 'the one we were expecting.'

# twenty-one

There was an atmosphere of tension in the offices of the Bundespolizeidirektion.

Marie-Anne Chahu was being held for the moment but Pel was worried and aware of a sickening disappointment. The links had been so clear, but they weren't links connected with drugs – only sex – and Kommissar Bakt had a look in his eye now that suggested his thoughts were dwelling on the strangeness of French morals.

They had moved too quickly. Darcy had been too keen and over-eager and the urgency had driven them into a mistake. Pel had allowed his anger at the Chief permitting Foussier to leave France to push him too far and they had arrived in Innsbrück expecting to pick up Marie-Anne Chahu for drug-trafficking. The fact that the charge looked like being a lot less had changed things quite considerably. The Director had gone to great lengths to accommodate them and was now showing his distaste in no small measure at the fact that they had only a vice case.

Pel was lighting cigarettes in quick succession. The odds had swung against him once more. The Chief would have a lot to say about it, he knew, and so would Judge Polverari. Somewhere the thing had gone sour on them. Yet he suspected even now that they were on the brink of working out the more major case and that the answer still rested somehow with Marie-Anne Chahu.

She remained defiant, however, because she knew that in the end they probably wouldn't even be able to charge her. They had no proof she was doing what she did for profit, and none that the girls had not been willing. And there were a lot of big guns on the other side, men with money and men with influence, and even in Republican France influence could still count.

This was a nasty one, Pel thought, and could have unfortunate effects on his career. Yet, he still felt Marie-Anne Chahu knew the answers and he had begged that a room be set aside for them to question her. Her career seemed to be finished because the thing would get around, and, despite the fact that he saw no harm in going to bed with her, Foussier would clearly not enjoy having his reputation sullied by what she'd been up to. He'd probably set her up safely somewhere, in Paris or the South, and would probably even be instrumental in finding her another equally well-paid post.

Meanwhile Pel's dinner date seemed to have vanished into the blue at full speed. It had become the most important meal in his life and he knew that if he threw his hand in, they could still be flown back in a matter of an hour or so. But he knew he couldn't go home yet, because he was still convinced the thing could be wound up here in Innsbrück.

He stared at the telephone, brooding and bitter, then abruptly he snatched it up and demanded Madame Faivre-Perret's home number. For a long time there was no reply and, with a sinking heart, he was just about to put the instrument down when he heard a click as the telephone at the other end was lifted. His heart skidded across his chest as he heard a female voice.

'Madame Faivre-Perret?'

'Who wants her?'

His heart sank again because it wasn't the voice he'd expected. 'My name is Inspector Pel,' he said.

'Oh, yes! She told me about you.'

Pel glared at the telephone, feeling his innermost secrets had become public. 'Who's that speaking?' he said desperately. 'I'd like to speak to Madame Faivre-Perret.'

'Well, you can't, Monsieur.' The voice sounded self-satisfied. 'She isn't here.'

Pel's stomach suddenly felt as though he hadn't eaten for a week. 'She's not?' He had firmly expected her to be.

'No. She went to Paris.'

'Surely she's back by now.'

'No, Monsieur. She has an old aunt at Vitteaux she always calls on when she goes to Paris. I expect she stopped there.'

'Do you have a telephone number?'

'No, Monsieur.'

Nor did she have a name. She was only the concierge who had been asked to call in to feed the cat.

So she had a cat! Pel grabbed at the titbit of information and stored it away. It was one more item about Madame Faivre-Perret he'd discovered.

'I think she must be going out tonight,' the voice went on in his ear. 'She's put out shoes and there's an evening coat. Pale blue.'

It made sense, Pel thought bitterly. Blue *would* suit her.

'Nothing else? No notes? Nothing?'

'She doesn't tell me her business, Monsieur. I expect she'll dash in and get ready at the last minute. She usually does. She's a busy woman.'

Pel replaced the receiver slowly and sat staring at it, baffled, bitter and faintly depressed. Why, he wondered, did God have it in for him so?

Madame Faivre-Perret was obviously looking forward to their dinner date, he decided – which at least was a faint consolation – but that would make the shock of his non-appearance all the more severe, especially if she'd made an effort to get back in time from Paris. He looked at his watch, alarmed at the way time was slipping by. How in God's name, he wondered, could he contact her? He could hardly sit at the end of a police telephone in Austria waiting for someone to turn up m France.

Bitterly, he lit a cigarette and began to pace the office that had been set aside for his use. A few hints had been dropped that it was needed, but he had shut his ears to them. The Innsbrück police could do without it just a little longer, he felt. And it was no good brooding about something he couldn't alter. His face bleak, his tongue feeling like charcoal after all the cigarettes he had smoked, he turned to the files Krauss had brought and moved the sheets of loose paper, the reports, the reminders, the photographs, one after the other. This was where it was, he felt sure. Among the details. Somewhere here was the connection with Paris or Marseilles, with Pépé le Cornet or Maurice Tagliacci. Unfortunately, his dinner at St Seine kept intruding with what they'd discovered about Marie-Anne Chahu's flat and he found it hard to concentrate.

Alongside him was the Innsbrück file on Alois Hofer. Bakt had been the officer who had led the raid on his home in the Nedergasse and he had pointed it out as the car that had met them at Dors had taken them to the Sudtyrolerhof. The Nedergasse was a narrow alley off the Mariatheresienstrasse, close to the great arch of the Triumphforte and overshadowed by the mountains that rose over the Goldenes Dachl and the old town. There had been tourists moving about under the arcades and Bakt had shrugged.

'He had vanished,' he had said. 'With all his family.'

Pel pulled the file towards him and began turning the items inside it. He was just wondering how long he could hold out against the combined disdain of Bakt and the Director when he realised he was looking at a photograph of a man wearing lederhosen and a feathered hat, who was standing by a woman dressed in the flowered print dress and apron of the Tyrol. She was tall with thick greying hair, flashing eyes and a wide smile, her face one that had become surprisingly familiar to Pel.

For a second longer he stared at it, his heart thumping with excitement, before slapping the desk and yelling for Krauss. 'Get Bakt,' he said.

When Bakt appeared, Pel jerked a hand at the photograph. 'Who's that?'

'Hofer.'

'And the woman?'

'His wife. She's French.'

Bakt made it sound like an insult. Pel glared.

'I know she's French,' he growled. 'What's her name?'

'Hofer.'

'Before her marriage?'

Bakt looked puzzled and indicated the file.

'It's in there somewhere.'

Pel was still searching when Darcy appeared. Pel shoved the photograph across.

'Take a look at that,' he said.

Darcy did so and raised startled eyes. By this time Pel was furiously searching through the material Krauss had brought with them and now he stopped and straightened up, holding two documents in his hands. It was the first time he had seen them side by side. For a while he studied them, his heart pounding, comparing words, letters, slopes and angles, excited but told by his common-sense that what he'd found wasn't enough. A good lawyer would have it thrown out of Court within minutes. It needed more.

Name of God, he thought, he ought to have listened to Didier Darras. He'd put it on a plate for him a couple of weeks before. I don't like letters, he had said. They give too much away. They certainly did.

He stared at the papers again, looking at the names on them, deep in thought, then he called for Krauss again.

'Find out if the lecture's still on,' he said.

Since there were no other telephones available and the Director, in a wave of contempt for French police methods, showed no inclination to provide them, Krauss had to use the one in Pel's room. Professor Rosschnigg seemed to be unavailable.

'He's in the building somewhere,' his assistant informed them. 'Please hold.'

As Krauss sat with the telephone to his ear, Pel jigged impatiently from one foot to another until a new voice came on the line. It was clear and loud and sounded as if it belonged to a very old man.

'Rosschnigg here!'

Krauss leapt into his explanation and the voice jabbered noisily in his ear. 'Yes, I organised the lecture. "Influences of Slavic Languages on the East German States." I provided some slides.'

'Is the lecture still being held?'

'Why? Are you French too? You sound French.'

Listening, Pel's thoughts were preoccupied. By this time, perhaps, Madame Faivre-Perret would be home at last, changing her clothes, attending to her hair, putting on make-up, perhaps even managing to be excited at the prospect of seeing Evariste Clovis Désiré Pel. Half an hour from now, though, she'd be wondering what the hell had happened to him, and half an hour later puzzled and more than likely sad, if not furiously angry. And, whether she were home or not, now wasn't the time to think about trying to telephone her again. Things had started happening and they were beginning to happen fast.

Krauss was still hard at it, growing red in the face with frustration, and in the end Pel snatched the telephone from him.

'Professor Foussier's lecture!' he yelled in French. 'Is it still on?'

To his surprise Rosschnigg switched languages at once. 'Of course. It's his speciality. I arranged it with him myself.

He'll be demonstrating his new system. We've just had it installed. It's worked electronically. It's in the Hofhalle.'

Pel slammed the telephone down and swung round to Krauss. 'Get me Nosjean,' he said.

'Back at the office?' Krauss looked unhappy. 'They don't seem very keen on us downstairs, Patron. It'll take a long time.'

'It had better not.'

Krauss pulled out all the stops and the call to Nosjean came through quickly.

'Patron?'

'Nosjean! The documents in the Cortot-Mortier case: You have them there?'

'In the file, Patron.'

'I want you to examine them carefully. There are one or two things I want you to look at.'

'Right, Patron.'

Pel described what he was looking for and went on quickly. 'I want you to compare them with the photocopies in the duplicate of the file we brought with us. The items are numbered and the original I have here is 354. Check it with the Mortier thing. See if the handwriting's the same. If it is, get Lagé to bring in the files of that half-baked photographic society of his.'

'The photographic society, Patron?' Nosjean sounded puzzled.

'You heard me, didn't you?' Pel snapped. 'You aren't deaf! I've never perceived an ear trumpet! Lagé's always boasting how he keeps everything. Let's hope he does, because he also has something I want you to check with Number 354. You'll know what, as soon as you've checked your own. Have the handwriting people look at that, too. And be quick. Ring me back at once with the answer.'

Holding on to his patience, smoking furiously, after a while Pel called Darcy in and talked to him long and earnestly.

'It was there,' he said. 'Among the details. As I knew it would be. We were looking so hard at Paris and Marseilles we didn't see what was on the end of our noses.' He looked at his watch. 'Nosjean will be at least an hour. You'd better get something to eat.'

From the window he watched Darcy leave the building and head for the old streets round the Imperial Summer Palace to find a beer and sandwich. He was frowning, and Pel knew he was as aware as Pel that something had to be pulled out of the bag to save their reputations.

Pel reached for the telephone and demanded his number again. It was going to cost him a fortune before he was done, he realised, and he had deliberately sent Darcy out because he preferred to be alone when he made his excuses.

'Sorry, sir. Line's engaged.'

Pel slammed the telephone down with a curse and sat staring at it as if he'd like to bite it. For God's sake, he asked himself bitterly, if she'd finally arrived home, why in the name of Heaven did she have to pick up the telephone and start ringing round all her friends just when he needed to contact her. He looked at his watch again, wondering what to do. Several more times he tried but the answer was the same every time until finally he was told the telephone was ringing out but that no one was answering.

'Merde!' By this time, he could only imagine she was in the bath.

Nosjean came through much more quickly than he had expected.

'The files on Cortot and Mortier, Patron,' he said. 'I found the note you wanted. The handwriting matched.'

'What about Lagé's files?'

'He made a lot of fuss, Patron. About keeping everything in order. I think he'd have liked a receipt.'

' Lagé's an ass. Did you find what you were looking for?'

'Yes, Patron. That matched, too.'

Pel gave a deep sigh. 'Have them photographed, Nosjean,' he said. 'Fast. And get them here. Fly them to Dors. You can explain to Judge Polverari. I think he'll accept the necessity. I'll have them met.'

By the time the photographs arrived, Pel and Darcy were on edge and the ashtrays were full of cigarette stubs. Bakt brought the packet in and laid it on the desk.

'You'd better stay, Kommissar,' Pel said. 'Then we'd better see the Director. These photographs may interest him.'

He began to talk, explaining everything they'd done, passing sheets of paper one after the other to Bakt who sat silently, frowning. Finally, he pushed across the photograph of the note that Nosjean had taken from his files on Cortot and Mortier.

Bakt's frown grew deeper. 'Are they connected, Inspector?'

'You bet your sweet life they are,' Darcy said.

He held out a packet of cigarettes and Pel took one. As he lit it, he had the feeling that things were going to be all right, after all. He'd continued to try to telephone Madame Faivre-Perret as they'd waited, but every time he'd been informed that there was no reply, and he could only imagine now that, as a businesswoman, she had no intention of getting involved in anything that might delay her date and was not answering. He had even been wondering if he would be wise to try again and – supposing that this time by the grace of God he got hold of her – whether he should with profuse apologies postpone his dinner date. But now, it seemed they might after all see things through to the point when he could leave it with Darcy and be flown back to arrive on the doorstep – even if a little late – to present them in person, together with a dozen red roses. The shops would all be shut when he arrived, he knew, but as a policeman, he had advantages over other people, and there were several florists for whom he'd done a good turn whom he felt he could persuade to open up their premises for him.

Marie-Anne Chahu looked a great deal less happy and considerably less self-assured when Darcy brought her up to Pel's office. She was no longer beautiful and poised. Her face was grey and her make-up had disappeared. Sweat – honest sweat – damped her dress between the shoulder blades and under the armpits. There were tears in her eyes, and she looked every day of her age.

Pel glanced at her, then at Bakt and the Director, who was sitting in a chair in the corner, his face grim.

'Would you like something to drink?' Pel asked. She shook her head.

'Coffee?'

'No.'

'Beer? It's cold.'

She hesitated then she nodded. 'I'd like a beer,' she said.

As Krauss left to get it, Pel leaned towards her and placed on the table the photographs of the slip of paper Nosjean had found in Mortier's wallet.

'Why was your telephone number in the wallet of Philippe Mortier, who committed suicide while under the influence of drugs?' he asked.

She stared at the paper. 'It's not my number,' she said. 'It's the office number where I work.'

'Why did Mortier have it?'

She shrugged. 'He was the one who lived with the Cortot boy, wasn't he? I gave it to him in case he needed help.'

'Do you know a man called Gilles Miollis?'

'He was murdered, wasn't he? I think I once had occasion to write a letter to him for the Professor. The Professor's a dedicated man. I think he'd discovered Miollis was involved with drugs. He had some strange contacts.'

Pel frowned. 'I'm sure he did. How about Archavanne? Louis-Arnold Archavanne?'

She moved limply in the chair. The heat stood in the room as menacing as an assassin. 'Yes. I know that name. When we moved to the new office, he carried the furniture.'

'He was running drugs.' Pel's voice grew sharper. 'Miollis helped him. So did Nincic.' He looked at Bakt and then at the Director, then he laid in front of her the sheets of paper he and Darcy had been studying. They were face down. Pel turned one of them over. It was the yellow slip Nosjean had found in Nincic's flat – the one on which they had found the imprint of the name and address of Alois Hofer in the Nedergasse.

As Marie-Anne Chahu stared at it tiredly, Pel pushed forward the second sheet. On one side was the list of names Foussier's wife had written out for Pel, the names of all the men at universities across Europe concerned with the drugs problem. Pel turned it over. On the other side was the beginning of a letter ... 'Ma chère Noëlle, Je suis heureux de t'informer...' He looked up at Marie-Anne Chahu but her face had suddenly become blank. He reached for a brown envelope and took out one of the photographs Nosjean had sent. It was a picture of a letter addressed to police head-quarters and began 'Mon cher Sergeant Nosjean ...' and con-tained the information Nosjean had sought on Cortot. Finally there was a photograph of a note from Lagé's photographic society's file that listed the things to be desired in a good photograph: Light. Position. Exposure. Lens. Naturalism. Each paragraph had its own heading, printed in capital letters and each had a few explanatory notes beneath.

'Someone was very generous with time,' Pel commented.

While she stared at them, he laid alongside them the note found in Nincic's flat, warning him of the arrival of drugs and advising him about distribution. To it, Nosjean had attached the envelope in which it had arrived. He looked at Marie-Anne Chahu. She returned his look with a hostile stare.

'Am I supposed to deduce something from these?' she asked.

'You are,' Pel said. 'Look at the "n"s. Noëlle. Nosjean. Nincic. Naturalism. Nedergasse. They're all the same, aren't they?'

'Of course. They are all written by the same hand.'

'Whose?'

She was silent for a while. 'Professor Foussier's,' she said and began to cry.

# twenty-two

'Mother of God,' Darcy growled. 'The arrogance of the damned man! He wrote notes to half the Hôtel de Police! At one time or another he'd been in touch with the whole of the PJ. The bastard trapped himself with his own self-importance.'

He did indeed, Pel thought. And Didier Darras had buttoned it up long since. He'd been right more than once, in fact. Dead right. Uncannily right. Even about Madame Faivre-Perret. Pel frowned as the thought of his lost date jabbed at his liver and he decided it was a pity he hadn't borne Didier's view in mind. Look out for the clever ones, he'd said. Taking notice of him might have saved the police a lot of trouble and himself a lot of telephoning.

Darcy was still raging on. 'I expect he thought he was so clever it wouldn't matter,' he was saying. 'We were all so stupid we'd never notice. All those damned degrees! All that assorted knowledge! Languages! Navigation! Electronics! Botany! Ornithology! History! Engineering! Finance! I expect he thought the poor old Flatfoots would never top that in a million years. After all, we only got our background tramping the streets and wallowing in other people's filth. We'd *never* catch on!'

'But we did, Darcy,' Pel said sharply. 'Because of a forgotten photograph. It wasn't Tagliacci or Pépé le Cornet who were setting up in our area. They were just trying to muscle into something they'd heard was beginning to look good.'

'It must have made him hoot with laughter when we gave him a bodyguard.' Darcy was angry, his face red. 'He set up his own route. And he wasn't worried about Pépé le Cornet or Maurice Tagliacci, because he could do something they *couldn't* do – he could go out and organise it himself. He had a few advantages over those baboons! He could fly an aeroplane, he had the foreign contacts, he could speak the languages, and above all he never needed to touch the stuff himself.'

Pel waited for him to calm down then he looked at Marie-Anne Chahu again. The muscles of her neck were taut, her face was thin with strain and her cheeks were wet with tears. He drew a deep breath. 'Ever heard of Alois Hofer?' he asked.

She stared at him. 'Yes,' she said cautiously. 'He was always writing for money.'

'What sort of money?'

'Hand-outs. He never worked. He's the Professor's sister's husband.'

'Yes.' Pel had felt like kicking himself as he had stared at the photograph found in Hofer's home and recognised the features of Hofer's wife. The brother-in-law who was dishonest! The brother-in-law who had a brother-in-law of his own in Hungary! Foussier must have started the thing in great glee, but then he'd found he'd raised a monster.

'He might have got away with it all, too,' Darcy said, 'if everyone hadn't wanted more than they were already getting.' He jerked a hand at Marie-Anne Chahu. 'Her, too. She led us to him in the end.'

Pel glanced at him. 'You were chasing the wrong rabbit, mon brave,' he said. 'Though, in the end, it led us down the right hole. He knew everything there was to know about students on drugs. He even wrote a thesis on it years ago. He had a wife who understood medicine, a father and a father-in-law who were doctors, and a brother-in-law who worked for a drugs manufacturing firm. There wasn't anything he couldn't find out if he wanted to. He also had expertise on a dozen subjects, including flying. You said it yourself: he was too clever by half. He was even clever enough to have thought up a happy habit to account for sudden disappearances to see his henchmen or when emergencies cropped up – his need to be alone to recharge his batteries. He even knew how to arrange a bomb on his car when we had our eyes on Paris and Marseilles and it was a good idea to encourage us. It was easy for him. He was clever enough to know everything. Nobody was after him. Pépé le Cornet and Tagliacci had never heard of him.'

Pel's mind was full of worms as they drove to the Hofhalle. Foussier: Hypocrite, liar, fornicator, cheat, murderer. The accusations pushed through his mind one after the other. Like his sister, he couldn't cope with his own brilliance. Perhaps he'd even started the thing up in the first place so he could pose as the man who could bring it down.

He was in no doubt now about what had happened. Foussier had thought it all so easy. He had his brother-in-law, Hofer, to set up the route, and Nincic, who was too fond of money, to supply him with the names of students who came to him looking for drugs. But then it had started to turn sour and when Nincic, who had had to get rid of Miollis, had also started demanding a bigger cut, this time he'd had to do the job himself – with Nincic's gun. By the time Treguy had blundered in, murder was growing easy and he'd finally been responsible for the deaths of three men. The only consolation was that none of them would be missed.

The Hofhalle was an ancient building redolent of the old Habsburg Empire. The entrance was magnificent, with a wide curving staircase running up either side of the hall. The place was studded with statues and the steps and balustrade appeared to be of marble.

'Used to be part of the Emperor's Summer Palace,' Bakt said.

Krauss was waiting in the doorway when the car stopped. 'Third floor,' he said. 'The lecture hall's in the old ballroom.'

As they started up the stairs, Pel touched Krauss' shoulder. 'Wait here,' he said. 'Just in case.'

On the third floor were two wide double doors, and as they pushed them open, a young man with a beard, spectacles and a great deal of hair put his fingers to his lips.

'Ruhig sein,' he whispered. 'Bitte, meine Herren.'

Foussier was standing on a platform at the end of the room. Under the lights he looked handsome and enormously tall. In front of him was a podium with his notes and behind him a screen showing a picture of a Mongol horseman. He was talking.

'Many of these languages,' he was saying, 'are monosyllabic. Chinese, which was once an agglutinating language, is not pure monosyllabic. Some Amerindian dialects are not only agglutinating but polysynthetic or incorporative, as may be seen in such names as "Montezuma" and "Moctezuma", or even "Montecuzomiaithuica-mina", which means "When the Chief is Angry he shoots from Heaven".'

There was a laugh and Foussier beamed. Then his smile died abruptly as his eyes fell on Pel standing at the back of the hall with Darcy and Bakt. For a moment he paused, then he drew a deep breath and they saw his hand move across his notes. 'Nevertheless,' he went on, more slowly, 'the agglutinating languages form the largest of the three groups. To it belong Japanese, Korean, the Caucasian forms of speech, the ancient Sumerian and Elamite, the Ural-Altoc family, various Amerindian groups and many others.'

As his hand moved again, Pel moved forward. 'Stop him,' he said.

They were too late. The lights went out and for a moment the room was in darkness. Then a slide flashed on the screen. It was a picture of a Caucasian soldier and, as it appeared, they saw that Foussier had vanished.

'The door at the rear,' Bakt snapped.

As they pushed their way down the centre aisle to the dais, there were immediate cries of annoyance and the young man with the hair by the door began to call out angrily. 'Ruhig sein, ruhig sein! Sich niedersetzen!'

Following Bakt, they clattered up the steps at the side of the dais. By this time everybody in the hall was on his feet, and the place was filled with angry voices. As they pushed through the door at the back of the dais, the hall lights came on and, by the reflection, they saw they were in a small room full of stacked chairs. To one side, a window stood ajar and, peering out, they saw it opened on to a corridor.

'The stairs!' Bakt snapped.

As they pushed back on to the dais and down the steps, hands snatched at them and angry faces turned. A youth grabbed hold of Bakt, who gave him a violent shove so that he staggered back, carrying several others with him. As he stumbled, there was the scrape and clatter of falling chairs.

As they reached the double doors, they saw Foussier pass. By the time they had fought their way free, he had almost reached the top of the stairs.

'Stop!' Bakt shouted. 'Stop right there or I shall tell my men to shoot!'

Foussier ignored the call and Pel yelled in French. 'We have the entrance guarded! You can't get out!'

As the uproar had started, Krauss had moved up from the ground floor and now, as Foussier hesitated, he began climbing the third flight of stairs with the lumbering run of an overweight man. As Foussier swung round, he saw Krauss for the first time and they glimpsed the glint of metal in his fist.

Krauss had reached him now and had grabbed his arm, to struggle with him against the balustrade. There was a report and Pel saw a puff of smoke drift away. Krauss' face, contorted with the struggle, changed and he staggered back, still gripping Foussier and dragging him with him. There was another shot, and Krauss pushed Foussier from him, as though trying to disable or disarm him by flinging him down the stairs.

As Krauss sagged by the wall, Foussier had staggered back against the low marble balustrade, half turned, off-balance after Krauss' shove, his body bowed backwards into space. For a moment, his hands flailed the air, searching for something to grasp as his feet slipped away from him and it was his very height that finished him. Transfixed, they saw him drop the gun as his body pivoted over the banister, sliding down the shiny marble under his own weight. As his feet rose, his head went down, and for one last wild second, they saw his eyes on them, agonised and accusing. A strangled shriek burst from his lungs to echo up to the roof of the building and ring round the ancient corridors, then they heard the crunch as his body struck the marble floor of the empty hall. There were shouts and questions behind them as the people in the lecture hall boiled out on to the landing, and Darcy and Bakt went down the stairs in a rush, their eyes empty and suddenly merciless. In the hall below, Darcy bent over the body then, after a moment, looked up and shook his head. Pel saw the gesture as he moved down the stairs. The Hofhalle was full of noise now, everybody talking at once, the landing outside the lecture hall packed with students, all hanging over the banister, staring downwards.

Nobody seemed to have noticed Krauss in the excitement. He had slumped down on the stairs in a sitting position against the wall, his knees drawn up, his hands holding his chest, blood oozing through his fingers, his head bent forward, his eyes wide open but empty. On the stairs alongside him was the gun that had shot him and, picking it up, Pel saw it was a Browning 7.65 mm – just as Leguyader had said – the same gun that Nincic had used to kill Miollis and then had used on himself, the same gun that had killed Treguy.

He felt weighed down by sadness. His dinner date and all it meant had shot off into the wild blue yonder. There had been no apology, no excuse, nothing, and he could imagine how he was regarded at that moment in the salon in the Rue de la Liberté. But, as he glanced again at Krauss, it suddenly didn't seem to matter very much. Whatever happened now, it wouldn't make any difference to Krauss. Nothing would make any difference to Krauss any more.

The irony of his death within a few weeks of his retirement was almost too much to bear. Krauss had never been brilliant and he had bored them all to tears with his talk of what he intended to do when he left the force, but the pathos of seeing him crouched there, his chin on his chest, seeing nothing, hearing nothing, feeling nothing, was almost too much. There'd be no dinner dates for Krauss. There'd be no fishing in his old age, no visits to Royan, no grandchildren, nothing.

Somebody had already contacted headquarters and an ambulance had arrived. Two men appeared with a stretcher and stared at Foussier. Darcy waved them away and indicated Pel standing on the stairs. As they began to climb towards him, they looked a little scared and bewildered. One of them bent over Krauss and shook his head.

Pel sighed again. He had still been hoping.

Placing Krauss on the stretcher, they laid a blanket over him and tucked it about him, securing him against the slope of the stairs with straps. Finally, they glanced at Pel then

lifted the folded end of the blanket and laid it over Krauss'
face.

Pel followed them as they began to descend in slow,
plodding steps, manoeuvring the stretcher cautiously round
the corners. Darcy was waiting at the bottom with Bakt, his
face taut, his eyes cold. He glanced questioningly at Pel, who
shook his head, then turned and stared at Foussier who was
still spreadeagled on his back, a small pool of blood beneath
his head. There wasn't an atom of compassion in his
expression.

'The bastard,' he said quietly.

'Yes.' Pel touched his arm and headed for the door. 'Come
on, Darcy. I think we'd better let the Chief know.'

# Mark Hebden

## Death Set to Music

The severely battered body of a murder victim turns up in provincial France and the sharp-tongued Chief Inspector Pel must use all his Gallic guile to understand the pile of clues building up around him, until a further murder and one small boy make the elusive truth all too apparent.

## The Errant Knights

Hector and Hetty Bartlelott go to Spain for a holiday, along with their nephew Alec and his wife Sibley. All is well under a Spanish sun until Hetty befriends a Spanish boy on the run from the police and passionate Spanish Anarchists. What follows is a hard-and-fast race across Spain, hot-tailed by the police and the anarchists, some light indulging in the Semana Santa festivities of Seville to throw off the pursuers, and a near miss in Toledo where the young Spanish fugitive is almost caught.

# MARK HEBDEN

## PEL AND THE BOMBERS

When five murders disturb his sleepy Burgundian city on Bastille night, Chief Inspector Evariste Clovis Désiré Pel has his work cut out for him. A terrorist group is at work and the President is due shortly on a State visit. Pel's problems with his tyrannical landlady must be put aside while he catches the criminals.

"...downbeat humour and some delightful dialogue."
*Financial Times*

## PEL AND THE PARIS MOB

In his beloved Burgundy, Chief Inspector Pel finds himself incensed by interference from Paris, but it isn't the flocking descent of rival policemen that makes Pel's blood boil – crimes are being committed by violent gangs from Paris and Marseilles. Pel unravels the riddle of the robbery on the road to Dijon airport as well as the mysterious shootings in an iron foundry. If that weren't enough, the Chief Inspector must deal with the misadventures of the delightfully handsome Sergeant Misset and his red-haired lover.

"...written with downbeat humour and some delightful dialogue which leaven the violence." *Financial Times*

# MARK HEBDEN

## PEL AND THE PREDATORS

There has been a spate of sudden murders around Burgundy where Pel has just been promoted to Chief Inspector. The irascible policeman receives a letter bomb, and these combined events threaten to overturn Pel's plans to marry Mme Faivre-Perret. Can Pel keep his life, his love and his career by solving the murder mysteries? Can Pel stave off the predators?

'...impeccable French provincial ambience.' *The Times*

## PORTRAIT IN A DUSTY FRAME

The sudden popularity of the poet, Christina Moray Tait, seventy years after her death, gives her great-grandson, Tennyson Moray Tait, a new-found notoriety. When approached by a man claiming he could reveal the true circumstances surrounding Christina's mysterious death, Tennyson decides to join him in Peru, facing the dark green extremes of the Amazon, a reluctant American freelance photographer, and a suspicious native guide.

## TITLES BY MARK HEBDEN AVAILABLE DIRECT
## FROM HOUSE OF STRATUS

| Quantity | | £ | $(US) | $(CAN) | € |
|---|---|---|---|---|---|
| | THE DARK SIDE OF THE ISLAND | 6.99 | 12.95 | 19.95 | 13.50 |
| | DEATH SET TO MUSIC | 6.99 | 12.95 | 19.95 | 13.50 |
| | THE ERRANT KNIGHTS | 6.99 | 12.95 | 19.95 | 13.50 |
| | EYEWITNESS | 6.99 | 12.95 | 19.95 | 13.50 |
| | A KILLER FOR THE CHAIRMAN | 6.99 | 12.95 | 19.95 | 13.50 |
| | LEAGUE OF EIGHTY-NINE | 6.99 | 12.95 | 19.95 | 13.50 |
| | MASK OF VIOLENCE | 6.99 | 12.95 | 19.95 | 13.50 |
| | PEL AMONG THE PUEBLOS | 6.99 | 12.95 | 19.95 | 13.50 |
| | PEL AND THE BOMBERS | 6.99 | 12.95 | 19.95 | 13.50 |
| | PEL AND THE FACELESS CORPSE | 6.99 | 12.95 | 19.95 | 13.50 |
| | PEL AND THE MISSING PERSONS | 6.99 | 12.95 | 19.95 | 13.50 |
| | PEL AND THE PARIS MOB | 6.99 | 12.95 | 19.95 | 13.50 |
| | PEL AND THE PARTY SPIRIT | 6.99 | 12.95 | 19.95 | 13.50 |
| | PEL AND THE PICTURE OF INNOCENCE | 6.99 | 12.95 | 19.95 | 13.50 |

ALL HOUSE OF STRATUS BOOKS ARE AVAILABLE FROM GOOD BOOKSHOPS
OR DIRECT FROM THE PUBLISHER:

Internet:   www.houseofstratus.com including synopses and features.

Email:   sales@houseofstratus.com
info@houseofstratus.com
(please quote author, title and credit card details.)

## TITLES BY MARK HEBDEN AVAILABLE DIRECT
## FROM HOUSE OF STRATUS

| Quantity | | £ | $(US) | $(CAN) | € |
|---|---|---|---|---|---|
| | PEL AND THE PIRATES | 6.99 | 12.95 | 19.95 | 13.50 |
| | PEL AND THE PREDATORS | 6.99 | 12.95 | 19.95 | 13.50 |
| | PEL AND THE PROMISED LAND | 6.99 | 12.95 | 19.95 | 13.50 |
| | PEL AND THE PROWLER | 6.99 | 12.95 | 19.95 | 13.50 |
| | PEL AND THE SEPULCHRE JOB | 6.99 | 12.95 | 19.95 | 13.50 |
| | PEL AND THE STAGHOUND | 6.99 | 12.95 | 19.95 | 13.50 |
| | PEL AND THE TOUCH OF PITCH | 6.99 | 12.95 | 19.95 | 13.50 |
| | PEL IS PUZZLED | 6.99 | 12.95 | 19.95 | 13.50 |
| | PORTRAIT IN A DUSTY FRAME | 6.99 | 12.95 | 19.95 | 13.50 |
| | A PRIDE OF DOLPHINS | 6.99 | 12.95 | 19.95 | 13.50 |
| | WHAT CHANGED CHARLEY FARTHING | 6.99 | 12.95 | 19.95 | 13.50 |

ALL HOUSE OF STRATUS BOOKS ARE AVAILABLE FROM GOOD BOOKSHOPS
OR DIRECT FROM THE PUBLISHER:

Tel:     Order Line
         0800 169 1780 (UK)
         1 800 724 1100 (USA)
         International
         +44 (0) 1845 527700 (UK)
         +01     845 463 1100 (USA)

Fax:     +44 (0) 1845 527711 (UK)
         +01     845 463 0018 (USA)
         (please quote author, title and credit card details.)

Send to: House of Stratus Sales Department    House of Stratus Inc.
         Thirsk Industrial Park                2 Neptune Road
         York Road, Thirsk                     Poughkeepsie
         North Yorkshire, YO7 3BX              NY 12601
         UK                                    USA

# PAYMENT

Please tick currency you wish to use:

☐ £ (Sterling)    ☐ $ (US)    ☐ $ (CAN)    ☐ € (Euros)

Allow for shipping costs charged per order plus an amount per book as set out in the tables below:

CURRENCY/DESTINATION

| | £(Sterling) | $(US) | $(CAN) | €(Euros) |
|---|---|---|---|---|
| **Cost per order** | | | | |
| UK | 1.50 | 2.25 | 3.50 | 2.50 |
| Europe | 3.00 | 4.50 | 6.75 | 5.00 |
| North America | 3.00 | 3.50 | 5.25 | 5.00 |
| Rest of World | 3.00 | 4.50 | 6.75 | 5.00 |
| **Additional cost per book** | | | | |
| UK | 0.50 | 0.75 | 1.15 | 0.85 |
| Europe | 1.00 | 1.50 | 2.25 | 1.70 |
| North America | 1.00 | 1.00 | 1.50 | 1.70 |
| Rest of World | 1.50 | 2.25 | 3.50 | 3.00 |

PLEASE SEND CHEQUE OR INTERNATIONAL MONEY ORDER
payable to: HOUSE OF STRATUS LTD or HOUSE OF STRATUS INC. or card payment as indicated

STERLING EXAMPLE

Cost of book(s):..................... Example: 3 x books at £6.99 each: £20.97
Cost of order:...................... Example: £1.50 (Delivery to UK address)
Additional cost per book:.............. Example: 3 x £0.50: £1.50
Order total including shipping:.......... Example: £23.97

## VISA, MASTERCARD, SWITCH, AMEX:

☐☐☐☐☐☐☐☐☐☐☐☐☐☐☐☐☐☐☐☐☐☐

Issue number (Switch only):

☐☐☐

**Start Date:**          **Expiry Date:**

☐☐/☐☐          ☐☐/☐☐

Signature: _____

NAME: _____

ADDRESS: _____

COUNTRY: _____

ZIP/POSTCODE: _____

Please allow 28 days for delivery. Despatch normally within 48 hours.

Prices subject to change without notice.
Please tick box if you do not wish to receive any additional information. ☐

House of Stratus publishes many other titles in this genre; please check our website (**www.houseofstratus.com**) for more details.